Reining in Never

CHELSEY FAY

Egan
Enjoy!

C Fay

BLAZING BOOKS PUBLISHING

To my husband, Chris. Thank you for helping me make all my dreams come true.

Contents

Prologue

Better As a Memory - Kenny Chesney

Wyatt

The October rain pounded down, soaking through my lined Carhartt jacket, as Finn and I struggled to repair the broken fence. My fingers were numb, the wire cutters slipping in my grasp as I tried to twist the rusted barbed wire back into place. It was a losing battle, just like everything else on this godforsaken farm.

"This is useless," I muttered, throwing down the cutters in frustration. "The posts are rotten. We need to replace the whole damn thing."

Finn wiped the rain from his eyes, his expression grim. "Your old man's really let things go."

I snorted. "That's an understatement. He's been too busy drowning himself in whiskey to give a damn about what's left of our cattle or the land."

We'd been out here for hours, trying to patch up the neglected fences, but it was like putting a band-aid on a bullet wound. The farm was falling apart, and my father seemed content to watch it crumble.

Finn dropped the tools he'd been holding. "Come on, let's go talk to him. Maybe we can knock some sense into him."

I shoved open the door to the old house, the scent of stale beer and regret filling my senses. My father lay sprawled on the couch, holding a half-empty bottle of whiskey in his hand, his eyes glazed over as he stared at the flickering television screen.

"We need new fence posts, Dad." My voice was tight. "And we need to buy hay soon."

He didn't even turn his head. "Nope. No need."

"What are you talking about?" I forced out the words between clenched teeth.

He finally turned, his bloodshot eyes fixing on me in a drunken haze. "I sold it. I sold it all."

My blood ran cold. "Sold what?"

"The farm," he slurred, a twisted smile playing on his lips. "I'm done. Richie's buying the whole damn thing."

The name hit me like a punch to the gut.

Richie Marcano was the loan shark my father had kept himself indebted to for years. The same man who'd had his thugs beat me to a pulp the last time my dad couldn't pay what he owed.

"You can't sell the farm," I protested, my voice rising in disbelief. "Especially to that monster."

"I can, and I did," he countered, his hand groping for a can of beer on the coffee table. "Go back to your rodeo. Hell, maybe I'll go back to the rodeo. Free myself of this shithole. Those were the days." He laughed—a hollow, broken sound.

"You son of a bitch." I lunged at him, driven by a surge of anger and betrayal. My hand clamped onto the front of his shirt to pull him off the couch, and my fist drew back, aiming for his smug, drunken face.

"Wyatt!" Finn's voice cut through my rage as he pulled me back, his grip firm on my arm.

My father, caught off guard, scrambled clumsily to his feet, his eyes wide with shock. "Get out." His voice was surprisingly sober for once.

"You really think you can make me leave, old man?" I towered over him, the advantage of height and sobriety on my side.

His gaze shifted to Finn, standing behind me, a silent plea in his eyes.

"You should leave." I told him. "You do nothing for this place."

"Wyatt." Finn's voice tone was warning.

"Richie's getting the paperwork ready. These fingers"—my father held up his trembling hands—"are signing it, and there's not one damn thing you can do about it."

My fists clenched and unclenched at my side, the urge to strike wrestling with the restraint Finn had on me.

"Wyatt, let's go." Finn's voice was calm but firm.

"Listen to him, son. Say goodbye to this place because you're never seeing it again," my father taunted, a cold finality in his tone.

We walked back out into the rain, loaded our horses and my meager belongings into my truck, and drove away. I was leaving behind the only home I'd ever known, the only place that had ever felt like mine. A place that *should*'ve been mine.

***

I entered the rodeo barn that would be home for the next week, tired after the long drive.

A blonde blur came barreling towards me.

Kinsley.

She launched herself into my arms, her laughter ringing in my ears as I caught her and breathed in her hair's sweet scent. My hands slid to her waist, pulling her flush against me as my mouth sought hers with a desperate urgency.

The moment our mouths met, the world fell away. Her lips were soft and pliant beneath mine, parting with a sigh that sent a shiver down my spine. I drank her in like a man starved, my tongue delving deep and tasting her sweetness. Her fingers tangled in my hair, tugging me closer, and I groaned into the kiss, the heat of her body seeping into my soul.

I needed her now more than ever.

I lost myself in the slide of her lips, the brush of her tongue, and the way she molded herself to me like we were two halves of a whole. In that stolen slice of time, there was only her.

But even as I savoured her presence, the ghosts of my father's betrayal and losing our farm haunted me like a cold shadow that not even Kinsley's light could fully chase away.

It all came rushing back: the tiredness, my bones aching with a weariness that went beyond the physical, and the strain of mustering a smile—even for her—felt like an impossible task.

Kinsley pulled back, oblivious, her blue eyes sparkling with excitement. "Wyatt, I've got the most amazing news! I've been talking to my dad, and he's willing to sponsor us both to go down to the States and hit the big circuits. Can you imagine? We could really make a name for ourselves!"

I paused, trying to process what she'd just told me.

Sponsorships. Her dad's money. Another reminder of everything I didn't have, everything I could never give her.

"I can't, Kins." My voice cracked under the weight of my emotions. "I can't take your dad's money. Especially not now, after everything that—"

Her brow furrowed in confusion. "What are you talking about, Wyatt? What happened?"

I shook my head. "I've lost the farm, Kinsley. My dad sold it to pay off his debts. I've got nothing left."

Shock and concern filled her eyes. "Oh, Wyatt, I'm so sorry. I had no idea. But this sponsorship could be a fresh start for us. A chance to build something new together."

I stepped back, my walls slamming up and shutting her out. "Don't you get it? I've lost everything, Kinsley. The farm, my family's legacy, and my goddamn self-respect. Now you want me to, what? Be your kept man? Ride on your daddy's coattails?"

Hurt flashed across her face, but I couldn't stop the words from pouring out, my pain and pride blinding me to what she was offering.

"I won't have it, Kinsley. If I'm going to make something of myself, I need to do it on my own. I won't be your charity case."

"That's not what this is," Kinsley argued, her face reddening. "I'm trying to help you, to support you. We could be together and build our careers together. Why can't you see that?"

"I don't need your help," I said. "I can do this on my own. I don't want to be known as the guy who only got a sponsorship because he was dating Cal Jackson's daughter."

"God, Wyatt, it's not that big of a deal."

"Yeah, it is Kinsley," I challenged, my voice rising. "I don't understand why you can't fucking see that."

"And I don't understand why you have to be so fucking stubborn all the time!"

"No, you clearly don't understand."

"Fine." Her voice went cold. "If that's how you feel, then we're done. I've really had enough of this. I'm done trying to help you, Wyatt. I'm done with all of this." She turned and walked away, her shoulders shaking with silent sobs.

I let her go, watching the best thing in my life slip through my fingers.

A part of me wanted to call out to her, to apologize and take it all back. But the words wouldn't come. Not this time. Every time we had this fight, it felt like getting slammed into the rails, the air knocked out of me. And right now, I was already spitting blood. My dad, the farm, this fight—it was all too much. I was too goddamn tired to even breathe, let alone chase after her and pretend I could fix a damn thing.

The ache in my chest grew—a hollow, gnawing emptiness that threatened to swallow me whole.

In a single day, I'd lost everything that had ever mattered to me. My home, my family, and now the love of my life. As I stood there, surrounded by the din of the rodeo, I'd never felt more alone. More broken.

It was the worst day of my life, and I had no one to blame but myself.

Chapter 1

FASTEST GIRL IN TOWN - MIRANDA LAMBERT

Kinsley

I t was love at first sight.

He was the most beautiful creature I had ever seen, with his deep and soulful brown eyes, shiny black hair, powerful muscles... I had to have him.

So, I bought him without a second thought.

Mr. Lucky Gambler was an eight-year-old black quarter horse gelding and the fastest horse I had ever ridden. But the honeymoon period was over by the time I had him on the trailer to bring him home.

I, of all people, knew better than to fall that hard and fast for a member of the male species. You'd think I would've learned my lesson the first time, but nope.

My frustration mounted as Gambler threw his head up for the umpteenth time, ignoring my cues to slow down. We circled the outdoor arena, kicking up dust under the warm spring Alberta sun. The endless cattle fields of my family's ranch stretched out around me.

"You overgrown turd!" I grumbled through gritted teeth, trying to rein him in.

Gambler snorted, his black coat glistening with sweat.

The sound of boots crunching on gravel drew my attention.

Dad leaned against the fence, a knowing smile on his sun-weathered face. "How's it going, Kins?"

I forced a grin. "Oh, he's being an angel. Just getting him used to the arena."

Dad raised an eyebrow. "Is that so? Looks like he's giving you a run for your money."

I shrugged, patting Gambler's neck. "We're working out some kinks. He's got a lot of spirit."

"Maybe you should give yourselves more time," Dad suggested. "Get to know each other better before hitting the rodeo circuit."

I shook my head, determination surging through me. "No way. We're ready. I can feel it."

Dad sighed. "Kinsley, I know you're eager to win, but rushing into things won't do you any favours. Take it slow; build that trust."

I met his gaze, my jaw set. "I appreciate the advice, Dad, but I know what I'm doing. Gambler and I are going to take the circuit by storm. Just you wait."

Dad held up his hands in surrender. "Alright, alright. Be careful out there. That's a lot of horse."

I grinned, imagining the upcoming competition, excitement already coursing through my veins. "Don't worry, Dad. We've got this."

Dad shook his head and waved as he strolled back to the big red barn that housed our string of ranch horses, as well as my and my sister's horses.

I guided Gambler around the barrels, my heart pounding with each mighty stride.

Barrel racing was all about speed, precision, and that unbreakable bond between the horse and the rider. The goal was simple: complete a cloverleaf pattern around three barrels in the fastest time possible. But simple didn't mean easy. Navigating those tight turns at breakneck speeds required razor-sharp focus and impeccable timing. The slightest miscalculation could mean losing precious seconds or even knocking barrels over, resulting in a loss.

As we approached the first barrel, Gambler overshot the turn, his hooves scrambling in the dirt. I cursed under my breath, pulling him back on course. We completed the pattern, but it was sloppy. I knew we could do better.

I brought Gambler to a stop, patting his neck. "Let's try that again, buddy. Nice and tight around those barrels, okay?"

We lined up for another run. This time, I kept my cues clear and consistent, guiding Gambler with my body and voice. We hit the first barrel, and though he still overshot, it was an improvement from before. Around the second barrel, we found our rhythm. Gambler responded beautifully to my cues, his athletic body coiled and ready for each turn. By the third barrel, we were flying, dirt kicking up behind us as we raced for the finish line. I let out a whoop as we crossed the line. It hadn't been a perfect run but still a damn good one. With a little more practice, Gambler and I would be unstoppable.

We ran the pattern again and again, each time smoothing out the rough edges. Gambler's overshoot at the first barrel became less pronounced, his turns tighter and more controlled. By the end of our session, sweat dampened his coat and my blue long-sleeve Henley clung to my back, but the satisfaction was undeniable.

I dismounted, leading Gambler out of the arena. My muscles ached in that pleasant way that came from a great workout. I unsaddled Gambler and brushed him down, ignoring the nagging in my stomach. Sure, we still had work to do, but we'd be ready for the first rodeo this weekend. Gambler had the speed, and I was the daughter of a rodeo legend.

We have what it takes to win, and nothing is going to stop us.

***

Gambler was kicking firmly and rhythmically into the rubber-coated door of the trailer.

"How did he load?" I asked our longtime ranch hand, Ben, as I approached the truck and threw my bag into the backseat.

"Oh, he knows every trick in the book to get out of loading, but unfortunately for him, so do I." Ben grinned at me through his salt-and-pepper whiskers. "Are you sure you don't want me to drive you and unload him on the other side?"

"Nah, I'll be fine." I loved to drive alone, hauling my horses to rodeos with windows down and music blaring. Gambler could kick along to the beat if he wanted to. There wasn't much damage he could do in that rig.

"I think that's a good idea!" My mother's voice called out from inside the barn. She emerged seconds later, frowning in disapproval, followed by my father. "Let him drive so that horse doesn't kill you."

"If he's going to kill me, it will not be by unloading him from the trailer; it'll be by coming around the third barrel and racing to home." I smiled sweetly at her, which only made her frown deeper.

My father tried his best to hide his grin but failed. He understood me and my need to win. Before settling into the ranch life, Cal Jackson had been a rodeo cowboy—the best of the best. He'd never backed down from any bucking bull.

Dad and I were so much alike, though my passion was barrel racing, not bulls. I'd given my mother some relief with that, at least.

"That doesn't make me feel better, Kinsley," she scolded. "Why can't you keep riding Cherokee? She ran so well for you last year."

"She did. And I will keep riding her. But I didn't finish first last year. Gambler will get me there."

I'd finished third in points overall last season, which of course was great, but it wasn't first. I was Cal Jackson's daughter. While my dad didn't put the pressure on me to win, the rest of the world did. I was good, even at a young age. I grew up on the rodeo scene with all eyes on me, constantly being told I had my father's talent, fearlessness, and drive. My bar had been set high right from day one, and I desperately wanted to scale it and be the best, just like he was. Just like everyone expected me to be.

Gambler was a recent impulse purchase. He was so fast, but he also had a reputation—he was kind of mean and unpredictable. If you got a good ride out of him, he was incredible, but he gave just as many bad rides, maybe more.

He'd sent his last owner to the hospital with a slew of injuries. That was why she'd sold him. *Lucky me!* I needed that speed if I was going to win, and I was positive that I could handle him.

The breeze blew a lock of my long blonde hair into my mouth, and I brushed it away.

"Do you want me to braid your hair for you before you go?" my mother asked, brushing her own blonde strands away from her face.

"How am I supposed to feel the wind in my hair if it's in a silly braid?" I teased.

"Stop fussin' over her, Marian." Dad wrapped his arm around his wife and pulled her into his side. "Kinsley is all grown up and knows what she's doing."

I resisted the urge to remind them that, at twenty-four, I'd been grown up for a while now.

Another loud kick sounded from inside the trailer. *Such an impatient boy.*

I peeked at Gambler through the window. "Hush now. We're going right away."

Another kick.

I opened the door of the trailer and let myself in. "Hey, grumpy man," I cooed at him.

He took my breath away every time I looked at him. Gambler was stunning—well, usually. At the moment, he had bits of hay sticking out of his mouth, and he must've rubbed his head on his hay net because hay was stuck in his forelock, making it look more like a bird's nest.

I laughed at his goofy appearance, pulled the hay out, and smoothed his mane. I ran my hands down his face, breathed in that wonderful sweet and earthy horse scent, and planted a kiss on his nose. "We're going to win together, aren't we, boy? You do what you do best and run like the wind."

He turned away from me and, with his teeth, pulled another mouthful of hay from his net as if to say, *I will if I feel like it.*

"Alright, Gambler, you're the boss. We'll head out." I peeked over him at my little red mare in the next stall, who was happily munching. "You good, Cher?"

Her ear flicked to me, but she went right on eating. She was a pro at travelling; she was a pro at everything. *My sassy girl.*

I stepped out of the trailer and secured the door behind me.

"All set?" Dad asked. "You can handle this rig?"

He'd bought me the new trailer for Christmas last year. It was a fifth-wheel trailer with living quarters up front, which included a queen-size bed, bathroom, and kitchenette. In the back, there was room for three horses, with padded walls and non-slip rubber mats. Only the best for his girl, Dad had said.

Yeah, I was a bit spoiled, but I didn't mind. This trailer was bigger than my last one and I hadn't driven it yet, but I wasn't worried. I'd grown up on a cattle ranch, and I had been driving since I was tall enough to see over the dashboard.

"Yep, no problem," I replied.

"Atta girl."

"Is Wyatt going to be there?" my mother asked, not looking me in the eye.

Why did she have to bring him up?

I balled up my fists. It would be so much easier if my mother didn't like my ex-boyfriend so much. But even I had to admit he was easy to like; he was always respectful, caring, and just had a simple charm to him.

"No idea." I lied, abruptly turning and heading for the truck to avoid further questions.

She got the hint.

To be honest, I'd finally given in and checked the rodeo website last night, to see if he was registered. He was. My heart had sunk then fluttered back up, then sunk again. It'd gone back and forth all night, and I'd barely slept.

My parents followed me to the driver's side door, and I hugged them both goodbye.

"Good luck, sweetie." My mother had tears in her eyes, as she always did when I left.

"It's a few months," I reminded her. "There should be a few opportunities for me to come back and visit when there's a break in the schedule."

The more rodeos you competed in, the more points you could earn. These points contributed to our overall standing in the rodeo circuit, and high standings could lead to qualifying for major events, like the Canadian Finals Rodeo.

When I was younger, she had come with me on the rodeo circuit, but now she stayed home with Dad to help run the ranch. They would come out to cheer me on whenever they could.

"Say goodbye to Abby for me." I told them. My younger sister was away at a riding clinic.

"We will," my mother answered.

"Keep your eyes up and always be looking where you want your horse to go, not down at his feet."

"Got it, Dad." I rolled my eyes and climbed into the truck.

I shoved the key into the ignition and started it up with a loud rumble, then I rolled down the window because what was even the point of driving with the window up?

Mom and Dad waved as I pulled away, the tires crunching on the long gravel driveway. Every acre of home was perfect, from the green pastures on either side of me to the cows grazing in the distance. But it was also quiet and still—two things I was not.

I needed to feel the adrenaline and the pure exhilaration every time I sat on a horse as I waited to burst across that start line and towards that first barrel. I loved my time at home with my family, but I also needed the thrill of the rodeo.

And the thrill that came with kissing Wyatt Collins.

I reminded myself that I couldn't think about him. *I. Will. Not. Think. About. Wyatt.*

So what if I could never resist him before? I would this time. Every time we'd gotten together over the last two years, it had ended in disaster and me broken-hearted.

I loved him, of that I had no doubt, but we were like fire and gasoline—we burned too fast. We weren't right for each other.

Love shouldn't be that hard, right?

I had to focus on my horses and my rides. That cowboy would not distract me from my goal. Winning mattered; it was all that mattered.

I turned up the volume on my stereo, blasting a Miranda Lambert album. With my right hand on the steering wheel, I put my left hand out the window and let it ride the waves on the wind. Up and down, up and down.

I let out a deep breath. This was all I needed. And Wyatt Collins? Never again.

Chapter 2

MAMMAS DON'T LET YOUR BABIES GROW UP TO BE COWBOYS - WAYLON JENNINGS & WILLIE NELSON

Wyatt

The engine of my beat-up old blue and white Ford F-150 rumbled beneath me—a vibration that had been absent for too long. After months of crashing at Finn's family's horse stable, helping with the chores, the winter training, and pretending I wasn't counting down the days until rodeo season, we were finally back to life on the road.

We got to the rodeo grounds earlier that morning, unloaded the horses, got them settled in, and unhitched my horse trailer. Then, we headed back out in search of food since the trucks that usually catered the rodeo hadn't arrived yet.

Beside me, Finn—my best friend and team roping partner—drummed his fingers on the dashboard to some unheard rhythm in his head. In the back, Grady, who always had trouble sitting still for too long, was getting fidgety while Rhett, his gaze steady on the road ahead, seemed to absorb the passing scenery with an almost zen-like calm. Nothing ever ruffled his feathers, not even Grady's restless energy beside him or the long hours already spent crammed in the truck that day.

I glanced in the rearview mirror. Grady was swiping his phone with one hand and dragging his other through his straight brown slicked-back hair. I rolled my eyes, got the attention of the other two guys, and motioned for them to brace themselves. Then I slammed on the brakes, coming to a screeching halt.

Grady's head jerked forward, colliding with the back of my seat. "Hey!" He rubbed his forehead. "That hurt!"

"Yeah, right," I retorted with a smirk. "The big bad bull rider got hurt? Maybe if you weren't so busy prowling for a date on your phone, you'd have seen it coming."

"I was not prowling for a date." Grady's guilty glance at his phone betrayed him.

"Yeah, you were," Rhett said from beside him, his blue eyes flickering towards Grady's phone screen. "I can see your phone."

Our laughter filled the truck until we opened our doors and stepped out into the fresh air.

"Okay, fine. I was. But you made me spill my drink all over your truck, so joke's on you." Grady threw his empty fast-food cup at me.

"Dammit." I bent to pick up the cup off the ground and tossed it into the truck with the rest of the garbage accumulated by life on the road.

"Ugh." Finn stretched his arms over his head. "I shouldn't have eaten that last burger."

"Your horse would agree," Grady said. "He's not going to like hauling your ass around tomorrow."

"Are you calling me fat?" Finn, who had always been lanky and lean, had filled out over the past couple of years, but slightly taller than my 6'1", it suited him fine.

"Not yet, but..." Grady shot Finn a knowing look.

Rhett and I smirked. We all ate a little too much fast food on the road, but driving from rodeo to rodeo, we didn't have a lot of options.

Finn and I had been partners since we were kids, and we'd always traveled together to rodeos. Last year, Grady and Rhett started joining us on the road to help save a bit of money. With the cost of gas, lodging, our horses, entry fees, and all the other expenses that came with the rodeo life, splitting cost between the four of us made things a little easier. The only way we made money was by winning, and I hadn't done a lot of that lately.

We stayed in cheap motels most of the time—the kind with half-lit neon signs and the rooms smelling like stale cigarettes. Whenever we could, we'd camp out under the stars, pitching a tent if the weather was good and the rodeo grounds allowed it. It wasn't luxurious, but it was our life, and we made it work.

"Let's go check the horses." I led the way towards the barns.

It was still fairly quiet on the grounds, but that would change soon as more trucks and trailers would pull in all afternoon.

"Are you seeing Kinsley tonight?" Grady asked.

For a second, my step faltered. "I told you guys. I'm done with all that."

"Yeah, you told us that, but we don't believe you," Finn said.

"I mean it. I'm done."

The guys exchanged glances, and my jaw clenched.

I had been in an on-and-off relationship with Kinsley Jackson for the last two years, but things had gotten complicated. We'd had a falling out the last time we were together, and I knew I hadn't handled it well. But as much as I cared for her, I couldn't help but think we were better off apart.

Now, with the new rodeo season starting, our paths would cross again. Our schedules would align for the next few months as we both traveled the same circuit. A part of me wished I could go south to compete and avoid the inevitable confrontation, but I knew I couldn't afford to be on my own. I needed the guys to make this work, to have any shot at making a living doing what I loved, and rodeo was all I knew how to do.

I'd just have to deal with Kinsley, be civil and professional, even if my heart felt anything but.

We entered the barn where the horses were stabled. I stopped in front of Drifter's stall, and he gave me a soft nicker.

"Hey, bud, how are you doing?"

I'd had Drifter since the day he was born. He was a big bay with a half moon crescent on his forehead and bred on my family's ranch. Best damn horse I'd ever ridden. I didn't have a ranch or a family anymore, but at least I still had him. He was the only family I needed—well, he and the guys.

I let myself in the stall and ran my hand down each of his legs; the trip had been long, and he had gone from the trailer straight to standing in a stall. His back legs felt a bit puffy. *What I wouldn't give for a grassy pasture to turn him out in.* I preferred him to live outside as much as possible, so he could keep himself moving, but that was difficult on the road.

"Let's go for a walk, buddy." I grabbed his halter from the hook and slipped it on over his ears.

He tossed his head a few times and pulled me towards the door of the stall, eager to be let out.

"He okay?" Finn came down the aisle towards me with a wheelbarrow and pitchfork.

"Yeah, he's fine. Needs to move and stretch his legs a bit."

Finn's scrutinising gaze wandered over my horse. "Are you su—"

"He's fine," I snapped and walked past him out the door.

Drifter wasn't just my horse; he was my livelihood. I made my living off his back, and if he wasn't okay, I was out of the rodeo. I couldn't afford to buy another horse, not with the tight margins we operated on.

There was a cool spring breeze, but the sun was trying hard to warm things up. I walked Drifter around for the better part of an hour, then found a patch of grass he approved of to let him graze–apparently, I wasn't the best judge of grass. While he grabbed mouthfuls, I lay down, letting his lead rope drop beside me—he wasn't going anywhere. I put my cowboy hat over my face, to block the sun from my eyes, but let it saturate the rest of me.

My mind was on my ride tomorrow.

Finn and I competed in team roping. It was a speed event where a steer got released from a chute, with us cowboys on either side. We raced after it, the header—Finn—roped the horns, and the heeler—I—roped the heels. The fastest time won.

There was a time where everyone touted us as the ones to beat and we were on our way to the big money. However, in the last couple of years, we'd hit a dry spell, and there didn't seem to be any rain in sight. If we couldn't start winning, I would have no choice but to quit. If I quit rodeo, I had nowhere to go.

I thought of the ranch. What I wouldn't give to have it back, call it mine, and have *something* to show for myself.

A winning streak, a sponsorship—those would turn things around for me. But I had to earn them on my own. I wouldn't take handouts because of whom I was dating. I wouldn't become Cal Jackson's puppet or Kinsley's project.

Rodeo was my life, my passion, and I'd worked too hard to get to where I was to let someone else call the shots. I needed to know that every win, every dollar I earned, was because of my own sweat and skills, not because of whom I knew or was sleeping with.

It was a matter of pride, sure, but it was more than that. It was about integrity, about being true to myself and the code I lived by. I'd seen too many guys get chewed up and spit out by this life, losing themselves. I wouldn't let that happen to me; I wouldn't compromise who I was for a quick buck or a moment of glory.

If I was going to make it, it would be on my own terms. I'd stand or fall by my own merits, and I'd do it with my head held high. That's just who I was, and no amount of money or fame could change that.

God, why did Kinsley have to be at this rodeo? She was nothing but a distraction—a beautiful, intoxicating distraction that turned my world upside down. I didn't want to admit to anyone that I missed her, but I did.

Warm breath hit my face. I lifted my hat and peered over at Drifter grazing right beside me.

"What do you think, boy? Is this our year? You and me; no girls allowed."

He gave a huff and a sneeze, spraying me with horse snot.

"Gee, thanks." I wiped my face on my sleeve. "Was that a yes or a no?"

A loud truck rolled by at that moment, blasting a Miranda Lambert song.

My stomach tied up in knots because I knew it was Kinsley; I could feel her presence in my bones.

Sure enough, I glimpsed long blonde hair whipping out of the driver's side window as the truck rambled over the gravel road next to our little patch of grass. My heart jumped in my chest. It was her truck, a black RAM Longhorn, but the trailer was new. A fancy brand-new Sundowner, complete with living quarters. I imagined what that thing had cost her daddy.

She focused on navigating through the bustling stable yard, so she didn't see us but would soon enough when she stopped to unload.

I rose to my feet and brushed the bits of grass off my jeans with my now sweaty palms. I needed to go hide or something.

I led Drifter back to the barn, going around the backside so I wouldn't run into her. The place was filling up, and voices—mostly gossip—carried through the air. I tried to tune it out, but when I heard Kinsley's name mentioned, I couldn't help myself; I paused outside a tack stall, where two girls were talking. They were barrel racers I didn't recognize.

"I can't believe she bought that horse!" one said.

"This is either going to make her unbeatable or take her out of the running altogether," the other responded.

On impulse, I barged into the stall. "What horse?" I demanded.

The two girls looked at me wide-eyed.

"What horse?"

"Uh, Mr. Lucky Gambler. He's, uh-uh—" the first girl stammered.

My pulse quickened, thrumming in my ears. "I know the one."

Fuck.

I turned and marched down the aisle, pulling Drifter along behind me.

Oh, I knew the horse. I saw him splatter Sherry what's-her-name into a barrel last year. That horse was dangerous. Everyone knew it.

What was Kinsley thinking?

Who was I kidding? I knew exactly what she was thinking.

Anything to win, right, Kins? Impulsive, reckless, and competitive-as-all hell girl.

I was so glad I was done with all her drama.

I put Drifter in his stall and tossed him a few flakes of hay and a scoop of his feed. After filling his water bucket, the anger I felt about Kinsley's foolishness still hadn't dissipated.

Maybe they'd had it wrong; maybe it was just a rumour. I had to see for myself.

I'll just wander over to the unloading area...

Chapter 3

WRANGLERS - MIRANDA LAMBERT

Kinsley

G ambler's kicking did not cease. It wasn't scared or even angry kicking. It was I'm-going-to-annoy-the-hell-out-of-Kins-
ley kicking. *Thank goodness for rubber-coated walls*, I thought for the
billionth time that trip, saving both my horse's legs and my trailer.

As I pulled into the rodeo grounds, I couldn't wait to get that horse
off the trailer and into a stall, then get out of earshot of him.

"You're a pain in the ass, Gambler!" I yelled back at him.

I put the truck into park in the lot outside the barns. Gambler let
out one last kick for good measure. I hopped out, the crunch of gravel
beneath my boots a familiar welcome. The scent of hay, horses, and
a hint of manure filled my nostrils, and I couldn't help the grin that
spread across my face.

This was where I belonged. This was my world, the place where I felt the most alive. The place where I could let everything else fall away and focus on my horses and my rides.

I took a deep breath, savouring the moment.

"It's about time you got here!" Maisey jogged over.

We hugged each other.

"How was the drive?" She tucked her straight shoulder-length brown hair behind her ears.

Maisey was a barrel racer, like me, so we were competitors in the arena but also best friends outside of it. We had an unspoken agreement to never let the sport come between us; no matter who won or lost, we'd always be there cheering each other on. Our friendship meant more to us than any buckle or title.

We'd grown up together on the rodeo circuit, spending long days training our horses side by side and pushing each other to be better riders. Sure, things got heated sometimes when we were neck and neck in a competition, with both of us competitive by nature. But at the end of the day, we left the rivalry in the arena. Win or lose, we'd crack open a couple of cold ones at the bar later, toasting to each other's success.

"Long," I said. "I need to get on a horse and *run*."

"Well, let's get you unloaded and saddle up!"

The kicking in the trailer grew louder and impatient. "Oh, enough already! I'll get you out."

"Is that him?" Maisey asked, her eyes round. She went up on her toes, trying to see through the small window of the trailer.

"Yep, letting the whole world know he's here." I rolled my eyes and walked to the back of the trailer.

"Geezus, Kinsley, what have you got in there, a dinosaur?" one of the rodeo regulars called from across the yard.

"Close enough!" I called back.

"She bought the demon horse!" Maisey shouted over to him.

"What? No way!" He strolled over. "Are you crazy?"

"I think demon is a bit of stretch." I unlocked the trailer.

Thanks to Maisey's announcement, more people wandered over to catch a glimpse of my monster.

Behave, I willed him as I opened the door.

His kicking stopped. He looked at me as if to say, *Finally.*

Gambler stood calmly, so I relaxed and unlatched his divider and secured it on the wall. I ran my hand down his neck and gave him a little scratch on his withers. It was his favourite spot.

"See, there's no reason to make a fuss; you're not new at this."

Originally, he'd trained for roping events and even did well for the cowboy who owned him, but then his speed caught the attention of the man's barrel racer wife, who retrained the horse. Gambler excelled at that too, but only when he wanted to. She got fed up with his moods and sold him. Sherry bought him and he really started getting a reputation, but we all knew how that had ended.

A lot of people would call me crazy for buying him, but I didn't care. I hadn't been able to resist him. Tall, dark, and handsome was just my type.

I tugged on the worn nylon lead rope, freeing it from the metal hook on the trailer wall, and urged Gambler to turn and follow me down the ramp. He suddenly leapt forward, charging out of the trailer in a blur, and pulled me along with him.

I barely had time to gasp before a large, calloused hand wrapped firmly around my bicep, halting what would have been an epic face-plant in the dirt. Gambler's lead rope was yanked from my grasp as I got pushed aside.

I stumbled, regaining my balance just in time to see Gambler's front hooves shoot upwards as he reared.

"Oh gawd, he is not rearing right now," I said under my breath, my heart pounding.

It couldn't get any worse than this, but one look at Wyatt Collins' hardened face as he held tight to Gambler's lead told me I was very wrong. His jaw was set, eyes blazing, and the muscles in his forearms corded from the effort of controlling my wild horse.

Yeah, this was definitely worse. Way worse. Wyatt Collins was pissed.

Here we go again, I thought. Not even a word to each other, and we were already in a fight.

"Hey, hey." His voice was deep, low, and soothing. But he was talking to the horse, not me.

I was staring like an idiot because no one had ever looked as good in a pair of Wrangler jeans as that man.

Wyatt was tall and tanned from the countless hours he spent outside on the back of a horse., He kept His thick dark brown hair—windswept from riding—pushed back off his forehead, the unruly locks held in place by his cowboy hat.

Wyatt's face bore a serious, intense expression, his deep brown eyes shadowed under a furrowed brow that never seemed to fully relax. His angular features and defined jawline gave him an edgy, grave look that was almost dangerous in its intensity.

He intimidated most people with his silent, brooding manner, but I always felt safe and grounded in his presence, reassured by his solid strength. With Wyatt, I was always cared for and protected. No matter how chaotic the world, he was my shelter from the storm. But right now, he looked like he *was* the storm.

Gambler came down and stood quietly, whatever he had flipped out about forgotten.

Pain-in-the-ass horse.

A small crowd had gathered around to take in the show.

I stalked over and tried to grab the lead from Wyatt, but he pulled it away.

"Give me my horse, Wyatt."

"I've got him."

"Wyatt," I warned.

"Get Cher off the trailer. Or have you forgotten about her now that you have a shiny, new horse?"

"Of course not," I seethed. What an arrogant asshat.

"What barn are you in?"

I hesitated a moment and glanced around at the people watching and whispering to each other. I pointed at the barn closest to us. Wyatt nodded and started leading Gambler towards it.

I looked for Maisey and found her, brow furrowed in concern.

Are you okay? she mouthed to me.

I nodded, then sighed and went back into the trailer to grab Cherokee. When I got into the barn, Wyatt already had Gambler in his stall and was filling his water bucket.

"Thanks," I mumbled, leading Cher into the stall next to him and taking off her halter.

"What the hell were you thinking?" he almost yelled.

"What are you talking about?" Startled, I looked up at him.

His face was hard and cold. "What would possess you to buy this horse?" He stepped closer to me, the muscles in his neck tense as he glared at me.

"Some of us like winning," I snapped.

It was a low blow. His jaw clenched, but he said nothing.

"I'm sorry, I didn't mean that," I sighed heavily, waving off my comment.

Wyatt was an incredible cowboy, but the last couple of years—basically, since we met—he'd been inconsistent in the arena. He'd been through a lot during that time, though, mostly with his dad. It was just bad luck, not a reflection of his skill.

"Yeah, you did." I opened my mouth to protest, but he spoke again. "He's dangerous, Kins," he said almost too softly.

I toed at the wood shavings around my feet. "He's a good horse. I can handle him." I bit the inside of my cheek.

Wyatt took off his hat and dragged his hand through his dark hair, blowing out a breath of air. He paced back and forth in front of the stall a few times.

I exited Cher's stall, hanging her halter on the hook beside the door.

Wyatt continued his pacing. He'd wear a trench in the dirt by the time he worked out whatever was going through his head.

I leaned against the door, crossing my arms over my chest. Apparently, I wasn't done waiting for Wyatt Collins to get his shit together.

He stopped and looked at me for a few seconds, then went back to pacing, tenser than a freshly tightened wire fence. He stopped, lifted his hat, and dragged his fingers through his hair yet again before placing the hat back on his head. "I don't like this."

"What? This?" I gestured to me and him. "Or this?" This time, I gestured to me and Gambler.

"The horse!" He threw up his hands, clearly exasperated with me, which was nothing new.

"Well then, it's a good thing we're not dating anymore, so it's none of your damn business!"

"Fuck, Kinsley!" He put his hands behind his neck and closed his eyes, his mouth drawn into a hard line.

"I appreciate your concern, Wyatt, but this isn't your problem. There is no problem. I'm going to ride Gambler, and I'm going to win."

We spent a few agonizing moments standing there, staring at each other. These moments allowed me to remember what it was like when those deep brown eyes looked at me like I was the only person in the world who mattered. The way his gaze bore into mine made my breath catch in my throat.

I couldn't tear my eyes from his. My heart raced for him once again, pounding against my ribcage as if it wanted to escape and close the distance between us. I ached to go to him, feel his strong arms wrap around me once more, and breathe in his familiar leather-and-pine scent. It had been months since I'd felt the comfort of his embrace, the safety and warmth only he provided.

My feet itched to move and take that step towards him. I wanted to tell him I missed him, that I still wanted him, that maybe we could make it work this time.

But before I gathered the courage to move, Wyatt shifted, his boots scraping against the barn's dirt floor. He took a step back, then another, his eyes never leaving mine. "Good luck out there." His voice was low. "Be careful with that horse." With that, he turned and walked away, his broad shoulders disappearing through the barn door.

I sank to the ground, my back sliding down the rough wooden wall of Gambler's stall. My knees pulled up to my chest as I wrapped my arms around them, trying to hold myself together.

The realization hit me like a ton of bricks—I wasn't over Wyatt. Not even close.

Chapter 4

You Proof - Morgan Wallen

Wyatt

I was so screwed. Did I think it would be easy to see her again? To see her and then walk away from her?

I couldn't believe she'd bought that damn horse. Gambler was a ticking time bomb, and she was playing with fire. Did she have any idea how dangerous he was? How capable he was of hurting her? The thought made my stomach roil.

Even as I fumed, I couldn't help but be drawn to the wildfire that burned so brightly within her. It was the same fire that had attracted me to her in the first place, that fearless, unstoppable spirit that made her take on challenges others would balk at.

I wanted to shake some sense into her, make her see the risks she was taking, but I knew Kinsley. She was stubborn as a mule and twice as headstrong.

I ran a hand through my hair, frustration coursing through me. I should've stayed away and let her handle Gambler on her own, but the thought of her getting hurt...

As I neared the campsite, the guys were all gathered around a fire, their tents pitched in the background.

"Hey, slacker, we set up your tent for you," Grady announced, pulling a hot dog on a stick from the fire. "You're welcome."

"Thanks." I sank into a folding chair with a heavy sigh, resting my head in my hand.

"Oh, bad mood. So, how's Kinsley?" Finn prodded.

The group shared an amused glance.

"She got a new horse," I said.

"Oh, yeah?" Grady asked.

"Mr. Lucky Gambler." The weight of those words settled like a stone in my stomach.

"Oh, shit," they chorused.

Silence fell over us then, broken only by the crackling fire. They understood what that girl meant to me—they'd had front row seats to the show—even if I kept denying it.

"You know," Grady started as we all sat around the campfire. "I think we're all going to see a lot more action with the ladies this year without Kinsley Jackson around."

I couldn't help but raise an eyebrow at him. "How do you figure that?" I was curious about where he was going with this.

"I'm glad you asked, Wyatt." Grady pointed his finger at me as if he was about to reveal one of the world's great mysteries. "I mean, Kinsley's great and all, but let's be honest—she's intimidating as hell."

There was no denying that. Kinsley had a way about her, like a force of nature, and yet she was every bit as graceful as a wild rose. Her eyes, strikingly blue, reminded me of the endless Alberta skies and could shift from fierce determination to playful mischief in a heartbeat. And that focus of hers was razor-sharp, whether she was racing barrels or fixing a broken fence. But it was her smile that captivated me, warm and bright enough to chase away the shadows. From the moment I first saw it, I was a goner.

Grady continued, oblivious to my trip down memory lane. "So, when she's on your arm and you're hanging out with us, it's like she scares all the other girls away. Now, when the four of us walk into a bar, the ladies will flock to us. Let me tell you." Grady leaned back in his chair, nodding his head like he'd made the most profound revelation.

The absurdity of his statement had us all bursting into laughter.

"You'll see," he said. "I'm right."

"I've had no trouble in that department," Rhett said.

Grady leaned in, scrutinizing Rhett with a puzzled frown. "That's what I don't get about you. You barely say a word all night, but despite that, you leave with someone's number."

"You ever think that the talking is your problem?" Rhett asked him.

Finn and I covered our mouths, trying hard not to laugh.

"No," Grady deadpanned.

We all lost the battle against laughter. Leave it to Grady to lighten the mood.

A couple of hours by the campfire with the guys was exactly what I needed to clear my head. I hit the sack feeling a lot better, deciding to focus solely on my rides the next day.

Drifter was stiff coming out of his stall the next morning, so I got him tacked up early and took him for a jog in the warm-up area to loosen his muscles. It took a bit, but soon enough, he was moving smoothly under me.

"How's he doing?" Finn rode up on his grey gelding, Ghost.

"He's good."

Ghost fell into step beside us. They were a well-matched team.

We pushed the horses up into a faster gait and circled the arena wide. As Finn and I loped around the perimeter, I couldn't help the excitement building in my chest. The rodeo grounds were coming to life around us: the sound of hooves against the dirt, the distant lowing of cattle, and the chatter of cowboys and cowgirls getting in some extra practice. The sun was just peeking over the horizon.

Finn pulled up beside me, his face serious. "Is your head in the game, Wyatt?" His blue eyes searched mine. "We need this win."

I met his gaze steadily. "I'm here, Finn. I'm focused."

We both knew how important this rodeo was. A win here meant the difference between money in our pockets or leaving empty-handed. I couldn't blame him for being worried. We used to be a solid team, regularly in the money, but then I met Kinsley and our luck changed. I had let her distract me in the past, and I had let Finn down. He'd eventually made peace with me dating her because he knew how much I loved her, but he had reason to think my mind was elsewhere when she was around.

"Good." He lingered in the quiet for a heartbeat longer than usual. "I think this is my last year on the circuit."

Surprise jolted through me, and I pivoted to face him, searching his expression for an explanation. "What do you mean?" I pressed.

He gave a casual shrug. "My folks, they're not up for the barn work much longer, and they're considering selling the place. Can't let that happen."

"You're going to take over? Full-time, with the boarding, lessons, and everything that goes with it?" I tried to picture Finn, with his love for independence, trading it all for day-to-day boarding barn management and teaching kids to ride.

"Yeah, I guess so," he muttered, his gaze fixed on something in the distance and deliberately avoiding mine.

"Is that really what you want?" I probed deeper.

Finn's passion for rodeo wasn't something easily set aside. It was in his blood, the same as it was in mine.

"All I know is that I don't want to lose the farm."

That, at least, I understood. The day my old man sold our ranch was the worst day of my life. I thought it would always be there, that it would be mine one day, but my dad had pulled the rug out from under me and, in a flash, it was all gone.

"Alright," I said, "I guess we better make this year count."

Our last year together riding as a team. I couldn't imagine doing this without Finn. Would I even try? Honestly, I didn't know if Drifter and I had much left to give. What did my future look like without rodeo? Thinking about it was like staring into a black hole. I had a lot to figure out.

Finn nodded. "We make it count," he echoed.

Chapter 5

THE RIDE - CHRIS LEDOUX

Wyatt

F inn and I strolled through the rodeo grounds, soaking up the surroundings we knew so well. We were in our element, a world that made sense when everything else was upside down.

Familiar gravelly voices caught my attention, drifting over from a worn wooden picnic table in a patch of shade. "Hey there, Collins! Winter! Get yer asses over here!"

Finn shot me a sidelong glance, and I shrugged. When the old-timers called, you answered. These faded cowboys might be retired, but they were walking encyclopedias in rodeo history and life on the circuit.

As we approached, a wave of nostalgia washed over me at the sight of their weathered faces carved with wrinkles earned from decades under the relentless prairie sun. These men had been bull riders, bronc riders, ropers, and even clowns back in their day. Now, they just lingered at the rodeos, chewing tobacco and swapping tales that got more embellished every year.

I imagined Finn and me riding until we physically couldn't anymore and then being the ones sitting here, reliving the good old days over and over. It was not an idea that excited me. I wanted more than that. A home. A family.

I pushed the thought out of my mind.

"Have a seat, boys," Big Jim rasped, patting the bench beside him. Despite his advanced age, a lively spark still danced in his pale blue eyes.

We slid onto the bench, and I could already feel the conversation sliding in a direction I wanted to avoid, as it always did with this crowd. Nothing was off limits or too personal for these guys.

"Seen your daddy lately, Wyatt?" Big Jim asked, his face crinkling like an old road map.

The old-timers were blunt and didn't beat around the bush. They asked what they wanted to ask, oblivious to anyone's feelings.

"No, sir. Jake... He's been gone a while." I tried to keep my voice steady. Dragging up memories of Jake Collins was like ripping off a scab before the wound healed.

"Damn shame, that." Big Jim shook his head with genuine regret. "Your father was one hell of a cowboy. Best damn roper I ever saw until—"

"Until he took up drinking and gambling," another cowboy chimed in. "We all like our whiskey, but ya got to know when to draw the line. Sad to see a good man fall like that."

A chorus of solemn nods and murmurs of agreement rippled through the gathered cowboys.

Finn gave me a sympathetic smile.

"Yeah," I muttered. "He was good, once." My jaw clenched as a knot formed in my gut.

"Married a city girl, didn't he? That's where he went wrong, I tell ya," another man added, his voice tinged with a knowing sadness. "Couldn't handle the ranch life. Took off and left him to his vices."

I dropped my gaze, unable to meet their eyes as flashes of memories assaulted me—the sound of my mother's suitcases thumping down the stairs as she fled in the night when I was just a kid, then Jake stumbling home late, reeking of cheap whiskey and even cheaper perfumes.

Thanks for reminding me, guys. I swallowed hard against the lump forming in my throat. I had been so young then, too young to understand why she left or why my dad spiraled out of control afterward.

"Used to have that little cattle farm, right?" Big Jim continued, oblivious to my discomfort. "Heard it got sold a while back. You ever think about getting it back? A man's gotta have some land."

Every day, I thought but didn't say. Instead, I nodded.

The dream of reclaiming my family's farm was always at the back of my mind. I imagined what it would be like to have Kinsley there, her laughter filling the wide-open spaces. But I quickly shoved that thought away. We were done, and there was no use dwelling on what couldn't be.

Finn jumped in. "Wyatt's doing fine on the circuit. He's got his sights set on bigger things now."

I appreciated Finn's attempt to steer the conversation away from the past. He knew all too well how much I struggled with my family history and losing the farm.

"Yeah, the circuit's been good to us," I agreed, forcing a smile I didn't quite feel. "But you never know what the future holds."

That seemed to satisfy the old cowboys, who launched into another wild tale.

As the sun stretched higher in the sky, I looked out across the arena. Rodeo was more than a sport; it was a community, a family. But even surrounded by friends and legends, a part of me felt like an outsider, carrying the weight of a legacy I wasn't sure I'd ever fulfill.

"Well, speaking of riding, we better get moving. Thanks for the stories, gentlemen." I stood up. "Big day tomorrow."

Finn rose as well, tipping his cowboy hat to the old guys. "Always a pleasure, gentlemen. I'll try to remember to send flowers next time."

A chorus of hearty guffaws followed us as we stepped away, their howls of amusement still ringing in my ears. I grinned and shook my head. Finn always had a way with those old codgers. He already fit in well with the senior crowd.

I caught sight of Kinsley across the grounds, her blonde hair shining in the sun as she laughed with some friends. A pang of longing hit me. The sight of her still made my heart kick against my ribcage in a way it shouldn't.

Finn and I navigated through the dwindling crowd, each lost in our thoughts, when a figure caught our attention.

Rhett stood a little way off, isolated from the rest of the rodeo's festivities. His phone was pressed to his ear, and even from a distance, the strain in his posture was clear. He paced back and forth, his movements sharp and agitated—very unlike his usual easygoing demeanour.

Finn nudged me, nodding towards Rhett. "Wonder what's got him all riled up," he murmured.

Rhett ended his call with a frustrated swipe. He rubbed a hand over his jaw—a gesture of stress we rarely saw from him.

I shrugged. "No idea. He never talks about his life away from the rodeo."

I was ashamed to admit that, even though we considered him a close friend, we knew little about him. We knew his record in the arena but nothing about his home, his family, or what he did when he wasn't throwing himself into the chaos of the rodeo circuit. It was odd, considering how much time we spent together travelling from one competition to the next, sharing wins and losses.

"Kind of strange, isn't it?" I said. "We see him almost every day, yet there's so much we don't know about him."

"I remember when he competed. It's been a long time, but damn was he good."

"Makes you think, doesn't it?" I said. "A guy like Rhett, with all that talent, just up and quits."

Rhett had given up competing years ago. No one knew why. The only reason he'd given was that he preferred the steady paycheck he got from working as a pickup man. We hadn't known him well back then—not that we did now—but we hadn't really been friends until this past year when he started travelling with us.

Rhett noticed us then, quickly masking his previous frustration with a practiced smile. He waved, walking over with a casual stride that hid the tension we'd witnessed.

"Everything alright?" I asked as he approached, trying to keep my voice neutral.

Rhett's smile didn't quite reach his eyes. "Yeah, family stuff. You know how it is."

We didn't know. Despite the countless days and nights spent together on the road, Rhett remained a mystery.

He glanced between Finn and me. "What about you two? Ready to show these folks what real roping looks like?"

I forced a grin, trying to match Rhett's lighthearted tone. "Absolutely."

Even as the words left my mouth, a flicker of doubt crept into my mind. The pressure to perform left me feeling like I was in quicksand, and I would just keep sinking. I needed a win, not just for the prize money but to prove to myself that I still had what it took to make it in this sport.

Rhett's gaze lingered on me for a moment as if he sensed my inner turmoil, but he didn't press the issue. Instead, he nodded towards the arena. "Well, I better get back to work. I have to be in the arena for the bronc riding."

I turned to Finn. "Let's go check on the horses, make sure they're ready for tomorrow."

Finn nodded, and we made our way towards the stables. The scent of hay and horse sweat filled my nostrils, grounding me in the moment. This was what I lived for—the thrill of the ride, the rush of the competition.

As I ran my hand along Drifter's flank, feeling the power and strength beneath his coat, I couldn't shake the nagging fear that I wasn't good enough anymore. That maybe my best days were behind me, and all that lay ahead was a slow, painful decline.

No, I thought, clenching my jaw. *I can do this. I* have to *do this.*

I had to believe that tomorrow would be different and I would turn things around. Because if I didn't, I didn't know how much longer I could keep going, keep chasing this dream that slipped further away with each passing day.

Chapter 6

IF I WAS A COWBOY - MIRANDA LAMBERT

Kinsley

Gambler was on edge. I sat hard in the saddle, gripping the reins until my knuckles turned white. I tried to walk him to the arena for our run, but he was bouncing around, pleading to be let loose. As we neared the arena, his agitation worsened.

A cowboy strode over and grabbed a rein, helping me steady him.

"Hey, Rhett," I said, trying to sound casual.

"Kinsley." Rhett tipped his hat, but his focus never left Gambler.

"What brings you here?" My left leg pressed against Gambler to prevent him from running Rhett over.

"Just helping out," he said, his voice steady.

"He didn't send you, did he?" A hint of suspicion entered my voice.

"I can't say I know what you're talking about," Rhett replied, but I caught a faint smile under his cowboy hat.

"Then I guess I owe you one, handsome." I winked at him as he guided us to the starting position.

"You sure about this?" He looked from Gambler to the arena.

"As sure as I'll ever be." I forced a confident smile onto my face despite the nerves twisting my stomach into knots.

I was never nervous before a ride. With Cher, I always knew what to expect.

We took our place in the long chute that led to the arena. I heard the announcer call my name over the booming loudspeaker, the sound echoing through the packed venue. I nodded to Rhett, signaling for him to release his grip on Gambler's bridle.

With the slightest nudge of my boot, Gambler sprang into motion, his powerful muscles propelling us towards the first barrel with a burst of speed that took my breath away. The wind whipped through my hair, and the adrenaline pumped through my veins as we raced across the arena. As we approached the barrel, I realized Gambler was shooting past it, losing those precious milliseconds that could make all the difference between victory and defeat in barrel racing.

"Damn it," I cursed under my breath, quickly correcting our path with a squeeze of my inside leg but slowing in the process.

Gambler responded, running to and pivoting around the second barrel with agility and precision. We flew towards the third barrel, determination burning in both of us to make up for lost time. Gambler's muscles strained beneath me as he gave it his all, but it would not be enough. As we crossed the finish line, I couldn't shake the sinking feeling in my bones that our time was too slow.

A wave of disappointment and frustration replaced the rush of the ride. We could do better than this, and the thought of letting down my family, especially my dad, was almost too much to bear. I pictured the inevitable photos that would surface later—my scowling face broadcast across rodeo news sites and social media. The frustration threatened to boil over, but I fought to compose myself as we made our way out of the arena, not wanting to show even a hint of weakness in front of the crowd. I could feel all the critical eyes on me and hear the whispers.

There would be plenty of time later to analyse what had gone wrong and how I could improve for the next competition. For now, I had to hold my head high despite the bitter taste of failure on my tongue.

I pulled Gambler up as I checked our time. It was worse than I'd thought.

"It's the first run. You'll do better tomorrow." Rhett came up beside me and took Gambler's reins as I dismounted.

"I lost it from the start," I admitted, deflated.

"Yep," he agreed, his honesty stinging a bit.

"Thanks for the vote of confidence," I half-joked. I should have focused on Gambler instead of flirting, even if it was in fun.

"He's new to you. You both need to learn each other's ways. You weren't ready for that, but keep at it, and you'll get there," Rhett advised, his voice firm but encouraging.

He was right. With Cherokee, I anticipated her every move, and she read me just as well. I'd been naïve to think Gambler and I would have that same connection so soon.

Rhett walked with me to cool Gambler down. I opened my mouth to speak but shut it before the words came out.

"Go ahead and ask." Rhett's voice was gentle.

"How's Wyatt really doing?" I asked, grateful for the opening.

"He's okay, but Drifter's slowing down, and he doesn't want to face it."

"Do you think Drifter needs to retire?"

"I do," he confirmed my fears.

Wyatt would be devastated. That horse was his world. He *needed* him.

"Wyatt thinks winning again will solve all his problems, but not on that horse."

"So, what's next?"

"He won't let anyone help," Rhett said, echoing the frustration I'd felt countless times. Wyatt had refused sponsorship from my family, which would've covered his expenses.

Stubborn man.

Maisey rode up on her palomino mare, Lexie. "Tough ride," she said to me, then turned to Rhett with a rosy blush to her pale cheeks. "Hey, Rhett."

He tipped his hat to her, and her flush deepened.

"I'll beat you tomorrow, though," I teased her. She would beat my time today easily.

"We'll see," Maisey replied, her confidence shining through. "I'm aiming to win a new saddle. Coming to watch?"

"Of course." I smiled. "Rhett?"

"Yeah, I'll come," he agreed.

"Great! Umm, I better get going," Maisey said, a hint of nervousness in her voice as she turned Lexie towards the arena.

I chuckled. "You're quite the heartthrob, Rhett."

"I am not," he protested, his cheeks tinting with a blush.

"So modest. It's adorable." I nudged him playfully.

"Stop." He laughed, his rare smile breaking through.

We watched the rest of the barrel racing together, Gambler now calmly standing at my side. Maisey was up next, and she flew through the pattern, setting a new fastest time.

"Wow," Rhett exclaimed. "That was impressive."

"Yeah, she's going to be hard to beat this year," I admitted with a twinge of jealousy. I was proud of Maisey, but I wanted to be the one impressing everyone. "Guess I have some catching up to do." I chewed the inside of my cheek.

As I led Gambler back to the stables, doubt crept in.

Had I rushed him into competition too soon? We weren't ready—that much was clear from our disastrous run. But I couldn't let one poor performance shake my confidence. We needed more time to get in sync, to learn each other's rhythms and cues.

I brushed Gambler down, my hands moving mechanically as my mind raced.

Maybe I should have stuck with Cherokee for this rodeo. She was reliable. We had a connection that came from years of working together. But Gambler... He was something special. I felt it in the way he moved; the power coiled in his muscles. We would figure out how to harness it.

"You'll do better next time," I murmured to him, running my hand along his neck.

He snorted as if in agreement. I smiled despite myself. We were a team now, for better or worse.

I thought back to what Rhett had said about Wyatt and Drifter. The idea of Wyatt losing his beloved horse made my heart ache in a way I didn't want to examine too closely. But I couldn't dwell on that now. I had my own challenges to focus on.

As I finished up with Gambler and headed back to my trailer, I pushed away the lingering doubts. So what if we'd had a rough start? Every partnership had its growing pains. We'd do better next time; I was sure of it. And if not, we'd keep trying until we got it right. I wasn't one to back down from a challenge, and Gambler was worth the effort.

I climbed into my trailer, the exhaustion of the day catching up with me. Tomorrow was a new day, a new chance to prove ourselves. And we'd take it, one ride at a time.

Chapter 7

OVER YOU - MIRANDA LAMBERT

Wyatt

No time.

The steer came out of the chute straight. Finn roped the horns beautifully and turned him just right, but I wasn't where I was supposed to be and I missed the hind feet. I was a second too late, but in this sport, every second mattered.

"And that is no time for Finn Winter and Wyatt Collins. Tough start for a usually consistent team," the announcer said over the loudspeaker.

Finn didn't look at me as we rode our horses out of the arena. I saw the disappointment on his face.

"I'm sorry. That was all on me. I'm not sure what—"

"It's fine," he said. "It happens."

I hated letting him down, especially since this was his last season on the circuit. Finn had been talking about retiring, but he wanted to go out on a high note.

As we dismounted, frustration clouded his eyes.

"Hey, I'm sorry about that. I don't know what happened, I—"

"Wyatt, I told you it's fine," Finn cut me off, his voice terse. "It's not the end of the world. We've had bad runs before."

I nodded, knowing he was right, but the guilt still weighed on me. Finn had been my best friend since we were kids rodeoing together. I couldn't stand the thought of letting him down, especially with his retirement looming. Or, our retirement, I should say...

"What the hell was that, Collins?" Travis Andersen, a long-time rival and not someone I wanted to see, strolled towards us with a couple of his buddies, smirking.

Ignoring him, we dismounted, and I hooked the stirrup around the horn to loosen the cinch.

"I knew your career was going down the drain, but after that performance, I think you're officially in the shitter."

My shoulders tensed, and I pulled them back. Finn caught my eye over the horses and gave a slight shake of his head.

"Word is Kinsley Jackson is done with you too. Can't say I blame her. Maybe she's ready to trade up for a winner."

"Shut up, Travis," I growled, my patience wearing thin.

But Travis was just getting started. "Or maybe it's not Kinsley. Maybe you're the one who can't keep up with her. I hear she's quite the handful in and out of the arena, if you know what I mean."

My blood boiled at his insinuation. "Watch your mouth, Andersen."

"Or what, Collins? You gonna miss me like you missed that steer?" Travis laughed, his buddies joining in. "Face it, you're washed up. Finished. It's only a matter of time before everyone else sees it too."

I wasn't a very aggressive guy, but it'd been one thing after another and I was ready to let something give. I turned to Travis, my fists balled up and ready.

Finn raced around the horses and put a hand to my chest, pushing me back. "Calm down, Wyatt."

Travis and his friends laughed.

"You wanna fight, Collins? I'm ready. After I leave you in the dirt, maybe I'll take a crack at that little barrel racer of yours and see what all the fuss is about."

"Dream on, Andersen." Her voice cut through me.

Of course, she had to show up at that moment. Kinsley walked over with Maisey, Rhett, and Grady.

"I'm not looking for a date, and if I were, I wouldn't be looking in your direction." She stood beside me, and her hand slid around my forearm. Her touch was both calming and igniting at the same time. She slipped her hand into mine.

Travis's gaze dipped to where our hands held. "Unbelievable." Travis shook his head. "You're going to regret hitching your cart to that loser one day, Kinsley."

"I'll be the judge of that." She squeezed my hand. Her skin was hot on mine, like it was about to catch fire, but I hung on and fixed Travis with a cool stare.

Travis and his friends left.

I ripped my hand from Kinsley's. I fought the urge to look down, sure I would see it scalded. "I didn't ask for your help, Kinsley."

"Of course not," she said dryly. "You would never ask for help. And God forbid somebody tries."

I clenched my jaw, the muscles tightening in my neck. "I don't need it." I took a step back.

Kinsley matched my movement and closed the distance between us again. "You do! You need help! Your horse does!" She gestured at Drifter.

"What the hell are you talking about?"

"Can't you feel him hesitate, coming out of the box? He can't get himself moving quickly enough anymore. That's why you missed today."

I shook my head. "You don't know what you're talking about."

"Oh, really? Ask your friends. Go ahead." She stepped back and held up her hands, gesturing to the surrounding group.

I glanced around at the guys, but they were all facing the ground, not saying a word.

"C'mon, guys, tell her she's wrong. Drifter is fine. It was an off day."

"I'm sorry, man." Finn stepped towards me.

I held up a hand, stopping him.

"I wanted to—"

"Don't." I looked over at Drifter. Kinsley was at his head, rubbing her hand over his face, and he was trying to get in her pocket where he knew she always kept some horse treats. *Traitor horse.*

I studied him. He was in good shape, had good weight, and was well-muscled. Had I hurt him? Was I hurting him? I replayed our rides in my head, searching for clues.

"He's getting older, Wyatt," Kinsley said quietly. "It's some old-timer stiffness. You have done nothing wrong." She knew me too well. Her gaze was on me, tears glistening in her eyes.

We stayed like that for a few long moments, Drifter grazing beside us. We didn't even notice that everyone else had walked away.

I didn't know what to say, so we stood there awkwardly, watching Drifter nibble at the grass. The sun beat down on the back of my neck, beads of sweat trickling beneath the collar of my shirt.

I could feel Kinsley's eyes on me, studying my face and searching for a reaction. My throat tightened; a lump that made it hard to swallow forming. I clenched my jaw, the muscles twitching beneath my skin as I fought to keep my emotions in check.

Kinsley stood perfectly still, her posture tense and guarded as if she was afraid one wrong move might shatter the fragile truce between us. The only sounds were the rodeo crowd's distant chatter and Drifter's content munching. He was oblivious to the tension crackling in the air.

"I should get him put away." I gave Drifter's reins a little tug, getting his attention away from the food, and he reluctantly followed me.

Kinsley fell into step beside us, her arm brushing against mine with each stride, sending sparks skittering across my skin.

"If you want to get the vet to... I mean, I could—"

Whatever she was going to offer, I didn't want to hear it.

I didn't want her rescuing me, so I interrupted her. "I'll figure it out," I said, my voice firm.

Kinsley's blue eyes searched my face, protest forming on her lips. She wanted to push me, convince me to accept her offer of help, but something in my expression must have stopped her. I saw the frustration and concern warring in her gaze, the way her brow furrowed as if she was physically biting back the words threatening to spill out. Pressing her mouth into a thin line, she swallowed back the argument I knew was on the tip of her tongue.

I felt a pang of guilt at shutting her down, but I refused to back down. This was my problem to handle, my mess to clean up. I would figure this out on my own, even as a small voice in the back of my mind wondered if I was making a mistake.

Kinsley's eyes searched my face a moment longer, likely looking for a crack in my resolve, but I kept my expression carefully neutral, and she gave a small nod of acceptance. Disappointment flickered across her face—there one moment and gone the next, replaced by a mask of composure.

"Right, okay." She moved to leave.

Suddenly, I couldn't stand the thought of her walking away. "How was your ride today?" I blurted, stopping her in her tracks.

She turned back to me, then rolled her eyes dramatically. "Ugh, a total disaster. Gambler and I are still trying to get on the same page."

I couldn't help the smirk that played across my lips at her exasperated tone. "The great Kinsley Jackson, struggling to handle a horse?"

"Oh, can it, Collins," she fired back, but there was no real venom behind her words. In fact, her bright eyes sparkled with amusement at our familiar back-and-forth. "Says the cowboy who couldn't even stay on the mechanical bull at Rhett's birthday party last year."

"Hey now, that bull was rigged!" I protested with a laugh. "Besides, I seem to recall you couldn't stop staring at this cowboy's ... skills ... that night."

The words hung between us, reigniting the lingering sparks of heated awareness that still crackled in the air whenever we got too close.

Kinsley's cheeks flushed, but she didn't look away and held my gaze boldly. "Well, you put on quite the show, cowboy." Her tone took on a sultry lilt. "As I recall, you rode me pretty hard later that night too."

It was my turn to feel the warmth of a blush creeping up my neck at her brazenly flirtatious words. Kinsley had never been shy. She said things that could bring me to my knees in an instant.

"Is that so?" I replied roughly, unable to resist playing along. "The way I remember it, you're the one who couldn't get enough—"

"Okay, okay!" Kinsley laughed as she held up her hands in surrender. "Let's just agree that we were both pretty ... insatiable back in the day."

The words "back in the day" caused a pang in my chest—a reminder of everything that had gone wrong between us despite our intense physical connection. As easily as we fell into this teasing affection, we always seemed to find our way to the same stumbling blocks that made our relationship crumble in the long run.

Some of that must've shown on my face because Kinsley's expression sobered, her smile slipping. We walked a few paces in tense silence before she finally spoke again. "You know, I missed this."

When I shot her a quizzical look, she waved a hand between us.

"The talking, joking, driving each other crazy..." A wistful smile played across her lips. "We were pretty good at that, weren't we?"

"Among other things," I agreed softly.

There had been times when Kinsley and just ... fit. When our combative energies aligned into something electric and intoxicating. Until real life got in the way, of course. Our dreams, our ambitions, our vastly different upbringings—they all eventually wedged an impassable divide between us, no matter how strong the physical connection was.

Kinsley's smiled turned melancholic. "Yeah, well, I guess we were good at some things but not so much at making it last, huh?"

The words struck me like a slap, not because they were cruel but because they rang so utterly true. Despite the spark that still burned between us, despite the comfort her presence brought me, Kinsley and I were a lighted match in a drought-stricken field. Eventually, we would burn everything in sight.

"I guess not," I agreed. The rueful moment between us shattered, bringing us crashing back to reality. "Which is why we're better off staying away."

Kinsley's shoulders slumped, but she still mustered up a tight smile and gave a small nod of acceptance. "Right. We just— We don't work."

"No, we don't," I said, more to convince myself than anything because, somewhere deep down, a nagging part of me wondered if that was really true. If Kinsley and I were just too stubborn to figure this out and make it last. Maybe if we just...

I shoved that thought aside, tucking it into a box on a shelf in my mind to let it gather dust. What-ifs and lingering thoughts wouldn't do either of us any favours. Kinsley and I had tried and failed. It was well past time we accepted that reality and moved on from the idea of there being an "us".

Still, I couldn't stop my gaze from dropping to her mouth one last time, remembering how her lips felt against mine and how her body felt pressed against me. With a silent curse, I gave myself a mental shake.

Pulling away was the right call, no matter how my body and heart might protest. Kinsley and I simply didn't work as a couple—at least, not in any lasting, permanent way. It was time I accepted that bitter truth once and for all.

"I got to get this guy put away for the night." I gestured to Drifter patiently standing at my side.

Kinsley nodded slowly, chewing the inside of her cheek. "Okay, well, I should get going anyway. I'll see you around, Wyatt." She hurried off before I could say anything else.

"Bye, Kinsley," I said, even though she was already out of earshot.

I got Drifter back to his stall and untacked him. I ran my hands slowly over each of his legs, checking for heat or swelling, but he felt good. "What are we going to do, old man?"

His ear flicked my way, and he eyed me as if to say, *Who are you calling an old man?*

I had no idea what I was going to do. Should I even ride him tomorrow and finish up this rodeo? Then what?

Damn, my life was a mess.

I filled Drifter's water bucket and tossed him hay and a scoop of grain. I wanted a bed to hide in until all my problems went away, but I would settle for my tent and a sleeping bag that night. When I woke up tomorrow, all my problems would still be there.

Chapter 8

VICE - MIRANDA LAMBERT

Wyatt

T he next morning, I decided a vet needed to check out Drifter to be sure he was okay. I didn't want him to suffer any more than he already had, so I made the call to one of the rodeo vets on-site.

Dr. Lawson looked Drifter over and said all his vitals were normal. He felt around his legs for heat and swelling and took him through a series of exercises. After a thorough examination, the vet told me that Drifter was getting older and might be developing a mild arthritis. I could still ride him, and light exercise would be good for him, but I would probably need to step back from competing because he wouldn't be able to go as hard as he used to.

The news didn't come as a surprise but hearing it out loud still stung a bit. It was the end of an era. My life with Drifter as my rodeo partner was ending.

The vet handed me the bill for the exam, and I shoved it in my pocket without looking at it. It would be more than I had in my bank account. I would deal with it later.

I thanked the vet for his time and gave Drifter one last pat on the neck before heading back to the camp with a heavy heart.

"What did the vet say?" Finn asked when I got back.

"Exactly what we thought—old age and arthritis." I sat down on a chair in front of the embers that remained from the fire we had at breakfast.

I saw the disappointment on Finn's face. As my partner, this affected him too. "So, what are we going to do?" he asked.

I took a deep breath and looked him in the eyes. "I'm going to have to pull out of the rodeo." With that, our dream of making a comeback was dead.

Finn nodded slowly, processing what that meant. He couldn't compete alone. I felt awful for letting him down.

"You could find a new partner," I pointed out.

"Yeah," he agreed. "But what's the point? I was going to be done at the end of the season." He slumped down into the chair next to me. "Wow. I didn't think we were going out like this."

"No kidding," I said. "It would've been nice to have a last hurrah or whatever."

"Go out a little nearer to the top." The corner of his mouth twitched.

I grinned. "Yeah, maybe a little."

"What's happening? Who died?" Grady emerged from his tent, rubbing his eyes. His normally straight, slicked-back hair was standing up. Not having a horse to take care of, he'd slept in later than the rest of us. He dragged his sleeping bag out of the tent, wrapped it around himself so only his face was visible, and sat down across from us.

"Our careers," I responded.

"Bad news from the vet?"

"Not good news."

"Incoming," Grady warned from his blanket cocoon, wrapping himself tighter and avoiding my eyes.

I turned my head to see Kinsley approaching the camp. I dragged my hand down my face. It was too early for this too.

Finn stood up. "Well, we better go ... check the horses." He looked down at Grady, who sat there, poking his boot out from under the blanket and nudging at the ashes from the fire. Finn rolled his eyes then tipped Grady's chair over, sending him sprawling to the dirt.

"Hey!" Grady cried. "What was that for? I don't have a horse!"

"You're a cowboy. Get one." Finn walked away.

Grady grumbled something under his breath, shoved his sleeping bag in the tent, then emerged wearing nothing but his tattered briefs. He pulled on his jeans without a care, oblivious to his state of undress.

Kinsley bit back a laugh at the shameless display while I glanced at Grady with a raised brow. Unfazed, Grady winked at Kinsley and followed Finn out of the camp.

Once they were gone, she sat down next to me. "Nice setup." She looked around the camp.

"Not everyone has a daddy who gives them fancy trailers."

"You know I didn't mean it like that."

"You're right. I'm sorry." I picked up a stick and pushed around the ashes. I tried not to look at her. Looking led to missing and wanting and bad decisions. "You really shouldn't be here. We just decided that we should stay a—"

"I know. That's not why I— I ran into Dr. Lawson in the barn," she went on. "I know it's none of my business, but I asked him— I'm sorry it wasn't better news."

"Thanks."

"Are you still competing today?"

"No, I'm done. And I don't want to talk about it."

She nodded but continued to sit there. She was biting her cheek, clearly wanting to say something else.

I sighed. "What is it?"

She hesitated, and something flashed in her eyes. "I paid your vet bill."

I snapped my head towards her, my eyes wide with disbelief. "You what?" The words burst out of me louder than intended.

I couldn't wrap my mind around what she had said. She'd paid my vet bill? I searched her face, trying to understand, but my shock and confusion made it hard to focus. It was a betrayal.

"Well, what was your plan, Wyatt?"

"That's none of your damn business, Kinsley! I'm not your charity case!" I stood up. I needed to move, to shake off the anger building up in me.

"I know that!" She rose from her chair. She could never just back off.

"No, you don't! I don't need your money or your family's sponsorships. Nothing! How many times do we have to fight about this? You don't get it!" My voice was getting louder, but I didn't care who heard.

"What I don't get is why you can't accept the fact that you need help! There are people who care about you that want to help you!" Her eyes shone with tears.

"I don't need help!" I yelled.

"Yes, you do!"

I was trapped in this never-ending loop with Kinsley, going around and around in circles with the same damn fight. She always had to push me, never content to let things be. It was like she couldn't help herself, constantly needling and prodding at me to get me to see things her way.

I shoved my hands through my hair roughly, pacing back and forth. The anger and frustration were building, expanding in my chest until I felt like I might explode. The more she pushed, the more I pulled away, digging my heels in. It was exhausting, but I didn't know how to break the cycle.

I wheeled around to face her, my fists clenching and unclenching at my sides. Those blue eyes I knew so well shimmered with unshed tears, and her arms wrapped protectively around her middle. It should've been my arms around her, protecting her. Instead, I was hurting her.

I cared about her more than I wanted to admit, but her relentless pressure made me feel cornered, like a caged animal. I just wanted her to back off, to let me breathe, but it seemed like every time we found some kind of balance, we ended up right back here, trapped in this endless argument neither of us could win.

Her hand reached out and touched my forearm—a soft plea—but I yanked my arm away, the flood of rage and pain within me needing some kind of release. My boots scraped against the dirt as I turned on my heel, putting distance between us. At that moment, what I felt was so ugly and wrong next to her.

Kinsley was a force of nature—vibrant, glowing, larger than life. And I was me, with all my flaws and shortcomings. She deserved better. I wished with my whole being that I was enough for her, that I could give her the life she wanted.

Sinking down into my chair, I dropped my head into my hands, fingers digging into my hair.

I would only disappoint her in the end. The fear of failing her, of letting her see how broken I still was inside, filled me with more anger and bitterness. It wasn't fair to take it out on her, but I didn't know any other way to protect us from the heartbreak I was sure would come if she stayed.

So, I pushed her away, despite the ache it caused me. I told myself it was for her own good, that this was the only way. Seeing the hurt in her eyes ripped right through me, making me hate myself even more.

Leaping back to my feet, I began pacing again, my restless energy thrumming. I had to break this cycle before I destroyed her real shot at happiness.

Voice hoarse, I said, "I can't do this with you anymore, Kinsley. I can't."

With that, I walked away.

Chapter 9

COWBOY TIL I DIE - THE ROAD HAMMERS

Kinsley

The bleachers were packed so tight I had to suck in my already thin stomach to squeeze through the rows. Popcorn crunched under my boots with each step. I clutched two bottles of water and a butter-soaked popcorn bucket, nabbing a few kernels with my tongue before handing one bottle to Maisey.

"Thanks." She shifted over as much as she could.

I wedged myself into the space, my shoulder pressing against some dude's beefy arm. You couldn't even slide a toothpick between us. The whole freaking town must have turned out for the bull riding. It was the last event of the day, and it always drew the biggest crowd. Even us girls racing at breakneck speeds couldn't compete with cowboys riding bulls.

We secured a spot close to the chutes, which gave us a prime view of the cowboys' faces as they descended onto the backs of their assigned bulls. I'd loved that vantage point ever since I was a young girl watching my dad compete. Seeing the exhilaration mixed with nerves flash across the riders' faces in the moments before the gate opened always gave me a thrill of anticipation.

I lived for the eight-second eternity—the ultimate test of man against beast. Daring cowboys clung on with all they had as those bulls twisted, bucked, and spun with cataclysmic force. When the buzzer finally blared, the rider went airborne before landing in the dirt. It didn't matter how many times I saw it; that heart-stopping moment before they hit the ground made the hair on my arms stand on end.

Though it had been years since my dad rode, I still got that same rush watching the new generation of cowboys try to conquer the rankest bulls on the circuit.

Wyatt stood at the bottom of the bleachers, forearms resting on the metal bars of the arena fence. He chatted with Finn but cut his eyes my way when Finn nodded towards me. Our stares locked for the briefest moment before Wyatt snapped his head back, jaw clenched tight as a vise grip.

"I'm guessing that it didn't go well this morning." Maisey nodded over at the guys.

"Nope," I replied. "Pretty much as I expected."

"Does he know what he's going to do? Is he even going to the next rodeo?"

I gave an exaggerated shrug. "I mean, I guess he has to stay with the other guys. They're travelling in his truck." I studied the tense lines of Wyatt's shoulders and the rigidness in his stance. "He'll have to haul poor Drifter around and pay his stabling costs, even though he's not even competing."

Maisey shook her head. "Man, that's rough."

Wyatt surveyed the bull riders with an intensity that bordered on envy.

A familiar ache tugged at my heart. It wasn't his sport, but knowing he wouldn't be out there at all would be hard on him. He was not meant for the sidelines. It frustrated me I couldn't do something; I wanted to, desperately.

My gaze traced the sharp angles of his jawline and the way his brow furrowed in concentration. I couldn't help but admire his rugged handsomeness. Even with the weight of his rodeo dreams crumbling around him, he carried himself with a solid strength that drew me in.

Our earlier argument replayed in my mind, the heated words we had exchanged still stinging. I'd meant well, but Wyatt saw my gesture as pity and had lashed out in that defensive way of his. I knew better than to take his words to heart—it was just Wyatt being Wyatt, pushing away anyone who tried to get too close. A part of me couldn't help but wonder if he'd ever let me in.

The announcer's voice boomed, calling out the first rider's name. His bull pawed and snorted in the chute; muscles coiled tight as a spring ready to explode. I crammed a mouthful of popcorn in my mouth, my eyes glued to the chute.

As soon as it flew open, the crowd detonated into cheers. The massive bull burst into the ring, a raging cyclone of hooves and muscle. The rider locked down, gripping the rope with every ounce of strength as the beast unleashed a merciless flurry of twists, bucks, and leaps.

My pulse thundered in my ears as I watched that death-defying dance unfold. This bone-jarring intensity, this raw danger—this was the lifeblood that coursed through my veins.

When that buzzer finally blared and they dismounted, I let out a breath, jumping to my feet with the rest of the crowd.

One by one, the riders took their turn, getting violently bucked, rag-dolled, and launched into the dirt. They scrambled like bats outta hell once they hit the ground, sprinting full-tilt toward the safety of the fence before the bull could wheel around and charge. A few had awfully close calls; one guy nearly got skewered before the bullfighters intervened, taunting the bull away.

The crowd gasped and cringed with every brutal blow, but we cheered louder. It was the gritty allure that drew us to the sport.

My gaze wandered over to the pickup men—the cowboys charged with protecting their fellow riders from those ill-tempered tons of muscle and horns. One had caught Maisey's undivided attention. Rhett.

His Mattel-like features were intensely focused as he snapped his rope, pushing the bull away from the cowboy sprawled in the dirt. Rhett maneuvered his horse with precision, every flick of wrist redirecting the bull and every rope swing driving the beast toward the exit. The crowd's roar faded into white noise as he zeroed in on that single, all-important task of getting that cowboy out of harm's way. Only once the bull disappeared did Rhett's stony expression finally crack, his shoulders dropping with relief now that the danger had passed. He looked like a freaking gunslinger after a high-noon showdown.

"Who are you here for?" I teased Maisey with an elbow to her ribs. "The bull riders or that pickup stud?"

She shrugged. "I don't know what you mean."

"Right." I laughed. "Well, I think we can both appreciate the next rider." I nodded towards the approaching not-quite cowboy, with his cocky swagger and full smile. Grady Martin.

"Amen," Maisey said. "He's so pretty." She sighed.

"Not datable."

"No, definitely not."

"But so pretty."

"So very pretty," Maisey agreed.

For once, Grady looked the part of a real cowboy instead of a wanna-be poser. From his scuffed boots and Wrangler jeans to the western-style shirt and cowboy hat somebody had probably lent him, he seemed more at home in that get-up than I'd ever seen him.

I glanced down at Wyatt and Finn, who were both smirking at their friend.

Grady lowered himself slowly onto the bull's back. Most cowboys in this moment had expressions of extreme focus and tension, but a whisper of a smile played across Grady's mouth. He was excited. And a total showboat.

Wyatt shouted something to Grady from his position on the rail, and Finn laughed.

Grady nodded that he was ready, and the gate flung open. The bull charged out, his back feet flying as he spun in circles.

Maisey gripped my forearm, probably as hard as Grady was gripping the rope.

His other hand was high in the air as he rode buck after buck.

I glanced at the ticking clock; it was taking its sweet time.

When it reached eight seconds, Grady swung his leg over in front of him and jumped swiftly down into the dirt. The bull fighters got the bull's attention away from the rider, and Grady tore the hat from his head and threw it hard into the ground with a big whoop.

The crowd went wild. He shot his arms in the air, beaming from ear to ear, and the roar of the crowd got even louder.

Damn, he was good.

The bull evaded the fighters and ran around the arena, not ready to leave yet. He, too, ate up the attention from the excited spectators. He made a run at Grady, who hadn't left the arena yet, and the crowd gasped, but Rhett steered his horse between them and swung his rope around the bull's neck. The bull took that as his cue and back to his pen ran through the open chute, his job done for the day.

Grady took a run and rear-mounted Rhett's horse, so he was sitting behind the man. He got the laughing crowd's attention and pointed at Rhett, encouraging a round of applause for the pickup man.

Rhett shook his head and elbowed Grady in the ribs. Still laughing, Grady jumped down, gave the horse a pat on the rump, and played to the crowd even more.

"Gawd, he's such a ham," Maisey shouted in my ear.

"The biggest." I chuckled, shaking my head as Grady basked in the adoring crowd like a star at a movie premiere.

When Grady left the arena, girls swarmed him, and he soaked up the attention like a sunbather soaking up the rays at the beach. Finn and Wyatt walked over to him, and two girls diverted their attention over to them.

Wyatt smiled at a cute redhead, and I felt a stab of jealousy.

"Hey." Maisey looked at me with concern. "He doesn't go for buckle bunnies, you know that."

"Yeah, I know."

My brow furrowed as Wyatt charmed that cute redhead. He was leaning in close, that crooked smile of his on full display as they talked.

A pang of jealousy twisted in my gut, no matter how much I tried to tell myself that he didn't go for buckle bunnies. The way his eyes crinkled at the corners when he laughed at something she'd said had me gritting my teeth. He was oblivious to female attention sometimes, but did he have to play right into it?

"Are we going dancing tonight?" Maisey asked.

"Absolutely," I said with a little too much force in my voice. If Wyatt was going to move on, then so was I. "Let's go find something hot to wear."

I grabbed Maisey's hand and tugged her to the bleacher stairs.

Chapter 10

KEROSENE - MIRANDA LAMBERT

Wyatt

The bar was packed to the rafters with folks boot-scooting to the twangy beats. The scuffed hardwood floors were littered with peanut shells, and the tables had damp circles left from sweating beer bottles. Neon signs flickered through the hazy darkness, barely illuminating the crowd swaying and spinning in the dim light.

I squeezed between wobbly tables and abandoned chairs, the smell of stale beer and sawdust thick in the air. Finally, pushing through to the corner, I found Finn hunched over the high-top, looking just as miserable as me while he nursed a longneck.

"We can haul him to the next few rodeos," Finn said, barely audible over the bar's pounding music. "Then maybe get him to my place."

I rested my elbows on the table, pressing my forehead into my palms.

The idea of leaving Drifter behind gnawed at me. For the millionth time, I cursed my father for selling our farm.

"Even if I could afford that, what am I going to do on the circuit without a horse?" I took a long sip of my beer.

The option of leaving him with Finn's parents was a small comfort. They would give me a deal on boarding him, like before, but I preferred to work off his keep. I didn't want handouts. The weight of my future pressed down on me like an anvil. With Drifter officially retired, I was a cowboy without a horse.

I took another long pull from my beer, but it was doing little to wash away the reality staring me in the face. How was I going to keep gas in the truck and food in my belly if I couldn't compete? Rodeoing was more than a way of life; it paid the bills too.

"Without team roping, maybe I should try tie-down again to finish the season." Finn shook his head, mouth twisting into a grimace. "But I'm too damn old for that shit."

"C'mon, man," I teased, trying to lighten the mood. "You're not that old."

Finn shot me a withering look, but the corners of his mouth twitched ever so slightly. "I'm not as young as I used to be, jackass. Hell, my knees creak tying my boots these days."

We were both almost thirty—not old at all—but in tie-down roping, you had to chase down the calf on horseback, jump out of the saddle, wrestle the calf to the ground, and tie up his legs as fast as possible. It was a lot harder on the body. At least in team roping, we stayed in the saddle.

"Why so glum, son?!" Grady placed four colourful drinks with little umbrellas on the table in front of us.

"What the fuck are those?" Finn eyed the drinks.

Grady laughed. "No clue. Compliments of those girls over there." He pointed to a group of cowgirl wannabes, who were watching us and giggling.

"I'm not drinking that," I declared. "It looks like unicorn piss."

"You are drinking it because it would be rude not to," Grady replied. "Bottoms up, my friend!" He lifted one glass to his mouth, took a big swig, and grimaced. "Shit, that's sweet. Like Kool-Aid mixed with cotton candy. Fuck, that's disgusting."

Finn and I chuckled.

Grady forced a smile and a thumbs-up at the girls. "Where's Rhett?"

"He said he had something to do. He'll be here later," I said.

The bar was filling up fast with a sea of fake cowboy hats and boots; the rodeo brought out the inner country in everybody. The DJ played a decent mix of the good 90s country and the newer radio hits. People's feet stomped on the dance floor, sending vibrations through the entire building.

"Why are we here?" I asked.

"Because here, we're the real deal," Grady answered. "Here, we are gods!" He threw his arms out and his head back, ready to be worshipped by the masses of rodeo fans.

"I need another beer." I got up.

"Get me one too," Finn said. "I'm going to need something to wash down this Barbie juice." He lifted a glass, peering into the contents.

I nodded and headed towards the bar. The bartender was busy at the other end, so I waited.

"Hey, cowboy," said a voice beside me.

It was the redhead I'd met at the bull riding. Had she told me her name? Shit, I couldn't remember.

"Hey, umm..."

"Natalie. We met earlier."

"Right. Of course." Nope, the name didn't ring a bell.

Her eyes travelled over me. I gave a polite smile and looked over to where the bartender was flirting instead of pouring drinks.

I eyed Natalie, taking in her made-up appearance. She was pretty enough, with her carefully styled hair and heavy makeup, but there was something artificial about her look, like she'd spent too much time in front of a mirror getting dolled up for a night out.

Kinsley was a natural beauty. She didn't need layers of makeup or hairspray to turn heads. With her sun-kissed skin, golden waves, and those striking blue eyes, she was stunning without even trying.

"Oh, I love this song!"

I listened for a second and groaned. Of course, it was a Miranda Lambert song.

"Dance with me?" Her smile was coy, and her eyes were bright. She gave a little tug on my shirt.

"Thanks, but I don't dance, and I hate this song."

Her face fell, and the guilt hit me. Places like this brought out my inner asshole.

"How about I buy you a drink instead?" The words were out of my mouth before I'd thought it through, but she was beaming at me and there was no going back now.

The bartender made his way over and looked at us. I gestured for her to order first.

"Umm, let's see..." She tapped her too-long, manicured fingernails on the bar. Could she even hold a drink with those things? "I'll have a strawberry daiquiri please."

"A beer for me. Whatever's on tap." I put some money down. "Make that two," I said, almost forgetting about Finn. I fished another bill out of my almost empty wallet. Hopefully, she was a cheap date. "This is for my buddy over there."

Natalie nodded, took a sip, and followed me back to the table.

Finn raised an eyebrow at me as we approached. "Finn," I introduced, "this is—" I hesitated. *Shit.*

"Natalie," she interjected.

I snapped my fingers. "Right. Natalie. Sorry." I sat down.

She took the stool next to me, not seeming to care too much that I couldn't remember her name. "So, are you guys bull riders too?"

"No, we are the much less exciting kind of cowboys," Finn piped up. "We compete in roping."

"Oh. Well, that's interesting too."

I didn't believe her. The disappointment on her face gave her away.

Finn smirked at me, and I rolled my eyes. *They always want the bull riders.*

"So, *Natalie*, what do you do?" Finn asked.

I meant to pay attention to her answer, but a familiar blonde head on the dance floor caught my attention, and below that, a very familiar denim-hugged ass moving to the beat of the music. There was no escaping her. She was laughing at something Maisey had said, head thrown back in that carefree way that made my heart stutter. Her golden hair was a halo of soft waves, glowing under the strobing lights.

Without thinking, I drank in every detail: the elegant curve of her neck, those full lips stretched in a radiant smile, and the tantalizing strip of toned midriff visible when she lifted her arms over her head. She looked so goddamn beautiful in that moment, unburdened and alive with a joy I ached to be a part of again.

Then her eyes met mine from across the crowd. The world seemed to grind to a halt. The pounding bass faded, and the flashing lights dimmed until there was nothing else but the blazing connection between us.

I felt the breath leave my lungs in a harsh exhale, like she'd just slammed into me at full speed.

Kinsley's smile faltered, shoulders tensing, but she didn't look away. Those striking blue eyes held my stare, searing into me with an intensity that was both exhilarating and terrifying. I watched a flash of emotions flicker over her delicate features—surprise, uncertainty, and an undeniable heat that punched straight through to my core.

In that heated moment, it was like the world had fallen away until there was nothing and no one else but her and me. I imagined crossing that space between us, backing her up against the nearest wall and caging her in with my body. I could almost feel the warmth of her soft skin under my calloused palms, taste the sweetness of her lips, and inhale the intoxicating apple scent of her shampoo.

My throat went bone dry at the thought of hauling her up into my arms, pinning her there with my hips as her legs wrapped around my waist, and finally sinking my hands into that glorious tangle of golden hair as I claimed her mouth.

A hard kick to my shin brought me back to reality. Finn was glowering at me from across the table.

"What the hell was that for?" I growled, rubbing the already-forming bruise.

"Your date just left, jackass."

"Huh? Oh, shit." Right, Natalie. Shit. "Where did she go?"

"Probably to find someone who would pay attention to her."

My eyes flickered back over to Kinsley and the guy who was getting too close for my comfort. He moved in nearer, his hands finding her hips as he pulled her against his body and whispered something in her ear.

My jaw clenched hard enough to crack molars, my knuckles straining white against the bottle as he pawed all over her. My every defensive instinct roared to life, screaming at me to go over and rip that asshole off her.

Finn's eyes followed my line of sight, and he shook his head. "Get used to that."

"I'll never get used to another guy's hands on her," I muttered, my grip tightening even more around the beer bottle.

"So, what are you going to do about it?"

My jaw ticked, and I scratched at the day-old stubble on my chin. I shouldn't do anything about it. I shouldn't. Kinsley was more than capable of taking care of herself; I knew that.

I needed to learn to walk away from her. I should leave right now...

Chapter 11

DRINKABYE - COLE SWINDELL ROULETTE ON THE HEART - CONNER SMITH (FEAT. HAILEY WHITTERS)

Kinsley

A body pressed in behind me.

I looked over my shoulder to a face I didn't recognize. The guy was smiling at me like a total sleazeball while his hands went to my hips. I was about to not-so-politely tell him to fuck off when another hand grabbed mine, yanking me forward, and twirled me around into a lively two-step.

"Cutting in!"

"What are you doing?" I laughed, moving my feet in the familiar quick-quick-slow-slow pattern.

"Saving some joker's life." Grady grinned back at me. "You can thank me by making me look good in front of those girls over there. No fancy moves, though; this honky-tonk dancing is hard."

"I'm thinking you don't need any help to look good. That performance in the ring tonight was pretty damn impressive."

"Right?! I was fucking awesome!"

I loved his non-existent modesty.

"Got your sights set on PBR?" My dad was one of the top Professional Bull Riders in his day.

"Yes, ma'am," he replied. "See what I did there? I'm learning to talk like a cowboy and everything!"

I shook off a laugh. "You should talk to my dad. He'll for sure have some advice for a career path."

"Wow, that would be amazing. I'll take any help I can get."

My face fell. "See? It's not that hard! Somebody offers help, and you take it! It doesn't have to be a big deal!"

Understanding flashed across Grady's face. "It's not a big deal for me, but it is for him."

"Why?" I stopped dancing and let my arms fall to my sides.

"It's a pride thing? I don't know. I don't get it, but that's just the way he is. It doesn't mean he doesn't love you."

I recoiled at Grady's words, my body tensing up. It wasn't a surprise to hear Wyatt loved me, but hearing it said out loud was like a punch to the gut.

My chest tightened, and I struggled to catch my breath for a moment. The sting of tears prickled at the corners of my eyes as a wave of emotion washed over me.

I loved him too. So damn much it hurt sometimes. But that wasn't our problem, was it? Love wasn't enough to make us work.

I blinked, forcing the tears back as I clenched my jaw. I would not cry over this—over him—again. Not here in this crowded bar, surrounded by strangers.

My hands balled into fists at my sides as I fought to regain my composure.

Grady was watching me closely, brow furrowed.

I forced a tight smile. "Yeah, well, love's overrated." The words tasted like ash in my mouth, a bitter lie, but saying them out loud made it feel a little truer and a little easier to swallow than the lump rising in my throat. "Ugh, forget it. I need a drink." I left Grady standing in the middle of the dance floor and headed to the bar.

I ordered a shot, downed it, and then downed two more.

"Are you okay?" Maisey came up beside me and eyed the empty glasses on the bar.

"Great!" I forced a smile. "Let's dance."

The song *Drinkaby* by Cole Swindell filled the room, and I grinned. *Perfect timing.* I pulled Maisey to the dance floor, right in the line of sight of the now four cowboys. Great, maybe I could get my friend noticed by one Rhett Parker. If anyone deserved a love story, it was her.

Maisey's eyes went wide when she saw him there watching us. She hesitated, a blush creeping over her cheeks as she tried to back herself into the crowd.

"No, you don't." I pulled her out into the open. "Time to shine, my friend."

The two of us ate up the dance floor. Maisey hardly glanced at Rhett; she was having so much fun.

The alcohol was well into my system, and I felt good. I wanted to stay in this country music induced trance where the rest of the world fell away, but it wasn't the world that fell away. It was me that got knocked on my ass, my balance seeming to have … disappeared.

What the hell?

A hand reached out to me, and I grabbed it, allowing it to pull me back to my feet. Oh, my arms felt heavy—or my head did? Something was heavy. The floor wasn't that bad. Maybe I should sit back down.

I tried to sink to the floor, but muscular arms circled my waist. I ran my hands up someone's biceps; I liked them a lot, these arms. They held me tight, and I decided I wanted to keep them.

My body relaxed and swayed, but my head was still heavy, so I rested it on a solid chest. Oh, that was so good too. It was warm and smelled like pine and horse—probably my favourite smell ever—and I breathed it in, closing my eyes.

"Mmm," I said. "This is wonderful. So much better than the floor. Can I stay here?"

"Kinsley," an exasperated but familiar voice said.

I looked up into Wyatt's deep brown eyes. He was looking down at me with an annoyed expression, but there was something else there too. Longing? Well, I should hope that's what it was.

"Kinsley," he said again.

"Shh. You're ruining it." I put my head back on his chest. Reaching up with my right hand, I put my fingers through the hair on the back of his head and rubbed a lock between my thumb and finger. I thought I heard him sigh over the beating of his heart before he rested his cheek on the top of my head.

Together, we swayed, and that was when the world fell away. I couldn't even hear the music anymore. I didn't know how long we stayed like that. Maybe I was even sleeping.

"Hey, Kins." Maisey's hand was on my shoulder. "Time to go."

"Nuh-uh," I mumbled, burying my face in Wyatt's chest.

"The bar is closing."

I lifted my head and looked around. The place was emptying.

"You girls have a ride?" Wyatt asked her while still keeping me on my feet.

"Umm, Reed. But where did he go?" She searched the room.

I wanted to go back to sleep.

"Let's go." Wyatt scooped me up into his arms.

Oh, this was nice. I could get used to this.

He carried me out to the parking lot.

"I think this is my new preferred method of transportation," I slurred.

Wyatt grunted in response. He put me in the front seat of his truck. Maisey got in the back with Finn. Grady and Rhett were across the parking lot, talking to a couple of girls.

"Aww, Mais, we should've asked Rhett to come with us! I'm such a bad wing ... something." I whined.

"Kinsley, shut up," Maisey said tightly.

Finn, beside her, hid his smirk under his hand.

"Oh, oops." I covered my mouth. "My bad."

Wyatt started the truck, and we drove out of the parking lot in silence.

I woke up to Wyatt unbuckling my seat belt. I blinked. We were in front of my trailer.

I stumbled out of the truck, my knees buckling underneath me. Wyatt grabbed me around my legs and threw me over his shoulder. His ass looked great. He carried me into the trailer, setting me down on one of the leather recliners.

He looked around my mobile home and scratched the back of his head. "Geez."

"Like it?" I threw my arms out, showing off my fancy new digs. "Wait, who am I kidding? Of course you don't. I'm a spoiled rich girl who hasn't earned any of it."

Wyatt's shoulders slumped. He sank down into the chair next to me, putting his face in his hands. I resisted the urge to run my fingers through his soft hair.

"I don't want to fight, Kins." Wyatt's voice was barely above a whisper.

"Yet that's all we ever do—fight or fuck." The words tumbled out, raw and honest.

Wyatt flinched as if stung, his eyes squeezing shut. The pain etched on his face made my heart ache. I wanted to smooth away the furrow between his brows and erase the hurt I'd caused.

Unsteadily, I pushed myself up from the couch, the room tilting slightly as I found my balance. I took a tentative step towards Wyatt, then another, until I was standing right in front of him. His eyes were still closed, his jaw clenched tight. I could see the rapid pulse at his throat and the way his chest rose and fell with each shallow breath.

Slowly, carefully, I lowered myself onto his lap, straddling his hips. The couch's leather creaked beneath our combined weight.

Wyatt's eyes flew open, his hands automatically coming up to rest on my hips, steadying me. The heat of his touch burned through the thin fabric of my dress.

I leaned in close, my lips brushing the shell of his ear as I whispered, "So, let's not fight."

Wyatt inhaled sharply, his fingers flexing against my hips. "Kinsley." My name was a plea and a warning all at once, his voice husky and strained.

"Hmm?" I nuzzled into the warm skin of his neck and placed a soft, open-mouthed kiss just below his ear, feeling his pulse jump beneath my lips.

"You need to go to bed." Wyatt's words were barely coherent, his voice a low rumble that vibrated against my mouth.

"I'm trying to," I murmured, trailing kisses down the column of his throat. I lingered at the hollow above his collarbone, tasting the salt on his skin.

Wyatt's breath came faster, his heart pounding against my chest.

Suddenly, he stood, his hands gripping my thighs as he brought me with him. I gasped in surprise, instinctively wrapping my legs around his waist. The world spun as Wyatt carried me the few steps to the bed, then gently lowered me onto the mattress.

For a moment, he hovered above me, his hands still on my hips, his eyes dark and intense. I could feel the heat rolling off his body, could hear the ragged sound of his breathing. I wanted to pull him down to me, to lose myself in his touch and taste.

But Wyatt pulled away, his hands leaving my body and the warmth of him disappearing. "Good night, Kinsley." His voice was thick with an emotion I couldn't name.

I reached for him, my fingers grazing the front of his shirt before he stepped back out of reach. My heart sank as he turned away, each step he took increasing the distance between us.

I watched him walk away.

"Wyatt, please." My voice was small and pleading, barely recognizable to my own ears. "Don't go."

He paused at the door, his shoulders tense, his hand gripping the handle. For a moment, I thought he might turn around and come back to me. But then he shook his head, and my hope withered.

"I can't, Kins." His voice was strained. "Not like this."

The finality in his words cut deep, and a familiar ache bloomed in my chest. This was how it always ended between us—with misunderstandings, hurt feelings, and unresolved tensions hanging in the air like a thick fog. I wanted to be angry, to lash out and blame him for all the problems between us, but it wasn't just his fault. We were both guilty of letting our pride and stubbornness get in the way of what we truly wanted.

As Wyatt slipped out of the trailer, I curled up on the bed, hugging a pillow to my chest. I squeezed my eyes shut, willing the tears not to fall.

I was tired of crying over Wyatt, tired of my heart being ripped apart every time he walked away from me. But no matter how hard I tried to steel myself against the pain, it always seeped through the cracks.

Tonight, I had allowed myself a moment of weakness, a moment of hope that maybe we would find our way back to each other. But as the cold, empty space in the bed beside me attested, that hope was fleeting.

I wanted to forget our problems, to ignore the baggage we carried and simply bask in the warmth of his love. But love alone wasn't enough to bridge the gap between us. And that gap grew larger with each passing day.

Chapter 12

HOW 'BOUT THEM COWGIRLS - GEORGE STRAIT

Wyatt

I trotted Drifter over a hill, looking down the rodeo grounds. My gut twisted.

What the hell am I doing here? The question nagged at me. I had already withdrawn my entry and had nothing to do all weekend. I'd driven the guys here, so my job was done.

A heavy sigh pushed past my lips, and I let my shoulders slump. At least I was still with my horse. He tugged at the reins, telling me he wanted to go faster, and I thought I needed that too.

That familiar ache twisted in my chest as I thought back to last night. No matter how much I tried pushing it down and burying it, the memory burned as brightly as a cattle brand. The way Kinsley had looked at me through those heavy-lidded eyes, face flushed, and lips parted in a way that goddamn near stopped my heart. The feel of her soft curves melting against me when I'd picked her up off that bar floor, all whiskey-warm and pliant in my arms. And later, when she'd settled onto my lap, those small hands dug into my chest with a desperation that mirrored my own...

The fantasy took on a life of its own, spiraling into forbidden territory despite my best efforts. I could almost feel the feather-light caress of her fingers as they danced down my stomach, those plump lips branding hot, open-mouthed kisses along the column of my neck. My chest heaved with each shallow pant, a familiar tightness building low in my belly.

As much as it killed me, I'd done the right thing walking away. Kinsley had been drunk, emotional, and not thinking straight. Taking advantage of her in that state would've been a new low even for a screw-up like me. But, Christ, had I wanted to.

My hands were shaking now, the muscles in my jaw pulsing from being clenched so damn tight. I tried forcing the image of her from my mind, but it was seared into the back of my eyelids, torturing me with every flutter of those long lashes and slight pout of those full lips.

With a harsh shake of my head, I forced myself to take stock of my surroundings. Drifter was pulling the reins from my hands, asking to be let loose.

"Alright, if you're up for it." I patted his neck and urged him forward.

He broke out into an easy lope, and I relaxed, enjoying the gentle rocking motion of the three-beat gait. Easy rides were all we were doing. He needed to move, but I let him decide how much and how fast. So far, he was happy and eager to go.

The morning sun was warming, and I was grateful for the shade of my hat. I let Drifter lope to his heart's content until he slowed himself to a walk. He tossed his head as if to say that had felt good.

"Back to your stall, buddy." I steered him back to the barn arena but wished it was a big, grassy pasture I was bringing him to.

We rode past the warm-up ring. It was full of barrel racers getting their horses ready for their event.

I scanned the arena until I spotted her. She had Gambler trotting calmly around the outside of the ring. I breathed out a sigh of relief. The horse looked good, really good. His well-muscled hind end was tucked neatly underneath him, propelling him forward. His head and neck were relaxed and reaching in a beautiful open frame. As beautiful as Kinsley was; that was what I had noticed about her first—the way she rode her horses. While so many riders were always yanking on their horses' faces and kicking them forward, that wasn't Kinsley's style. She was an exceptionally kind rider. She let her horses move in a way that was free and natural.

Our philosophy on riding was one of the first things we'd bonded over, but it hadn't taken long for me to fall in love with everything about her, especially her smile. She was always smiling; she was always *happy*. I had never met anyone like that.

For as long as I could remember, my mother had been miserable. She hated life on the farm, hated rodeo, and hated my father. Though, my father was an alcoholic with a gambling problem, so I couldn't blame her too much for that last one.

She was young when she met him, a girl from the city who thought it would be fun to go to the rodeo and flirt with the cowboys. She got pregnant by one of those cowboys and suddenly found herself stuck on a small-town farm that was barely getting by while her husband was off at rodeos every weekend. She stuck it out for as long as she could before she packed a bag and left.

Unfortunately, she forgot to pack me. I stayed with my father, who had no choice but to take me on the circuit with him.

My father had been a great cowboy, but the more he drank, the worse he got, which meant prize money was not coming in. The pitying looks I got from people still haunted me, so I'd learned to hold my head up high and pull myself up by my bootstraps.

I loved life on the circuit. My dad wasn't too concerned about where I was or what I was doing, so I had a lot of freedom. I met Finn and followed him and his parents around; sometimes I would even jump in their truck to ride to the next rodeo, and I didn't think my dad even noticed when I didn't ride with him and just showed up in another town.

I watched Kinsley ride for a while, making sure that horse of hers was behaving, then took Drifter back to his stall and brushed him down.

"What's our plan?" I asked him. "We're going to need one pretty soon." His ear flicked towards me, but that was all I got. "I know. My responsibility. A horse is for life." I would have to figure out how to take care of him. I owed him that.

When he was settled, I went to find the other guys. They were already ring side for the barrel racing, which would start right away. I joined them on the rail.

"Good ride?" Finn asked.

"Yeah, he felt good."

The first rider was announced—a rookie who knocked over the first barrel. It hurt her time quite a bit. Rider after rider made decent time, but nothing spectacular, not until Maisey. She *flew*.

"Holy shit," Finn said. "Where did that come from?"

"Didn't you see her last weekend?" Rhett asked. "Incredible. She's killing it this year."

"You know, Rhett," Finn started, but I elbowed him in the ribs. "Hey!"

I looked at him and shook my head. I was not about to let him reveal Maisey's crush on Rhett, which was exactly what he'd been about to do.

"Never mind," Finn mumbled.

I thought they would make a cute couple. Maisey was a sweetheart, and Rhett was a good guy, but he was also complicated, and Maisey probably didn't need that.

Maisey's time was the one to beat, but nobody came close. When Kinsley's turn was up, I went up on my toes trying to see her in the chute. Gambler's head was up in the air, the whites of his eyes showing. Kinsley was trying to hold him back. Her lips were moving; she was talking to him and patting his neck, trying to get him to calm down.

"Shit."

A loud clang rang out as he sent a hard kick into the metal dividers.

"That horse is all strung out," Finn murmured.

Get off, Kinsley. Please.

The girl didn't know fear, and it sometimes made her reckless. She walked Gambler in a tight circle, continuing to speak softly to him. It did the trick. He was calming down. She stopped and stood facing the arena, waiting for her cue to go.

"That's better," Finn said.

I nodded in agreement, but I still wasn't breathing.

At the cue, Kinsley and Gambler took off for the first barrel, but it was too fast. He was going to overshoot it, like he had last weekend. Kinsley tried to rein him in tighter, get him around closer to the barrel, but he was going too fast.

Time slowed down as I watched the scene unfold before me, every detail etched into my mind with painful clarity. Gambler's shoulder fell in, and I saw the moment his balance shifted, the way his hooves scrambled for purchase on the dirt. My heart seized in my chest, a cold fist of dread squeezing the air from my lungs.

Kinsley pitched to the side; her body thrown off balance by Gambler's misstep. Her blonde hair whipped around her face, obscuring her features, but I could imagine the look of surprise and fear in her blue eyes that always seemed so fearless, so alive with determination and fire.

And then, with a sickening crack that echoed through the arena, Kinsley's head slammed into the barrel. The sound reverberated through my bones, turning my blood to ice. I watched, frozen in horror, as her body went limp and crumpled to the ground like a marionette with its strings cut.

There was a collective inhale of breath throughout the crowd, but I couldn't breathe at all. My lungs constricted, and my throat closed as panic gripped my body. The world around me faded away. The silence of the crowd was a deafening roar in my ears. All I could see was Kinsley, lying motionless in the dirt, terrifyingly still.

Memories flashed through my mind in rapid succession: Kinsley's laugh, her teasing smile, and the way her eyes sparkled when she looked at me. The thought of losing her, of never seeing that light in her eyes again, sent a wave of nausea rolling through my gut.

The horse got up, but Kinsley didn't move.

Without hesitation, I jumped over the rail and sprinted across the arena. My feet pounded against the ground, each step feeling like an eternity as I raced towards her. I couldn't think, couldn't feel anything beyond the overwhelming need to get to her and make sure she was okay.

The medics were right behind me, shouting things I couldn't comprehend over the ringing in my ears. Shock had taken over my body, muting the chaotic scene around me. All that mattered was Kinsley, and the desperate prayer in my mind. *Please, let her be okay. I can't lose her. Not like this. Not ever.*

The medics carefully loaded Kinsley onto a stretcher, securing her neck in a brace. Her eyes were closed, her beautiful face smudged with dirt. I grasped her limp hand in both of mine, refusing to let go even as the medics lifted her into the ambulance.

The medic stopped me from climbing in with a hand to the chest. "Are you family?"

"She's my girlfriend. Please, I have to go with her. Her family isn't even in town."

He considered a moment, studying my face, which must have told him something because he nodded and allowed me to climb into the ambulance.

The wail of the siren barely registered in my stunned mind as we sped toward the hospital.

My heart raced as I sat in the back of the ambulance, my eyes never leaving Kinsley's face. The medics worked around me, attaching various monitors and an IV. All I could focus on was the steady rise and fall of her chest—the only sign that she was still with me.

I clutched her hand tighter, silently willing her to wake up, to flash me that dazzling smile and tell me everything would be alright. But her eyes remained closed, her face unnaturally still.

A lump formed in my throat as I realized how much I needed her, how empty my life would be without her light. Memories flooded my mind again: the first time we met, the way her laughter filled the air, and the stolen glances and electric touches that always left me wanting more. I had tried to deny it for so long, to push her away and protect my battered heart, but in that moment, with the very real possibility of losing her forever, I couldn't lie to myself anymore.

I loved her.

I loved the way she saw the world, always finding joy and beauty in the simplest things. I loved her fierce determination; she never backed down from a challenge. I loved how she made me feel alive, like I could conquer anything if she was by my side.

Regret washed over me as I thought of all the times I had pushed her away, too afraid to let her in. I had wasted so much time, so many opportunities to tell her how I felt. And now, as the ambulance raced towards the hospital, I prayed that I would have the chance to make it right, to hold her in my arms and never let go.

Chapter 13

TIN MAN - MIRANDA LAMBERT

Wyatt

The steady beep of the heart monitor nearly drowned out the hushed voices somewhere behind me. I leaned forward in the hard plastic chair, elbows digging into my thighs as I stared at Kinsley's unconscious form.

She looked so fragile and small lying there, blankets pulled up to her chin. Dark smudges of exhaustion clung to the delicate skin under her eyes.

Seeing her like this, stripped of her radiant, almost blinding vitality, made something twist deep in my gut. My fingers twitched with the urge to reach out, to grasp that motionless hand and will some of my own strength into her still body. But I couldn't bring myself to close that distance, not yet.

A nurse's hushed voice carried over from the hallway, all business, as she updated Kinsley's parents on her condition over the phone. They were already on their way but kept calling.

Head trauma. Concussion symptoms. Possible fractures.

My chest constricted hearing those clinical terms applied to her. All because of that damn horse.

My jaw clenched hard enough to grind molars as the memory played out again. The way Gambler's shoulder dipped at the last second, pitching Kinsley straight into that unforgiving steel barrel. The sickening thud when her head struck the metal, reverberating through the stunned silence of the arena. And me, helpless to do anything but watch it happen in horror, muscles locked and lungs forgetting how to draw air. Even now, the memory made my throat burn with the bitter taste of failure. I'd failed to protect her.

I dragged a hand down my face, fingertips catching on the coarse stubble shading my jaw. I'd warned her about that horse, tried to make her realize how dangerous he was, but she'd just waved off my concerns, like always, too bullheaded and stubborn to listen to reason.

A harsh snort escaped my nose because God knew that was the quintessential Kinsley Jackson—beautifully, recklessly, and almost infuriatingly self-assured. No amount of pleading or logic could ever deter her from a path once she set her mind to it.

Maybe that was why I'd always found her so damn irresistible. That fearless, unbreakable spirit shone as bright as the sun itself, daring me to try to rein her in even as I got burned at every turn. Kinsley was wild, passionate, and thrillingly unpredictable in a way that should've terrified any sane man. Yet I kept circling back, craving the warmth and chaos she brought into my life with every blazing smile and silken caress. Even knowing the inevitable scorch that awaited, I was powerless to resist the pull of her light.

Please wake up, darlin'. Please, just open those baby blues for me.

The words formed on my tongue, but I choked them back. Begging whoever might be listening wouldn't do a damn bit of good. All I could do was wait, holding vigil at her bedside like a prisoner awaiting his sentence.

I wasn't sure how long I sat there losing myself in the steady rhythm of her shallow breaths and that damn beeping monitor, but it'd been long enough for the daylight filtering through the blinds to fade, casting the room in eery shadows.

Then, so slight I almost missed hem, a subtle twitch of her fingers against the sheets and a faint flutter of those dark lashes. My whole body went rigid, frozen in place as I watched her thick throat work to swallow.

"Kins?" The name slipped past my lips in a hoarse rasp.

Those beautiful eyes finally blinked open, pupils blown wide in confusion and pain as they darted around the dimly lit room. When they landed on me, some of the wild panic seemed to recede. Her rigid body unwound slightly.

I sat up straight, hands clenched in tight fists to keep from reaching out towards her. God, how I ached to gather her up and never let go. But for now, just seeing that spark of life flicker back into her gaze was enough to loosen the crushing weight on my chest.

"Hey there, darlin'." The old endearment rolled off my tongue before I could stop it. "You really know how to make an entrance, huh?"

Her brow furrowed slightly at the sound of my voice, those full lips parting like she wanted to speak but couldn't find the words. Then her eyes squeezed shut, a tear slipping from the corner to streak down her pale cheek.

Something inside me shattered at the sight. Before I could think better of it, I reached out, fingers ghosting along her cheekbone to catch that solitary tear. I felt her go utterly still under my touch, breath hitching sharply.

"Don't you worry now," I murmured, throat so thick I could barely force the words out. "I've got you, Kins. You're going to be just fine."

Those impossibly blue eyes fluttered open again, shining with a vulnerability I wasn't used to seeing from her. Just like that, the fight went out of me. Every scrap of anger, resentment, and bitter hurt burned away until there was nothing left but the naked relief of having her back.

I shifted closer until our faces were just inches apart. I was close enough that I could see the faint smattering of freckles dancing across the bridge of her nose, the soft curve of those parted lips that had haunted my dreams for far too long, and the rapid flutter of her pulse thrumming in her throat, almost in sync with the jackhammer beating of my heart.

"You had me scared half to death, you know that?" My voice came out gruffer than I'd intended, cracking under the weight of the emotions welling up. "Don't you ever pull a stunt like that again, you hear?"

She held my stare, eyes shining and lips trembling. Whatever she saw in my gaze seemed to reach her because some of the fear melted from her features. A slight nod was her only response, but it was enough to unravel the knot of dread inside me.

With a shuddering exhale, I allowed my fingers to trail from her cheek, blazing a path down the curve of her jaw and along the slender column of her neck. Her pulse fluttered wildly under my touch, those blue eyes slipping closed as she let out a soft, trembling sigh. Just like that, the last two years of anguish and bitterness between us melted away, leaving only the raw need to feel her warmth and know she was truly here and alive.

My hand came to rest against the side of her neck, fingers tangling in her silky hair. As her eyes slid open again, I drank in every detail, lingering on the slight uptick of her lips and the delicate flutter of her lashes. That spark between us, the one I'd tried so hard to smother, flared back to life, white-hot and scorching, consuming every rational thought until there was nothing left but her.

I could've lost her today. Could've missed my chance to...

I drew in a harsh breath, forcing myself to let go of that dangerous notion before it swallowed me whole. This wasn't about me and what I wanted. It was about her, making sure she was okay and that she'd recover.

Slowly, reluctantly, I pried my hand away from those golden strands, letting it fall back into my lap. Kinsley's eyes fluttered open again, glassy with confusion and something deeper I couldn't let myself dwell on. Not now, not when she was hurting and vulnerable like this.

"Just rest now, okay?" I murmured, my voice sounding wrecked even to my own ears. "I'll be right here when you wake up."

Her eyelids were already drooping, her body surrendering to the pull of medication and exhaustion. But not before her gaze locked onto mine one last time, unspoken words passing between us in that blinding soul-merge of a moment.

Like every other time in our tumultuous history, I felt that undeniable pull toward her light. That irresistible craving to bask in her radiance, even though I knew the blazing intensity would ultimately reduce me to ash.

Because no matter how many times I got burned, I would never stop chasing the sun.

Chapter 14

COWGIRLS - MORGAN WALLEN

Kinsley

I woke with a start, my head pounding. This time, the pain was sharper, more insistent, as if it wanted to make sure I didn't forget the price I'd paid for my recklessness.

Grimacing, I squinted at the clock that read 3:12 PM. It was the day after my accident. Yesterday, I had been groggy and disoriented. I didn't remember much of what had happened, except that Wyatt was there when I woke up.

Nausea churned in my stomach as I forced myself into a sitting position, the room spinning momentarily. Wyatt was slumped in the chair beside my bed, legs stretched out, with his boots resting on the edge of my mattress. His hat was pulled low over his eyes.

A faint smile tugged at my lips, despite the throbbing ache. Wyatt had been a constant presence, refusing to leave my side.

The doctor had labeled my condition a "lucky escape from a worse fate" with a tinge of disapproval. I knew the risks of riding horses all too well; I didn't need to be reminded. Yet the sport, with its lessons in discipline, integrity, and humility, gave purpose to both my and my horses' lives. They would never know a day where they weren't loved and taken care of. Together, we were doing something special. Nothing would ever stop me.

A knock came at the door, and my parents stuck their heads in. My mom was already crying, of course. They came into the room, followed by my sister, Abby—younger than me by only a couple years—who was staring at me wide-eyed and tense. I was always struck by how much she looked like our dad, with the chestnut hair and deep brown eyes, while my mom and I were spitting images of each other, with blonde hair and blue eyes. We look like two different families. Abby and I might as well be.

"Oh, my goodness! Look at you!" Mom cried. Her blue eyes were rimmed red, so I knew she had been crying long before now and knowing that only aggravated the nausea in my stomach.

"Shh!" I gestured towards Wyatt, who stirred but remained asleep.

"Oh, sorry!" Mom covered her mouth and looked sheepish. "I see you and Wyatt not getting back together didn't stick for very long."

"We're not together."

"Right." She rolled her eyes. "How are you feeling, honey?"

"Hey, honey." Dad planted a soft kiss on the top of my head.

Abby offered a tight smile. I didn't bother smiling back. She'd probably been dragged here against her will.

"I'm fine," I reassured them. "Just a headache. I'll be up and about in no time. You guys didn't need to drive down here."

"When your kid is in the hospital, you go to said kid," dad said.

Mom nodded in agreement and pulled my blanket up around me. "You look cold. Are you cold?"

"No, Mom, I'm fine. I promise."

"How's the horse?" Dad asked.

I was grateful for the subject change. "He's good. Wyatt said the guys got him checked out by the vet and he got a clean bill of health, no injuries. He'll be ready to go for the next one."

"Absolutely not!" Mom exclaimed. "You tried him, and he already got you injured. You need to sell him."

"No way." I looked to Dad for help. He usually took my side in this kind of thing, but he was thoughtful for a moment.

"Cal..." Mom started.

"Hold on," he said. "We're not selling the horse."

I sighed in relief.

"However, you're not getting back on him anytime soon."

I sat up straighter at that. "What?"

Dad held up his hand. "Kinsley, you have a concussion. You will not be getting on any horse for at least a few weeks."

I opened my mouth to protest.

"Agreed."

I whipped my head around to look at Wyatt, who was awake, his mouth a hard line. My vision blurred from the movement and the nausea rolled through my stomach again. How long had he been awake? *Traitorous bastard.*

"Gambler stumbled," I told them. "It wasn't his fault!"

"He was worked up before the race. You didn't have him under control. He went way too fast and overshot the barrel, just like he had last weekend." Wyatt's eyes bore into mine.

I was going to kill Wyatt. I shot him a murderous look, so he knew it was coming, but he only looked back at me coolly.

"I'll get it worked out," I promised them, my eyes pleading.

"No, Kinsley. The horse is dangerous," Mom said in her no-non-sense tone.

"He's not!"

"Regardless of whether he is or isn't, you're not riding him right now," Dad said.

"If he's not exercised regularly, he'll be way worse when I do get on again."

"We'll get someone to—"

"Wyatt," I blurted.

Confusion flashed across their faces.

I turned to Wyatt. "Can you ride him for me? Keep him going and fit so he's ready for me?"

He frowned and hesitated. Seconds ticked by as I held his stare. I could see thoughts swirling in his eyes, turning over and over. I silently pleaded with him, willing him to accept.

"Please?" I begged, not caring about my pride.

He looked at my dad for approval, and I rolled my eyes.

"Hey! This is between you and me, cowboy," I told Wyatt. "I don't need you two"—I jerked my finger back and forth between them—"teaming up to manage me." *Stupid men.* "I need you to ride my horse while I recover. When I'm better, I will get back on him." I shot my mom a look that said I didn't want to hear anything about it and then looked expectantly at Wyatt, who hesitated but finally nodded tersely.

"Alright," he agreed.

"Fine," Dad said.

My mom threw her hands up in surrender and pouted.

I leaned back on my pillows, satisfied. And queasy again.

"Hey! Can we get in on this party?" Grady entered the room, holding flowers, followed by Finn, Rhett, and Maisey, all with gifts of some sort. They couldn't have had better timing.

"Hey!" I smiled and hugged each of them.

I introduced Grady and Rhett to my parents and Abby, who still hadn't said a word. Big surprise. They already knew Finn and Maisey.

It might have been my imagination, but I swear Grady did a double-take at Abby, which I found amusing because my uptight sister would never go for a guy like that in a million years. I thought an accountant or something would be more her type.

"How are you?" Maisey hugged me.

"Oh, so much better," I assured her. "How's Gambler?"

"Spoiled and pampered, and munching away in his stall." Finn winked at me. "We'll take care of him for as long as you need."

"I'll walk him tomorrow," Maisey added.

"Thanks," I said, "but no need. Wyatt is going to be riding him for a while."

Some brows were raised at that, but it was Finn I was looking at.

"Really?" Finn said curiously.

"Yep. Just till I'm better."

Finn studied my face, the wheels turning in his head. I gave him the whisper of a smirk so no one else saw, and when a smile spread over his face, I knew he understood. He nodded slowly.

Yep, I'm a genius.

Chapter 15

HORSEPOWER - CHRIS LEDOUX

Wyatt

I sat on the dirt floor of the barn aisle across from Gambler's stall. *The Demon Horse.*

He was ignoring me, focused on his hay. Despite his reputation, I couldn't deny that he was a beautiful horse, athletically built, and a part of me was excited to ride him. However, a knot of apprehension twisted in my stomach at the thought.

"Did he already throw you?" Finn's voice echoed down the aisle as he approached.

"No, we're bonding. Can't you tell?" I picked up a piece of hay and twiddled it between my fingers.

"Is that what you call this? Looks more like you're avoiding getting on him." Finn slid down to the ground beside me. "Not nervous, are you?" he teased.

I laughed. "No, not nervous. Just something. I don't know what."

"Could it be it's been forever since you've ridden a horse besides Drifter, and with him retiring, it's making you think about a future with another horse? And that maybe scares you a little?" Finn suggested.

I turned to look at him, one eyebrow raised. "Are you for real right now? When did you become a shrink?"

Finn shrugged. "Just a thought I had."

"This isn't my new horse. I'm just exercising him for Kins," I clarified.

"Ah, yes, there's that too. The ex-girlfriend you vowed to stay away from, yet you're still drawn to, and the horse that is forcing you together to face your feelings..."

"You can fuck right off," I snapped.

Finn chuckled. "I call it as I see it! You can't make this shit up!"

I punched him in the arm, but he kept laughing.

"Get on the damn horse!" He stood up and left.

I shook my head. He was right; I was overthinking this.

I got up, dusted off my jeans, and grabbed my saddle.

As I opened the stall door, Gambler eyed me and the saddle as if to say, *You're kidding, right?*

"Nope," I told him. "You and I are going for a ride. I know you don't know me, but I promise I'm not that bad, and Kinsley will be out to visit you soon. You know, you gave her quite the bump on the head? So, I'm kind of inclined not to like you very much. That's my girl you hurt." I slung the saddle onto Gambler's back, and he blew out his nose. "I mean, I know the point of barrel racing is to go fast, but you're a little extra? You need to learn to focus." Gambler shook out his mane. "We'll work on it."

I did up the cinch loosely, then went to grab his bridle. He took the bit easily, and I slid the crown piece over his ears, then led him out of the stall and walked out of the barn. He acted like a champ.

"You know exactly what you're doing, don't you?" I mused as we left the barn area. Stopping him, I tightened the cinch. "Do you like to play games, is that it?"

Putting a foot in the stirrup, I swung a leg over and sat down in the saddle. He didn't move a muscle.

"You're trying to trick me into a false sense of security, aren't you?"

He sighed, looking bored.

"No need to answer. I'm on to you. I will not be easy to get rid of." I urged him forward into a leisurely walk.

As we passed the riding rings, where other people were working their horses, Gambler pinned his ears at the horses passing us on the other side of the fence.

"Oh, don't be a grump. They're not bothering you."

When we got to a nearby field, I let him trot at a nice, easy pace. He was happy out here, super responsive to cues, and a nice horse to ride. I did a few laps around the perimeter of the field at a trot and then at a lope. I had to admit I was enjoying him.

"Okay, so you're not that bad. But you don't want to be a trail horse, do you? There's nothing wrong with that, of course, but do you think that'll be enough for you? I think you like to go fast."

Walking him back to the arena, I stopped him outside the ring and watched the riders inside go around the barrel pattern.

The guys approached, so I raised a hand.

"How did he do?" Finn asked.

"Great," I replied. "He'd make an excellent trail horse."

"So, try him in there," Finn suggested, pointing to the now nearly empty arena.

I liked ending on a good note, but part of me wanted to see what he'd do. Maybe I could figure out the issue, fix it, and make him a little safer for Kinsley.

"Do it!" Grady hollered.

"Cowboy up," Finn added.

As the last rider left the ring, I took the opportunity.

Gambler saw the barrels and perked right up. He pawed the ground and tossed his head, yanking the reins from my hands. He was eager to go.

Here goes nothing.

When I let him loose, he took off towards the first barrel too damn fast. I tried to hold him back, but he wasn't having it. I barely got him around the barrel; he had to dig in deep to make it, but fortunately, it slowed him a bit. He took the second and third barrels easier, then flew home.

I was breathless when I pulled him up. "Fuck," I breathed out.

The guys were hollering and grinning from where they perched on the rail.

"Damn, he's fast," I told them.

"It's just that first barrel that's the problem, eh?" Rhett observed, studying the horse. "That's always where Kinsley had the issue too."

I nodded. I took him around a couple more times, and the same thing happened.

"He takes off like a bat out of hell for that first barrel, but once he's around it, he finds his focus and he's good," I explained.

"It's not like he doesn't know it's coming," Finn said. "I'm not sure how you can prepare him any more for it."

"Maybe forcing him to take it real slow for a while?" Rhett suggested.

I wasn't sure how well that would go over with Gambler, and going slow was a little counterproductive to the sport.

"I'm sticking to bulls," Grady declared. "Horses are way too complicated."

I wanted to argue, but I didn't have a leg to stand on right now.

I patted Gambler's neck, and he relaxed under my touch. "You are a conundrum, aren't you?"

Chapter 16

HEART LIKE MINE - MIRANDA LAMBERT

Kinsley

"Why can't I stay in my trailer?" I complained to my parents from the back seat of their truck. I'd just been released from the hospital and it couldn't have come soon enough. I'd been going stir crazy in there.

"Because you'll be all alone," my mother replied. "You can spend a few days with us at the hotel, so we can watch over you."

I sounded like a child, and I was more than old enough to make this decision myself, but it was hard to argue with your parents when they paid for everything. In that regard, I saw why Wyatt didn't like taking money from people; that way, he didn't have to answer to anybody. On the other hand, if you couldn't go on without the help...

It wasn't like I didn't have any of my own money. I'd won a fair bit of prize money and gotten some sponsorship deals. I'd earned those, but I got that far because my parents had always gotten me the best horses, which didn't come cheap, so I was very grateful to them.

"I won't be alone if Abby stays with me," I suggested, trying to find a compromise.

"Huh?" Abby sputtered from her seat. "I don't think so."

"Really? You'd rather stay in a hotel with them than on the rodeo grounds surrounded by horses and hot cowboys?" I teased, trying to tempt her with the allure of the rodeo life.

I saw both my parents smirking in the front seat; even they thought Abby needed to loosen up.

"Sounds like a fine idea," Dad chimed in supportively.

"But—" Abby protested.

"It's the rodeo, sweetheart, not a prison cell. The rodeo is in your blood; embrace it," Dad encouraged.

I snorted, imagining Abby amidst the rodeo chaos in her fitted riding breeches and crisp polo shirt. She would look so out of place it wasn't even funny, but whatever; it would be good for her.

Abby crossed her arms over her chest and slumped back in her seat, scowling.

"Watch your posture there, Dressage Queen, or you'll turn into a hunchback."

Abby shot daggers at me with her eyes. She was mad, but she'd get over it. We got along sometimes.

Dad pulled the truck into the rodeo grounds, and I leaped out the second it stopped with a quick goodbye thrown over my shoulder. I had horses to see.

I found both Gambler and Cherokee dozing in their stalls, both clean and shiny. I made a mental note to thank my friends for taking such great care of them.

"Hey, guys!" I cooed.

I let myself into Cher's stall first and gave her a big hug, planting a kiss on her nose. Two days without seeing them had been too long. I didn't do "no horse" days.

Cher nosed at my pockets, looking for treats.

"Did you miss me or the treats?" I teased her.

When I entered Gambler's stall, he merely flicked an ear in my direction. He was much too dignified to beg for treats, but I gave him some, and he didn't object.

"Just so you know"—I ran my fingers through his long black mane— "there are no hard feelings, okay?"

"I saw your accident." Abby's voice caught me off guard. I hadn't heard her approach the stall. She stood with her arms crossed over the door, looking in. "Somebody posted it online."

"Of course they did. It was epic," I replied.

Abby rolled her eyes. "Hardly." She rubbed her hand up and down Gambler's face, fiddling with his forelock. Her eyes softened as she looked at him.

My sister and I had little in common, but we both loved horses.

Gambler's head jerked up, startling us both, but it was just the approach of four smoking hot cowboys.

"She's back!" Grady's smile was wide and grew even wider when his eyes landed on my sister.

Nope, I hadn't imagined that. Good luck to him.

My heart skipped a beat when my eyes landed on Wyatt. I felt the fluttering in my stomach like a girl with a schoolyard crush.

"Well, you guys are a sight for scrambled brains," I greeted them.

They laughed, except for Wyatt, who scowled at my joke.

I let myself out of the stall and elbowed him in the stomach. "Lighten up," I teased and gave each of them a hug.

"So, how's my boy been behaving?" I nodded towards Gambler.

Finn started, "The horse? Or Wyatt? Both could use some tuning—"

"Great on the trail, same old in the arena," Wyatt interrupted, his eyes dark, intense, and unreadable. I didn't miss the way his walls seemed to be firmly in place, like he had retreated to a fortress.

"Did you try him on the barrels?"

"Yeah, he tried to overshoot the first one every time," Wyatt answered.

I nodded and chewed the inside of my cheek. So, it wasn't just me who had this issue with Gambler.

"We'll figure him out." Finn throwing an arm around Wyatt's shoulders. "He needs something to do."

"I trust you guys." I eyed the men with a rush of gratitude for how they'd stepped up to help me out. "Let me buy you all a round at the bar," I offered, grinning. "As a thank you for taking care of the horses."

The reaction wasn't what I'd expected. They all exchanged shifty glances, their eyes darting to Wyatt like they were waiting for his cue.

Grady cleared his throat. "I was thinking we should have a bonfire instead. You know, hang out, relax..."

I raised an eyebrow. Since when did these guys turn down a chance to hit the bar?

"Uh, sure, I guess. I can bring the beer," I suggested, still trying to figure out what was up with them.

Rhett chimed in, "Or something non-alcoholic? And some snacks? Personally, I'm starving." He patted his stomach.

Now, I was confused. These guys were notorious for their love of beer, and now they wanted a quiet night in? I studied their faces, noticing how they all seemed to look to Wyatt for approval like they were trying to show him they were following some kind of plan.

Wyatt shifted under their gazes, his jaw clenching. He caught my eye for a moment before looking away, and I could've sworn I saw a flicker of guilt there.

"Okay, what's going on?" I demanded, crossing my arms over my chest. "Since when do you guys pass up a chance to go to the bar? And why do you keep looking at Wyatt like he's the boss of you?"

"No reason at all," Grady said. "We've been talking about having a bonfire all day."

I didn't believe him, but I also didn't feel like starting a fight with Wyatt because whatever was going on was coming from him.

"Alright, well, I'll text Maisey." I pulled out my phone from my back pocket. After sending the message, I inquired, "You guys haven't seen her, have you?"

"She was in the ring riding a little while ago," Rhett replied.

Is she, now? I thought, barely containing my smile.

My phone dinged with Maisey's enthusiastic reply of emojis. I linked my arm through Abby's. "Let's go."

"Umm, maybe I should..." Abby hesitated, looking for an excuse to bail.

"Nope, you shouldn't. You're coming," I declared.

"Of course you are!" Grady put his arm around my sister. He began pulling her down the aisle.

Although she was stiff, she went along. She looked back at me with round, concerned eyes, but I only shrugged and winked at her.

Together, we all made our way out of the barn, the surrounding air laden with the comforting scent of hay and horses. Tension rolled off Wyatt as I slipped into stride beside him.

He shifted away from me as if afraid he might break me. "How are you?" he asked.

"I'm fine," I assured him. "You worry too much."

"Nope, I don't," he replied, his statement tugging at my heart. "What?" he asked.

The memory of my drunken advances still burned with embarrassment. Maybe that was why he was so closed off, despite him being there for me in the hospital. "Umm, last weekend in my trailer... I'm sorry—"

Wyatt cut me off. "It's not a big deal."

I instantly regretted bringing it up. Why did I have to make things awkward?

"I just wanted to thank you for being there for me after my accident," I said quickly, trying to regain some ground. "And for riding Gambler for me. It really means a lot."

"It was the least I could do," Wyatt muttered, still not meeting my gaze. "After everything..." His voice trailed off, leaving the weight of "everything" hanging heavily between us.

I studied his expression, searching for a hint of what he'd meant by that. After everything we had meant to each other? After everything we had put each other through? What?

The silence stretched uncomfortably. Part of me desperately wanted to ask him to clarify, to rip open that door we'd been slamming shut on each other for so long and finally lay everything out in the open. But the other part feared his answer, that "everything" might be his way of saying we were truly done.

As I looked at Wyatt, really looked at him, I saw something flicker across his features. A conflict, an internal war, was being waged behind those rugged walls he always insisted on keeping up.

He opened his mouth, closed it, then opened it again, seeming to struggle with what to say. "Kins, I..." He ran a hand through his hair in frustration. "Dammit, this is harder than I thought."

My heart kicked into high gear as I waited with bated breath. Could it be... Did he not want us to be over after all? Or was it the opposite? Did he want to end us for good?

Wyatt blew out a harsh breath, squaring those broad shoulders as if bracing himself. "Seeing you get hurt like that, it made me realize..." He trailed off again, jaw tensing.

I laid a hand on his arm. "What? Realize what?"

Wyatt's jaw clenched. He shook his head minutely. "Never mind. Doesn't matter."

Just like that, the glimmer of hope that had sparked inside me sputtered and died. He was shutting me out again, the door slamming shut once more.

I opened my mouth, not even sure what I planned to say, but the words never came. The shuttered look on Wyatt's face told me it would be no use. Not tonight, at least.

With an imperceptible shake of my head, I let out a frustrated breath. Fine, if that's how he wanted to play it. I was sick of constantly running into this damn brick wall between us.

"Okay, well, I'm going to catch up with the others," I muttered, jogging ahead and falling into step beside Rhett.

Rhett gave me a concerned look. "You good?" He glanced behind us to Wyatt.

I managed a tight smile and a nod, but my mind was racing.

When were Wyatt and I going to stop dancing around...whatever this was? The tension, the heated glances, the aborted attempts to open up—it was exhausting.

As we headed to the fire pit at the guys' camp, I stole a glance back at Wyatt. He lingered behind, shoulders tense and jaw set in that stubborn line I knew so well. Our eyes met briefly, and I felt that same intense jolt—the kind that could ignite something deeper between us if we ever stopped stomping it out.

But then Finn called his name, breaking the moment, and Wyatt turned away.

Huffing an irritated sigh, I faced forward again. It wasn't over between us, not really. But clearly, we were still stuck, trapped in this cycle of starting and stopping, opening up and slamming shut. When were we finally going to kick through this door between us instead of just rattling the handle?

One of these days, something had to finally give between us. One way or another, a door was going to open. I'd be damned if I was going to stop pushing against it, not when I could still feel that fire burning on the other side.

Chapter 17

SMALL TOWN SOMETHING - HIGH VALLEY

Wyatt

The flickering flames of the bonfire danced mockingly before my eyes, every crackle and pop seeming to taunt me. *Idiot. Coward.* I scrubbed a hand down my face, the heat from the fire doing nothing to burn away the disgusted feeling burning in my gut.

What the hell was wrong with me? The words had been right there, sitting on the tip of my tongue. *I can't lose you. You're too important.* After Kinsley's accident, after realizing how easily I could have lost her for good, it was like all the bullshit between us just melted away. And she had been right there, those big blue eyes locked on mine practically pulling the truth out of me. I had been a hairsbreadth away from finally laying it all on the line.

Then, what? I choked? Got spooked by my own damned honesty? Let my typical emotionally constipated male pride get in the way of finally saying how I really felt?

"Stupid son of a bitch," I muttered under my breath.

I could still see it playing out—Kinsley's hopeful expression crumbling as I deflected and slammed that door shut yet again for no good reason.

Groaning, I buried my face in my hands, trying in vain to physically wipe away the image of the hurt look in her eyes as she'd turned away without another word, leaving me rooted in place like an idiot. She had every right to be pissed at me.

Kinsley sat as far away from me as she could, and I didn't blame her; I was a jackass. She and Maisey had spread out a blanket on the ground next to Rhett. Grady set up a chair next to the girls for Abby to sit in, and he sat next to her, though she looked like she might bolt any minute. Finn and I sat across the fire from them.

"Should I welcome you to the forever bachelor club now or...?" Finn said.

"I don't think I'm there quite yet," I replied.

"No? Sure looks like it to me. Just think, you and I can grow old together with all our horses. Is that a thing? Crazy old horsemen? You know, like crazy cat ladies, only men with horses," he joked.

"I get it. That doesn't sound appealing."

"No, it doesn't. I don't think I could live with your cranky ass, so you better figure your shit out because I plan to be a lone bachelor," he said.

"I can't wait for you to fall in love and then mess it up," I told Finn before clamping my mouth shut. *Fuck.* "I don't know why I said that. I'm sorry." I couldn't believe I'd said that to him.

Finn shifted in his seat. "Don't worry about it," he brushed me off, but I knew him better than that. That one stupid comment was going to drag him down.

Kinsley chatted with Rhett and Maisey. I was captivated as her hands moved animatedly, accentuating her words with vibrant gestures. The firelight cast a warm glow on her face, making her eyes sparkle like stars in the night sky.

I strained my ears, desperate to catch a snippet of what she was saying, to know what was making her light up like a Christmas tree. I remembered when I used to be the reason for that radiant smile, the cause of that infectious laughter. I longed for those moments and craved her undivided attention on me. It was like basking in the sun after a long, cold winter.

Kinsley leaned closer to Maisey, her grin turning mischievous. Maisey's cheeks flushed a deep crimson, and she ducked her head, trying to hide her smile. I chuckled to myself, realizing that Kinsley was probably talking up Maisey to Rhett. Kinsley had a heart of gold.

As if sensing my gaze, Kinsley's gaze flickered in my direction. Our stares locked, and for a moment, the world faded away. The corners of my lips twitched upwards in a small smile, and she mirrored it with a dazzling grin of her own. Kinsley did nothing halfway; her smile was as bright as a supernova, threatening to blind me with its intensity.

In that instant, a wave of desire crashed over me, stealing the breath from my lungs. I wanted her, needed her like a drowning man needed air. My fingers itched to tangle in her golden hair, to pull her close and never let go.

"Hey, Kinsley! Speak up! We're getting bored over here!" Finn called out over the fire, pulling me out of my daydream.

"Well, that's what you get for being boring!" Kinsley retorted.

Finn faked offense. "I'm not boring."

"Oh, really?" Kinsley asked.

"Is there a reason we're sitting so close to the fire when it's this hot out?" Maisey questioned—a valid point, given the hot, sticky night, unusual for spring.

"Go jump in the creek," Finn dared.

"After you, Mr. Not Boring." Kinsley's eyes twinkled as she stared down Finn over the flames, bringing him back to life with a challenge.

"There's a creek?" Maisey inquired, sounding interested.

"Back through the trees there." Rhett gestured behind him.

"Well, Finn?" Kinsley raised an eyebrow.

"Let's go." Finn stood up, grinning.

I dropped my head into my hands.

"Swimming?" Grady clapped his hands together. "I'm in." He grabbed Abby's hand and pulled her to her feet.

"No, no, no," Abby protested, shaking her head and digging her heels in. "I'm not swimming."

Everybody got up, and we made our way through the trees to a wide, still creek. There were large, smooth rocks beside it.

Kinsley sat down, put her feet in the water, and moaned. "Oh my gawd, that feels good." She kicked her legs, sending up a splash. The cool drops landed on my face, offering a brief respite from the heat.

"Grady," Finn called out. "Race you in."

After a brief pause, both guys stripped down to their boxers, ran to the edge, and jumped into the water, creating a big enough splash to make the girls shriek.

"Who won?" Finn asked when his head broke the surface.

"Me," Grady declared, slicking his wet hair out of his face.

"It looked like a tie to me," Maisey commented. She was sitting beside Kinsley, dangling her feet in the water.

"Unacceptable. To the other side and back," Finn challenged him, and they were off, kicking hard to splash the girls.

"Well, we're already wet." Kinsley peeled her shirt off and then stood up to wiggle out of her cutoffs.

The other guys looked away, but I couldn't. My eyes took in every inch of her smooth, bare skin, and a surge of heat swelled inside me.

Kinsley looked back at me, catching me staring, but still, I didn't look away. I couldn't. I devoured her with my eyes. God, she was so beautiful it hurt.

Kinsley smirked at me and dove in, wearing just her bra and underwear. I only averted my eyes when Maisey moved to follow.

"I think you're going to need that cold water." Rhett patted me on the back before joining the girls in the water.

Fuck. I stripped and jumped in to cool off before my blood started flowing in directions I didn't want it to.

Only Abby stayed on the shore, dipping one foot in the water while pulling her other knee up. She wrapped her arms around her leg and rested her chin on her knee.

"I won!" Grady called out.

"You did not! You were two feet behind me!" Finn yelled back.

"Liar! You saw I won, right?" Grady asked Abby as he pushed himself out of the water and sat down beside her, shaking the droplets from his hair.

"It was pretty close, but..." Abby smiled. She was looking a little more relaxed.

"Okay, never mind. I'll get him next time," Grady conceded with a shrug.

The water was cold and refreshing. I dipped my head back to get my hair wet.

"Do not float on your back," Finn warned me. "I do not want to see any masts up."

I glanced at Kinsley, who was trying to hold back her laughter.

"Got it," I said. "It's under control. The cold water is doing wonders."

Kinsley burst out laughing. That was better. I grinned at her, and she bit her bottom lip the way I liked, though I would've preferred biting it myself.

Reaching over, I grabbed her wrist and yanked her toward me so her chest was flush against mine. "We're playing chicken," I announced.

She threw up her arms in celebration. God, I loved making her happy.

I looked over at Maisey. "Up for the challenge?"

Maisey looked back and forth between Finn and Rhett.

"Rhett, I'm going to let you take this one. All this winning is going to my head," Finn said, stepping aside.

Kinsley bounced beside me in excitement. The girls climbed onto our shoulders, and I wrapped my hands around Kinsley's smooth, toned thighs.

"Three, two, one, go!" Finn shouted.

Rhett and I stepped towards each other, and the girls began wrestling and screaming. I held on tight to Kinsley's legs, trying to keep her from falling over. A guy had definitely invented this game. Kinsley and Maisey were well-matched in strength and were stuck in a deadlock.

"Ready to give up?" I asked Rhett.

"Not a chance." Rhett grimaced as Kinsley pushed Maisey backwards, but he held on, and she regained her balance.

"Harder," I urged Kinsley.

"That's my line," she retorted.

Rhett choked back a cough. *Well, shit.*

"Sails up yet, Wyatt?" Finn called out.

"Getting there," I shot back, trying to focus on the game and not on being between Kinsley's legs, which gripped tighter around my head. "That's not helping." I patted her thigh.

"You can deal with it later. I want to win," she replied, determined.

"How are you handling this?" I asked Rhett.

"Who says I am?" he replied.

Then, splash! Maisey fell into the water and came up sputtering. Rhett helped steady her, which only made her turn a deep shade of red.

"Yes!" Kinsley cheered, her hands threading into my hair and digging blissfully into my scalp.

Okay, we were done.

I dumped her into the water. "I'm out of here," I declared, swimming away from the victorious chaos.

Chapter 18

MY SISTER - REBA MCENTIRE

Kinsley

Leaving the creek, Abby and I walked back to my trailer, the moon lighting our way.

After the chill of the water, the breeze was warm on my skin. I was feeling good. I'd finally gotten a bit of the old Wyatt back, the one who could smile, laugh, and have fun with me. I wanted more of that, so much more.

I'd hated saying goodnight and walking away from him. I'd really wanted to invite him back to my trailer, but I was stuck spending the night with my sister.

Abby and I had always been different, but lately, it was like we were worlds apart.

When we were young, we had been inseparable, our lives revolving around the ranch and our horses. Those early days were filled with so much joy and simplicity. I remembered us as little girls, giggling as we brushed our horse's manes, dreaming of the day we'd compete together. Dad had set up a barrel racing pattern for us in the sand ring. Abby and I had been buzzing with excitement, taking turns weaving our horses through the barrels.

I remembered the thrill of that first run, the wind whipping through my hair as my little quarter horse ran his heart out for me. Abby had been right behind me, whooping and hollering, her face flushed with pure exhilaration.

"We're going to be the best barrel racers ever, Kins!" Abby had exclaimed, her smile stretching from ear to ear.

In that moment, I had believed her. But it hadn't lasted.

Things had changed. The innocent dreams of our childhood had faded, replaced by diverging interests and priorities. While I'd become more consumed by the sport, living the rodeo life, Abby had drifted away. She'd called it a ridiculous sport and wanted no part of it.

The sting of her words had cut deep, and no amount of pleading on my part would change her mind. Abby had turned her back on our shared passion, leaving me to navigate the rodeo world alone, and I had no idea why.

From that point on, a chasm had grown between us, widening with each passing year. The bond we had once cherished frayed until it was barely recognizable, replaced by awkward silences and unspoken resentments.

"Did you have fun tonight?" I asked Abby.

She only shrugged.

I rolled my eyes. Once inside, I tried to shake off the awkwardness, tossing my damp clothes into a corner. "You know, Grady was pretty interested in you," I ventured as I wrapped a towel around myself.

"Not everyone enjoys the constant attention of your cowboy friends," she snapped, her voice tight with annoyance as she flopped down onto a chair at the kitchenette table.

The towel half-secured, I paused, taken aback by her sharpness. "Hey, I was just messing around. Besides, it wouldn't kill you to have a little fun now and then." My words, meant to be light, were full of judgement I hadn't intended.

Abby stood up, the chair screeching against the floor. "My idea of fun isn't the same as yours, Kinsley. Not everyone needs to be the centre of attention all the time," she retorted, her eyes blazing with a mixture of defiance and something else. Was it hurt?

"Abby, I didn't mean it like that. I just thought—"

"What? Because a bull rider shows a little interest, I should be flattered? That I should be more like you?" Her voice broke a little on the last word.

The hurt in her voice made me pause, my defences crumbling. "No, Abby, that's not what I'm saying. I just thought you might like someone noticing you. You know, someone as ... outgoing as Grady."

"Oh, right, because no one ever notices me. Not when Kinsley Jackson is around."

"You know that's not what I meant!"

Angry, I retreated to my bed. Abby, with a quiet huff, gathered blankets from a cupboard and began making a makeshift bed on the couch.

The trailer was quiet except for the occasional shift of fabric or sigh.

Abby broke the silence, her voice low but clear. "I've started seeing someone."

Surprised, I rolled over to face her, my interest piqued. "Oh? Who's the lucky guy?"

She hesitated, a flicker of uncertainty crossing her features, before she replied, "Evan Morris."

The name hit me like a cold splash of water. Memories of high school flooded back. He was popular, handsome, and knew it, flirting his way through parties, always surrounded by admirers. He was the type who never took anything seriously, including the string of girls at his side. I remembered him hitting on me a few times at parties, always with that confident smirk, assuming I'd be another notch on his belt. I had never been interested; his type had never appealed to me.

"Evan Morris?" I tried to keep my voice neutral despite the whirlwind of thoughts. "From high school?"

Abby nodded. She sat up with a slight defensiveness in her posture as if bracing for judgement. "Yes, that Evan."

I processed this, trying to imagine the Evan I remembered with my quiet, reserved sister. Abby had always been the antithesis of guys like Evan—loud, outgoing, and always surrounded by a crowd. She preferred to keep to herself and her horses, staying clear of the drama that followed Evan and his friends. It baffled me why Evan would even pursue Abby. Of course, Abby was beautiful—any guy would see that—but their personalities were so different.

I couldn't believe I had, even jokingly, entertained the notion of Grady and Abby, which was even more ludicrous if that was possible. Grady, with his wild rodeo lifestyle and his easy charm, represented everything Abby stayed away from. The rodeo circuit, the late nights, the constant travel—none of it was her. Abby had never shown the slightest interest in rodeo or the cowboys who came with it. And Evan, well... That didn't seem to be the right direction either. I saw her with someone more reserved. Someone serious but kind.

"That's ... interesting," I managed, choosing my words carefully, but I knew as soon as the words left my mouth that I had chosen wrong. "I hope he's good to you, Abby," I offered.

Abby bristled, her voice tightening. "He is. But you wouldn't understand, would you? You wouldn't know a healthy relationship if it smacked you in the face."

I recoiled. "What the fuck, Abby?" My patience with my sister was wearing thin.

Abby's expression hardened. "He's a lawyer now, Kinsley. People change. Or is that concept too foreign for you, given your endless dance with Wyatt?"

Her words stung. "Abby, that's not fair. Things are complicated with Wyatt—"

"Complicated?" She scoffed. "Is that what you call it when you spend the entire night clinging to each other? Seems pretty straightforward to me."

"It's not like that with Wyatt. We're friends and—"

"Friends?" Abby interrupted, her voice rising with incredulity. "So, the way you two flirted with each other tonight, that's how 'friends' act? Please, Kinsley, who are you trying to fool?"

The accusation hit hard, forcing me to confront the blurred lines between Wyatt and me. "It's not the same, Abby. Evan—"

"With Evan, I'm happy," she cut in, her voice firm. "Can you say the same about you and Wyatt? Off again, on again. It's exhausting, Kinsley." The roll of her eyes was pointed and patronising.

I felt a flush of anger at her words, a fire that pushed back against her judgement. "At least I'm not pretending to be someone I'm not. Unlike some people who date guys because they tick all the 'perfect' boxes."

Her comeback was swift but with a sharper edge. "You think Wyatt is box-free? Let's see... Bad boy cowboy? Check. Perpetually broke? Check. Oh, and let's not forget the charming habit of disappearing when things get tough. Check. Anything else you'd like to add to the list?"

"That's low," I shot back. "I'm trying to be supportive here, but you're making it really hard."

"Supportive? This from the sister who's always in the spotlight and leaves no room for anyone else? Maybe I wanted something different, Kinsley. Maybe Evan's exactly what I need."

The implication that I was somehow the cause of her choices, her retreat into the shadows, ignited a fresh wave of frustration within me. "Or maybe you're scared, Abby. Scared to really live, so you choose the safest option. Evan Morris might look good on paper, but is he what you want, or is he just another part of the 'perfect life' façade?"

"You think you're so brave because you ride fast horses and have a chaotic love life? At least I'm trying to find real happiness, not just the thrill of the next ride or the next argument with Wyatt."

The trailer felt small, a pressure cooker set to explode. "Real happiness?" I challenged. "By always playing it safe?"

"We're not talking about me anymore," Abby snapped, her voice tight. "We're talking about you and Wyatt. How many times will you go back to him before you realize it's not going to work?"

Her words struck deep. I lay back on the bed, staring at the trailer's ceiling, the weight of her accusation settling heavily on my chest.

Was it the thrill of the ride, the rush of the argument that kept me going back to him? Abby's words replayed in my mind, taunting me.

I rolled over, burying my face in the pillow, trying to block out the thoughts that swirled in my head. But they wouldn't leave me alone; they wouldn't let me rest.

As I stared into the darkness of the trailer, I couldn't help but mourn the loss of the closeness Abby and I used to have, that unbreakable sisterly bond we had once shared. Somewhere along the way, we had become strangers, two people leading parallel lives that rarely intersected.

I didn't understand her choices, her desire for a life so different from mine. But maybe that was the problem. Maybe I'd been so focused on my own path, my own dreams, that I'd forgotten to see hers. I wished I could figure out where hers was leading. I had a hard time believing even she knew that.

Chapter 19

Take Me to the Rodeo - Chris LeDoux

Kinsley

"What the hell do you think you're doing?" Wyatt's voice rang out as he and Finn pulled their horses up beside me.

I halted Cher and patted her neck, offering them my most endearing smile.

The previous night's argument with Abby still lingered in my mind, leaving a residue of tension that I was eager to shake off.

"You're not supposed to be riding yet," Wyatt said.

"I think the deal was that I don't ride him." I pointed at Gambler, who looked half asleep under Wyatt. "I'm walking around, not running barrels, and it's Cher. She's always good."

Wyatt didn't look pleased, but he didn't argue either, so I counted it as a victory. After last night's creek escapades, I wasn't sure where we stood. One minute he was pushing me away, the next flirting. It was hard to keep up.

"You're putting my horse to sleep."

Wyatt shrugged and slouched in the saddle like a defeated cowboy, which wasn't a good look for him. "He'll perk up once we get out in the field." He smoothed down Gambler's unruly mane.

"More trail riding? I think he needs more of a challenge," I suggested.

"Let's go rope some cows," Finn chimed in.

I kept a straight face, even though Wyatt shook his head.

"What for?" Wyatt asked, sounding unenthused.

"Because it's fun?" Finn replied, not convincingly.

I groaned inwardly. "I was told he was trained on cows before they started racing him," I added. "I bet he'd enjoy it."

"Please?" Finn implored, sticking out his bottom lip and batting his eyelashes at Wyatt, who couldn't help but laugh.

"Fine, just don't look at me like that," Wyatt conceded.

"It's turning you on, isn't it? The whole 'damsel in distress' look?" Finn teased.

"Yeah, no." Wyatt urged Gambler forward. "Let's go."

Finn shot me a triumphant look, clearly pleased with himself.

The guys warmed the horses up in the arena while I talked some wranglers into helping us out with some steers. I parked Cher and myself at the fence to watch. I wasn't quite ready to get out of the saddle yet, and I welcomed the distraction from the restless thoughts of my sister. She and my parents had left that morning, and I wasn't sure if I was happy to see her go or not.

I relaxed in my saddle and played with strands of Cher's coppery mane as Wyatt and Finn prepared for their run. Gambler pranced in place in the box, ears perked forward, almost like he knew what was coming.

A small smile tugged at the corner of my mouth—this was Wyatt's element. His shoulders were relaxed, the constant crease between his brows smoothed out. For once, he didn't look burdened by the weight of the world.

The wrangler nodded, opening the gate to release the steer. Finn surged forward, his loop sailing through the air to catch the horns. I held my breath as Wyatt followed, his rope flying, catching the steer's heels and snapping taut. Gambler didn't even flinch; he was locked in and focused like I'd never seen before. He dug his haunches in, muscles rippling beneath his black coat as he held the steer steady.

A whoop escaped my lips.

Wyatt glanced over, his face split by a grin that reached all the way to the crinkles around his eyes. In that moment, he was lighter, happier. Free.

"Holy shit!" Finn hollered. He patted his horse, Ghost, on the neck.

Wyatt rode over to me. "Did you know he could do that?" He leaned back in his saddle and ran his hand over Gambler's hindquarters.

I shrugged. "I guess he likes cows. Go again."

They ran it a few more times, each as flawless as the last. Gambler was a completely different horse, calm and responsive to Wyatt's cues. It was like the steer grounded him and gave him purpose beyond running in circles.

I couldn't help the pang of jealousy that twisted in my gut. My horse went better for Wyatt than he ever had for me. All those dreams of championships, of making my family proud, slipped further away with every perfect run Wyatt did.

But then Wyatt caught my eye, that smile still playing on his lips, and maybe—just maybe—it would be worth it.

"Alright, Cher, it's you and me again. I'm sorry I was being so stupid and let a handsome boy come between us. Girl power all the way." I patted her.

Cher turned her head and touched her nose to my foot, signaling her forgiveness. She probably even appreciated the break, knowing I would come back to my senses eventually.

"Now, to convince Wyatt of this plan..."

That might not be so easy. Sure, we had convinced Wyatt to mess around and try Gambler, but now we had to persuade him to rodeo with the horse, and Wyatt was stubborn.

They rode out of the arena, breathless and smiling.

"Wow," I said. "Impressive. It's like you guys have done that before."

"I know, right?" Finn replied, laying it on a little too thick. "It'd sure be nice to have a partner again for the team roping event next weekend." He looked directly at me as he said it.

I feigned surprise and pretended to consider it.

"Finn, no—" Wyatt began.

I interrupted. "Sure, why not?"

Wyatt, taken aback, turned to me. "Kins, he's your horse."

"I'm not riding him right now. Besides, after seeing that, I'm not sure I have him on the right career path."

Those words were harder to get out than I'd thought they would be. It was obvious Gambler was a cattle horse but handing him over to Wyatt was like giving up a part of me.

I swallowed hard, forcing a smile onto my face as Wyatt's brow furrowed.

"Are you sure about this, Kins?" His eyes searched mine, always able to see right through my bravado.

"Of course," I lied, praying he wouldn't call my bluff. "I'm not riding him right now. He should be kept busy, and he obviously enjoys this."

Wyatt studied me for a long moment before nodding slowly. "Alright, if that's what you want." He reached over, his calloused fingers brushing my cheek in the softest of caresses. "Thank you."

My heart fluttered at his touch, warmth spreading through me. This was worth it, I told myself. Seeing that look of pure joy on Wyatt's face as he rode Gambler was all I could ask for after the heartache we'd been through.

Finn cleared his throat, breaking the moment. "Well, I'm going to go get our entry in." He swung off Ghost and headed towards the registration booth.

Wyatt turned Gambler to follow but paused, glancing back at me over his shoulder. "You coming?"

I shook my head. "I'll catch up in a bit. I want some more time with this girl." I patted Cher's neck, her coat's familiar scent calming me.

Wyatt's expression softened. "Don't be too long." With that, he nudged Gambler forward, falling into step beside Finn.

An ache settled deep in my chest. Cher shifted beneath me as if sensing my unease.

I leaned forward, burying my face in her mane to hide the tears that threatened to spill over. "I'm doing the right thing, aren't I, girl?"

I pulled back from Cher's mane, wiping at my damp cheeks with the back of my hand. What was I thinking? How could I hand over Gambler like that? He was my horse, my dream.

Finn shot me a subtle wink over his shoulder, letting me know he was in on the scheme to get Wyatt roping again.

I couldn't help but wonder if we'd thought this through, though. Wyatt wasn't an idiot. He was bound to figure out eventually that Finn and I had cooked this whole thing up behind his back. I imagined the stormy look that would cloud his face when he realized we'd manipulated him, even if our intentions were good. That crease would appear between his brows, and his jaw would tighten in that way that meant he was fighting to keep his emotions in check.

He hated feeling out of control or like decisions were being made for him. It went against every fibre of his being. I knew that better than anyone after our years of being ... well, whatever we were. He would see this as me overstepping again, trying to control his life.

It wasn't like that at all, but I understood why he might view it that way, given our history. I was trying to give him a new lease on the rodeo life he loved so much, a chance to rekindle that passion I saw burning in his eyes when he rode Gambler.

Then again, maybe I was getting ahead of myself. Maybe Wyatt would surprise me and be grateful for the opportunity, not getting bogged down in questioning the intentions behind it all. Maybe he'd accept this gift with grace instead of second-guessing every motive.

I knew that was just wishful thinking. I could only hope the risk would be worth it.

I sighed, resting my forehead against Cher's neck as I tried to push those doubts aside. Only time would tell how Wyatt would react when the truth came out. For now, I had to focus on being supportive, on not letting my selfish desires get in the way of his potential for happiness.

If giving up my prized horse and risking my own rodeo dreams for a little while was what it took, well ... I'd have to woman up and deal with it. Wyatt's smile was worth that and more.

Chapter 20

COWBOYS AND PLOWBOYS - JON PARDI & LUKE BRYAN

Wyatt

The coppery tang of dust and horse sweat permeated the air as I swung the rope in tight loops, letting the weight and rhythm steady my newfound nerves. This old, small-town arena might have been a far cry from the big pro circuits, but the dry Alberta air still thrummed with an edge of anticipation before a competition, and it was the perfect rodeo to dip my boots back into.

"Easy, big guy." I patted Gambler's thick neck, feeling the coiled power vibrating through his muscular body as he danced beneath me.

Despite our week of hard prep work, those first-run jitters still had my heart hammering in my chest.

Finn rode up on Ghost, the gelding's smoky coat gleaming with a fine sheen of sweat.

A wave of nostalgia washed over me, taking me back to all the times we'd geared up together for a competition. It felt like coming home after a long stint on the road, and it hadn't even been that long.

"Just like old times, eh?" Finn remarked with a grin.

I allowed myself a rare full-blown smile as I nodded. "Good to be back."

My brief moment of contented ease was interrupted as another rider approached, giving Gambler an appraising look.

"Hell of a nice horse you got there." He tipped his hat. "New mount?"

I shifted in the saddle, avoiding his eyes. "Nah, just riding him for now."

The cowboy's expression shifted as understanding dawned. Studying Gambler more intently, he asked, "Wait a minute, ain't that Kinsley Jackson's horse? Mr. Lucky Gambler?"

My jaw clenched hard, and I forced out a clipped, "That's right."

He left it hanging there. I could practically hear the unspoken thoughts whirring through his head: *How'd a busted-ass cowboy like you score a ride on a horse like that? Must be nice having a rich rodeo princess girlfriend to buy your way onto a top-dollar mount.*

"We're up next." Finn's voice sliced through the uncomfortable silence, mercifully redirecting my attention.

I gave Gambler an extra pat as we headed toward the boxes, forcing aside the gnawing twist of unease. No point dwelling on what that jackass—or anyone else—might assume about my situation. I was just here to ride, same as always.

As we settled in on either side of the chute, my and Gambler's focus resharpening. Gambler eyed the steer through the bars and went still, poised and ready.

On the other side of the steer, Finn's eyes were alight with that fire we'd stoked for so many years, the unspoken vow to leave it all out there passing between us in a single nod.

Then the gate flew open with a metallic clang, and just like that, the world stripped away until nothing existed but this moment.

Gambler exploded into powerful strides the second that steer moved from the chute, his bunched muscles transitioning into an unstoppable burst of forward momentum. Finn surged forward on the other side. Three swings of his rope, and he had the horns, turning the steer just right for me to do my job.

My awareness narrowed to the rope whipping through the air and the hoofbeats' rumbling drumbeat reverberating through my bones. As the steer veered left, I let the loop sail in a low arc, wincing as it cinched perfectly around the hind legs. Gambler dropped back on his haunches, front hooves digging in as he threw his weight against the jarring strain. Finn's end went taut, and just like that, the big animal was locked down.

The clock flashed a time that had my pulse pounding harder than Gambler's feet hitting the dirt. A triumphant whoop burst from me before I could rein it in. Finn echoed the cry as we basked in the rush of a flawless run.

Riding that wave of adrenaline, we exited the arena, and I slid from the saddle with a grounding thud, just in time to catch an airborne mass of golden locks and denim barreling into me like a little blonde hurricane.

"Wyatt!" Kinsley crashed against my chest with a breathless laugh, knocking the wind out of me.

Her slender frame fitted against mine like she was made to be there. My arms closed around her waist as I breathed in her crisp, sweet apple scent. Just for a moment, I allowed myself to indulge in the pure, uncomplicated thrill of having her in my embrace.

Then she pulled back just enough to beam up at me, blue eyes sparkling with excitement. "Oh my god, you two were amazing out there!" Spinning in my arms, she ran her hands along Gambler's neck and settled on his face. "And you, big guy! You were such a good boy. Yes, you were."

I watched her fawn over the big gelding—her horse, I had to remind myself—with a strange, unsettled feeling twisting my gut.

Kinsley turned that blazing smile back on me, happier than a kid at Christmas. "That time, Wyatt! Did you see it? You guys smoked the competition!"

I couldn't resist grinning back at her infectious enthusiasm. "We did alright."

She rolled her eyes, giving me a playful shove. "Alright? That was phenomenal!" Stepping in close, she pinned me with a look that damn near sizzled me from the inside out. "I knew you two would be unstoppable as a team."

The way she looked at me, all bright-eyed admiration and shining belief, hit me harder than a punch to the gut. A slow coil of want unfurled low in my belly as I drank in the flush of her cheeks, the tousled disarray of her hair, and the slightly parted lips that were just begging for...

"Couldn't have done it without this big guy," I managed as I patted Gambler's shoulder.

"Is that so?" She drifted closer until I could feel the heat radiating from her body. Her sweet, mouthwatering scent enveloped me as her fingers trailed up my arm in a feather-light touches, leaving goosebumps in their wake. "Or maybe you're just that good."

My throat went dry as her words carried that raspy edge of pure sin. "Kins..."

"I've missed watching you ride," she breathed, stepping even closer so her front was brushing mine. Her voice dropped to a gravelly whisper that had me fully hardening against my wishes. "You're one hell of a sight out there, cowboy."

I squeezed my eyes shut against the dizzying wave of want that slammed into me hard enough to damn near buckle my knees. This woman would be the death of me, no doubt about it.

"Am I interrupting something?" Finn's amused drawl pierced our little two-person bubble.

Kinsley jerked back, colour flooding her cheeks as she smoothed back her wild hair. "Not at all," she replied in a breezy tone. Clearing her throat, she went on, "Just congratulating you boys on a spectacular run."

One brow inched up as Finn's too-knowing gaze slid between us. "I'm sure."

Kinsley flashed him a bright smile before turning to greet Maisey when she approached. As the two wandered off, chatting and laughing, Kinsley glanced back over her shoulder, blue eyes still shining with that same heated promise.

Part of me wanted nothing more than to chase after her, to haul her back against me and slant my mouth over hers. But the other part felt a strange sense of relief at having that blinding, all-consuming blaze between us banked for now.

"Look away from the witch and her magic powers," Finn said.

"What?"

"You're getting that dopey, Kinsley-whipped look on your face again," Finn remarked with a shake of his head as he clapped me on the shoulder.

"Shut up." I scowled at him, resisting the impulse to look back over my shoulder for another glimpse of her swaying hips.

"Do you want me to get you a mirror?"

As we started walking the horses back toward the barn, Grady and Rhett caught up.

"Damn, boys, what're we doing to celebrate that nice, fat payday?" Grady slapped me on the back, grinning.

"Going to bed." I led Gambler into his stall.

"You're a good friend, but no thanks, buddy," Grady replied.

Rolling my eyes, I snagged a flake of hay from a nearby bale and chucked it at his face. "Here, make yourself useful for once."

He batted the clinging bits of hay off him, still grinning as he tossed the flake into Gambler's stall. I followed it up with a couple more.

"Hey, we should get signed up for the next string of rodeos now that we're back in the running," Finn said from the next stall.

I paused. "I should probably check with Kinsley first, make sure she's good with me riding Gambler for a while longer."

Finn shot me an exasperated look, already anticipating the argument. "She already said it was fine. You're overthinking again."

He was right, but it didn't change the fact that this wasn't my horse we were making plans with. What was our timeline on this? I couldn't ride him forever. Kinsley and I should have some sort of agreement. Maybe I could give her a cut of the winnings. This wasn't just any horse; this was her horse, her parents' cold, hard cash underfoot every time I swung a leg over that saddle.

"Let's go get those entries squared away." Finn drew me from my thoughts. "First round's on us after that win."

Grady perked up like a dog catching a whiff of fresh steak. "Well, now you're talking! Let the meal train start rolling!"

"Yeah, you just keep riding our coattails, you bum," I shot back, shoving his shoulder as we made our way out of the barn.

"Hey, I'll be first in line kissing both your boot heels if you start raking in the real dough."

Our laughter and trash talk carried across the dusty parking lot as we wove between the maze of trailers and rigs towards my truck.

Despite myself, I found my gaze scanning the crowd, searching unconsciously for any glimpse of Kinsley. But she was nowhere to be found, slipping through my grasp as easily as smoke between my fingers.

"Dude, I'm starving." Grady groaned as we finally reached the truck. "Can we hit a buffet or something? I just want to eat for, like, five hours straight."

"Best idea you've ever had," I said, my stomach grumbling.

Chapter 21

I Grew Up On Farm - The Reklaws

Kinsley

"Any persistent symptoms?" The doctor checked my eyes.

The paper on the exam table crinkled beneath me as I shifted and tried to keep my eyes open. "Nope," I answered. "Nothing for almost three weeks now."

Wyatt stood at the other end of the room, arms crossed over his chest, scrutinizing every move the doctor made. He had insisted on coming with me to hear from the doctor himself that I was fine.

"Well, everything looks good. I don't see why you can't start riding again, as long as you're careful."

"Oh, I will be!"

"You're sure, Doc? You don't think a couple more weeks—" Wyatt began.

I interrupted. "Ignore him."

The doctor chuckled and made a note on my chart. "I promise you everything checks out. I wouldn't give her the okay to ride if I didn't think it was safe," the doctor assured Wyatt. "My daughter would kill me if I did; she's a big fan of yours and wants to be a barrel racer too."

"Bring her to a rodeo sometime soon and come say hi!" I offered.

"I'll do that. Good luck to both of you and come back if you have any concerns." He smiled as he left the room.

Wyatt gave him a brusque nod.

"You're pulling that 'overprotective man' shit again," I commented.

"Yup," he replied, unapologetically.

"It's sexy as hell."

The comment cracked his stern façade, eliciting a small grin from him. "Let's go." He took my hand and pulled me off the table.

We got to his truck, and he opened my door. I slid into the passenger seat and sank into it, thinking about all the memories this truck carried. *That time on the side of the highway in the pouring rain...* A shiver ran up my spine.

He got into the driver's side and started it up.

"Where are we going now?" I asked.

He raised a brow. "What did you have in mind?"

"I don't know. I feel like all we ever do is go from rodeo to rodeo. Don't you want to go out into the real world every once in a while?"

"Not really."

"You would live in a barn."

"If only I had a barn to live in," he muttered.

Damn, I'd walked into that one.

Wyatt pulled out of the parking lot, and I stared out my window, unsure of what to say next. There was a time when talking to him had been so easy. On our first date, we'd done nothing but talk and laugh. That was also the last time things had been easy between us. Yeah, of course we'd had good times since then, but our relationship was like a carnival ride that went up and down—sometimes your belly filled with butterflies, and the next moment nausea took over.

Instead of leaving the city, he drove further in towards downtown.

"Where are we going?" I asked.

"Out into the world," he replied.

We parked the truck on a busy street and got out. The area was lined with small trendy shops, cafés, and restaurants. I bounced with excitement.

Wyatt looked around and scratched the back of his head. He stood out in this area with his dirty boots, Wrangler jeans, plaid shirt, and trucker cap. "At least you dressed up for the occasion." He eyed my attire.

I had opted for a pale blue sundress that day, a change from my regular jeans.

"Oh, c'mon, cowboy. I'll be beating them off you with a stick," I joked, grabbing his hand and tugging him along down the street.

We popped into a few stores, browsing through clothes and trinkets. Or, I browsed while Wyatt wandered around looking bored.

I chose a few items—a cute blouse with sunflowers printed on it and a couple pairs of jeans. I took them up to the register.

The cashier rang me up. "$191.25."

I pulled out my credit card and handed it over. Out of the corner of my eye, I saw Wyatt's gaze lock on the card. His brow furrowed and his lips drew back into a thin line, but he didn't say anything.

The cashier ran my card and handed it back to me, along with my purchase tucked into a bag. "Thanks! Have a great day."

"You too!"

I looped my arm through Wyatt's as we stepped back out onto the sidewalk. His body was tense beside mine, and I sensed the unease radiating off him. I didn't need to ask what was bothering him; I already knew.

We passed several restaurants, but Wyatt turned up his nose at menus advertising sushi or vegan options. A burger joint caught his approval, and if I was being honest, as much as I liked to think of myself as open-minded, nothing beat a good burger. I was cattle rancher's daughter, after all.

We wolfed down burgers and fries, and I kept quiet while he paid for the food. It was nice to see him open his wallet without a pained expression on his face. He had won his last three rodeos, so I knew he had been cashing some pretty good checks. I was so proud of how well he was doing, even if it was on the horse that should have been putting me in the money.

"Where to now?" he asked as we walked out of the restaurant.

I looked up and down the street, and then pointed to an old building displaying a marquee adorned with glowing lights.

"A movie?"

"Yep, c'mon." I jogged across the street when there was an opening in traffic.

Wyatt followed behind me. The theatre boasted retro matinees and was playing one of my favourite films.

"Two for *Cat Ballou* please," I told the box office attendant.

Wyatt pulled out his wallet again and paid for the tickets. After we loaded up with popcorn and drinks, we found seats in the nearly empty theatre.

"I think you're the only one who likes this movie," Wyatt remarked, surveying the deserted room.

"Jane Fonda playing a schoolteacher turned outlaw? What's not to like?" I settled into the seat, which Wyatt was a little too big for, and started munching on my popcorn.

"You're still hungry?"

"No, but you can't go to a movie and not eat popcorn. It's a rule."

"Is it?" He smirked at me.

The lights dimmed, and the screen came to life as the movie started.

"You've never seen this?" I asked.

He shook his head, but I wasn't surprised, considering the movie was from 1965.

"Wow, Jane Fonda was hot," Wyatt said.

I laughed. "I know, right? She totally still is. I used to watch this movie all the time when I was a kid, and I wanted to be her so badly."

We munched on our popcorn in silence for a while, absorbed in the film. I got through half my bag before I was ready to burst, so I put it on the seat next to me. This left me with free hands, and I wasn't sure what to do with them. This wasn't exactly a date, but it kind of was. I mean, it was Wyatt. I was tempted to make out with him.

He didn't seem to feel any of my awkwardness because he didn't hesitate to put an arm around my shoulders and draw me to his side. He was the most confusing guy ever. This dance we were doing was giving me whiplash. I had never been so unsure around him before.

We'd broken up and gotten back together a few times, but everything about this time felt different. It was like this was our last chance; we were going to make this work and be together forever, or we wouldn't, and this would be the end for us.

I laid my head on his shoulder and snuggled in close. His fingers brushed lightly up and down my arm, sending shivers through me.

I would not let him go without a fight.

The movie ended, and we stood up and stretched, blinking as the lights came back on. Wyatt smiled at me.

"Were you awake for the whole movie?" I asked.

"Umm, I'm not sure," he answered. "It was good, though."

I rolled my eyes at him. "Well, I guess we ought to get back and take care of the horses."

He nodded, and we made our way out of the theatre. We left the city and returned to the homey and familiar country landscape.

"Oh, look! Horses!" I pointed out my window at the small herd grazing in a pasture beside the highway.

"I love that you still do that," he said.

"Do what?"

"You own horses. Your whole life is horses, but you still get excited like a little kid when you see them."

"Every horse is worth getting excited over."

"Isn't that the truth."

He took my hand across the seat, and we drove back to the rodeo grounds, enjoying the view of green fields and distant mountains blurring along beside us.

Chapter 22

I'll Be Your Small Town - Cole Swindell

Wyatt

"So, you guys went on a date?" Grady asked.

We were sitting in the empty bleachers overlooking an outdoor sand ring, watching the barrel racing practice. Kinsley had Cherokee out and was warming her up at a nice, easy trot around the perimeter.

"Yeah, I guess. It wasn't planned or anything," I replied.

"Are you guys back together?"

The sun beat down on my neck as I leaned forward, my elbows resting on my knees. I couldn't take my eyes off Kinsley as she guided Cherokee around the barrels, a small, fierce smile playing across her lips.

"I don't know," I mumbled more to myself than to Grady.

It had been so easy, so natural, to fall back into our old rhythm. The way she'd laughed at my jokes, the way her hand had fit perfectly in mine as we'd walked down the street. It was like no time had passed at all.

But that was the problem, wasn't it? Time had passed, and things had changed. We had changed. Hadn't we?

I rubbed my jaw, feeling the stubble that had grown in over the past few days. I had probably given Kinsley the impression that we were back together. The way I had looked at her, held her close in the dark theatre... Since her accident, we just sort of started falling back into a relationship. But I honestly didn't know if I meant it. I thought I did. I hoped I did. But doubt still played around in the back of my mind, and I didn't know if I was ready to dive back into that particular rodeo.

And yet, I couldn't deny the way my heart had skipped a beat when she smiled at me over that burger. The way my skin had tingled when her fingers would trail over my arm. It was good to be with her again, to feel that connection that had always been there between us.

Kinsley guided Cherokee to a stop, patted the horse's neck, and whispered something in her ear. She looked up then, her blue eyes finding mine across the distance.

My breath caught in my throat, and I felt that tug in my chest, that longing for something I wasn't sure I could have.

"But you're on good terms, right?"

"Yeah, why?"

"Would you happen to have her sister's phone number?"

Grady's question caught me off guard.

"Really? Abby?" I turned to him in disbelief.

"I liked her."

"Then why didn't you ask her for her number?"

"I did. She said no."

I couldn't help but laugh because he looked so perplexed.

"Well, you have your answer. She doesn't like you and giving you her number would cross a line or something."

"See, I think she does like me, but she's in denial."

"I'm not sure the denial lies on her side."

I was a bit surprised at Grady's persistence. I didn't think he and Abby had that much in common. I didn't know Abby all that well; she and Kinsley weren't close, and she rarely came out to rodeos.

"I don't see you two together. You're a bull rider; she does dressage."

"That's the word! She mentioned it, but I couldn't remember. Dressage." He mulled over the word. "What is it?"

"Uh..." I scratched the back of my head. "It's like horse dancing or something."

"Huh?"

"Google it."

He whipped out his phone and started watching YouTube videos. "What the fuck?" he exclaimed after a moment.

"I know."

"This is a sport?"

"Yep."

"I don't get it."

"Like I said, you two are very different."

"Oh, look at this one go! He's dancing to the music!" He tilted the phone so I could see, but I only glanced down briefly.

"What are you guys watching?" Finn said as he and Rhett came over and sat down beside us.

"Grady has a hard-on for Abby Jackson, so he's learning about dressage," I explained.

"Oh gawd." Finn shook his head. "Good luck with that."

Kinsley's turn came up, and she held Cher outside the arena. Suddenly, Cher leaped from her mark and raced towards the first barrel. I held my breath, but they took the turn beautifully, and the next two as well.

"There you go. She survived," Finn said.

I stood up, swatting his hat off his head as I walked by them. Jogging down the bleacher steps, I made my way over to Kinsley. She was standing beside Cher, talking to a couple of cowboys I didn't recognize, which only made me quicken my pace.

"Hey, you," she greeted when she saw me.

I brushed by the cowboys without a care that I was interrupting and took my place at her side.

"Well, good run, Kinsley," one of them said, and they both waved and retreated.

"You scared them away." She turned and smiled up at me.

"They'll get over it."

"Jealous?"

"Who wouldn't be?"

"Good answer. Ready to win again today?"

I nodded and gazed down at her, drinking in her face. "How do you want to celebrate tonight?"

"Ooh, getting a little cocky, are ya?"

"Something about that question rings true."

Her laugh burst forth, contagious and bright. "C'mon, cowboy, walk us back to the barn."

I helped her get Cher untacked and started brushing her soft, coppery coat. Kinsley brushed her from the other side, and I found my eyes drawn to her delicate wrists and her precise flicking motions.

"What's got your concentration, cowboy?"

"Your wrists," I blurted without thinking.

"My wrists, huh? Interesting choice. He's a wrist man." She was smirking at me, and I couldn't suppress my smile. "Do you want to come home with me in a couple of weeks?" she asked suddenly.

"What?"

"We have a break in the schedule coming up. I thought maybe you would want to come back to the ranch with me for a while. Bring Drifter, maybe leave him there? We could turn him out with our horses for the summer; he'd love it."

I thought it over. It would be nice for him to spend the summer grazing instead of being hauled around from rodeo to rodeo. I wouldn't mind the break either, to sit still for a while.

If I agreed to go home with Kinsley, it would mean something to her. I wouldn't be able to keep pretending we were just friends. But I wanted to be close to her again and make her happy.

"Sure, I'll come." My voice came out softer than I'd intended.

Kinsley's face lit up, her smile brighter than the sun streaming through the barn windows. "You will?" She bounced on her toes in excitement. "Oh, this is going to be so much fun! Drifter will love it there. We have this big pasture with a creek running through it, and the grass is so green and lush..." She rambled on, her words tumbling over each other in her enthusiasm.

A smile tugged at the corners of my mouth. It was impossible not to get caught up in her energy.

"I'll call my parents and let them know." She pulled out her phone.

My smile tightened at the mention of her parents. Not that I didn't like them—quite the opposite. They had always been kind to me, welcoming me into their home with open arms, but they were a class above me with their sprawling ranch and their expensive horses. It made me uncomfortable, like I didn't quite fit in their world.

Kinsley paused, her finger hovering over the call button. "You okay?" Her brow furrowed.

"Yeah, I'm fine." I forced my smile back into place. "Just thinking about how happy Drifter is going to be."

She grinned, then hit the call button and put the phone to her ear. As she talked to her mom, I leaned against the stall door, watching the way the light played off her hair and the way her eyes sparkled when she laughed.

I knew I was in trouble, that this trip would change things between us, but for the first time in a long time, I looked forward to the future, whatever it might bring.

Chapter 23

WE WERE US - KEITH URBAN & MIRANDA LAMBERT

Kinsley

We loaded Gambler, Drifter, and Cher into my trailer. Wyatt insisted on driving, so I handed over the keys to my truck; he'd left his with Finn and Grady. Rhett had to go home for a while.

The drive to the ranch took a few hours, and we fell into a comfortable silence except for Gambler's kicking.

"Does he always do that?" Wyatt's eyes darted to the rearview mirror as if expecting to see a horse jumping out of the trailer any second.

"Yep." I turned up the music to a song he liked.

His head just barely moved to the beat. I gazed at him unabashedly, and when he glanced over at me, the corner of his mouth quirked up.

"What?" he asked.

I shrugged, shaking my head. "Nothing," I said, but I couldn't hide my smirk. "I'm happy you're coming with me."

"Me too."

"Really?" I bit down hard on my lip.

"Of course, why?" He looked puzzled.

"Because we're technically still broken up, aren't we? Friends, or I don't know what."

Wyatt sighed and dragged his fingers through his hair, his expression conflicted. He was quiet for a long moment, the only sounds the hum of the engine and the faint music playing in the background.

Finally, he spoke. "I don't know what we're doing, Kins." He paused, swallowing hard before continuing. "I don't know how to not love you, to not be in love with you."

The words hung in the air between us, heavy with meaning. Time seemed to slow as I processed what he'd said, my heart pounding in my chest. I studied his profile intently: the firm line of his jaw, the furrow in his brow, and the way his fingers tightened on the steering wheel. His confession had stripped away his usual guard, leaving him raw and vulnerable. I could see the struggle playing out on his face, the desire to protect himself warring with the depth of his feelings for me.

I held my breath, afraid to shatter this fragile moment. My mind raced, replaying his words over and over. The intensity of his admission made my skin tingle, hope blooming in my chest.

Slowly, I exhaled, gathering my courage. "Wyatt," I whispered, my voice barely audible over the rumble of the road beneath us.

He glanced at me briefly, his eyes dark with longing and uncertainty, before returning his gaze to the road. The air between us crackled.

I wished desperately that I could close the physical distance between us. My fingers twitched with the urge to reach out and touch him, to trace the familiar lines of his face and reassure us both that this was real. I wished the console between us would vanish so I could slide closer to him. *Stupid fancy truck.*

"We should have taken your truck," I mumbled.

A low chuckle rumbled from Wyatt's chest, surprising me. "Why?"

"Because it's much more conducive to snuggling."

He looked over at me, amused. He reached his hand over the console and rested it on my thigh, his thumb rubbing over the denim of my jeans.

As we pulled into the ranch's long driveway, Wyatt's entire demeanour shifted. An unease settled over him as he took in the endless fields, the mountains in the distance, and our family home, which was a large, rustic, lodge-style house. There were a couple of barns—one for the horses and a calving barn—a machine shop for the tractors, a bunkhouse for staff, a hay shed, and a little further down the road, my grandparents' old house, which had been empty since they passed.

As soon as we stopped the truck, my parents came out of the house to greet us. I hugged them both.

"Wyatt, we're so glad to see you again." Mom pulled him in for a warm hug too.

"You too. Thanks for inviting me."

"You're welcome anytime," Mom replied. She'd always had a soft spot for him. She was the nurturing type and seemed to sense he needed nurturing. I didn't think she was wrong, even though he resisted it.

"Mr. Jackson." Wyatt walked over to my dad and held out his hand. "Thanks for letting me bring my horse for a while." I had filled Dad in on the situation with Drifter over the phone before we came. "I'll pay for his upkeep, of course—"

"The horse is more than welcome to stay, but I don't need your money." Wyatt opened his mouth to speak, but Dad held up a hand to stop him. "What I do need is help driving the herd to another pasture. And some other chores done around here. Can I count on your help?"

"Yes, sir, absolutely."

"Great. You two get settled in the house, and then we'll have some lunch."

"I have your room made up with fresh linens, Kinsley," Mom said.

"Okay, thanks, Mom!"

We unloaded the horses from the trailer and put them into stalls in the barn to settle in and have a drink. After grabbing our bags from the truck, I eagerly dragged Wyatt into the house, navigating through the familiar hallways and up the stairs until we reached the sanctuary of my bedroom.

My bedroom was decorated in country chic style, with a soothing palette of blues and whites. The walls were adorned with framed photographs of my horses while a vintage-inspired quilt covered the plush, oversized bed. A weathered wooden dresser and nightstand completed the rustic yet elegant look.

As we stepped inside, a sudden realisation hit me, and I turned to him, a hint of uncertainty in my voice. "Did you want your own room?" My eyes searched his. "My mom kind of assumed—"

His response was immediate and unwavering. "No, I don't."

His words were filled with a quiet intensity that sent a shiver down my spine and ignited a warmth in my cheeks, which spread to other parts of my body.

"Okay," I breathed out, my heart racing at the implications of his decision.

Despite our impromptu date we had shared and the rekindled connection, Wyatt hadn't so much as attempted to kiss me. Yet the thought of him sharing my bed tonight unleashed a torrent of fantasies that went far beyond the realm of innocent kisses. My mind wandered to the possibilities of tangled sheets, heated touches, and the pleasure of rediscovering each other in the most intimate way possible.

Mom had a big lunch ready for us when we went back downstairs, and Wyatt's stomach rumbled at the sight of food, making us all laugh.

"Sorry," he said, a bit embarrassed. "I'm starving, and that looks amazing." On the table were barbecue ribs, baked potatoes, corn on the cob, and coleslaw. "All this is for lunch?" he asked in disbelief.

"I figured you guys would be hungry after the drive, so I made the big meal for lunch, and we'll have a nice stew for supper later," Mom explained.

"More food later?"

"Yes, there's three meals a day around here," I teased. "We don't starve our cowboys."

"We can't when we work them as hard as we do," Dad added.

We all dug into the food, and I watched, amused, as Wyatt shovelled it in.

Mom looked especially pleased; she loved feeding people. "How is it?" she asked Wyatt.

"The best meal I have ever had."

"Good. I don't like leftovers, so have more."

Wyatt nodded and helped himself to more of everything. Mom raised an eyebrow at me, and I shrugged and smiled.

Abby came into the kitchen in her riding clothes—white breeches a navy polo shirt tucked in with a thin leather belt, and tall black boots. Her brown hair was pulled back from her face in a French braid.

Her presence changed the atmosphere. She greeted everyone politely, but her eyes lingered on Wyatt with a hint of curiosity. Taking a seat, she ate quietly.

"How was your ride?" I asked her.

"It was fine."

I waited for her to elaborate, but she didn't. I guess we weren't past our fight at the rodeo.

When we were all stuffed to capacity, Dad stood up and said it was time for a walk. "Walking after meals is good for digestion," he said. "I can show you some of the stuff I want to get done while you're here."

Wyatt followed him outside after Mom shooed us away, refusing help with the cleanup.

"We're a little short-staffed right now," Dad explained, "so your timing couldn't be better."

"I'm happy to help."

"Good, good. I hear you're doing well with Gambler."

"They're amazing together," I said.

"I appreciate Kinsley letting me use him. I know I need to look at getting another horse of my own. I will. I—"

"There's no hurry," I assured him. "Cher and I are doing great. You and Gambler are a great team."

"Yeah, but..." He struggled; the conflict blatant on his face.

I wanted to end this conversation before we ended up in another fight.

"We'll get that sorted out later," Dad said, coming to my rescue. "Come look at these cows, will you?"

Wyatt clamped his mouth shut, drawing it into a hard line, and to my relief, he followed Dad without another word.

Chapter 24

SHE'S EVERYTHING - BRAD PAISLEY

Wyatt

I woke early the next morning, my eyes opening to the sight of Kinsley sleeping beside me.

A pang hit my chest. Last night, after turning in, Kinsley had gone to the bathroom to wash up. I had pretended to be asleep when she returned, just lying there. The waves of disappointment had poured off her as she climbed into bed beside me. It wasn't that I didn't want her; I always wanted her. But something inside me was holding back, despite letting her believe we were trying again.

With a gentle touch, I kissed her forehead then quietly slipped out of bed. Pulling on my jeans and t-shirt, I tiptoed out of the room, making my way down the stairs and out the front door. The morning breeze greeted me as I headed over to the barn to start chores. If I was going to stay here, I was determined to be useful.

"Morning, Drifter," I greeted my horse in his stall, throwing him some hay before fetching his grain.

"Morning," Ben, the farmhand, called out as he walked down the aisle, an insulated mug of coffee in his hand. "You're out early."

I nodded. "Here to help."

"Great." Ben grabbed a cart of hay. "Get some coffee from the tack room."

Once I had a few gulps of coffee, I started scooping pelleted feed into the horses' buckets.

"You want your horse turned out with the others today?" Ben asked.

"Yeah, let's try it."

"We don't have any real aggressive ones, except Gambler, but we'll keep him separate."

I nodded in agreement as we set about haltering the horses and leading them to the pasture behind the barn.

When I released Drifter, his head shot up, eyes wide as he surveyed his surroundings. He stood still, sniffing the air.

Smirking at him, I said, "It's called freedom, boy. Enjoy."

Heeding my advice, Drifter took off running, giving a few spirited kicks and squeals. I laughed, watching him embrace his newfound liberty. He galloped up to the nearest group of horses, and they greeted one another by blowing into each other's noses before taking off running together.

Watching them, I felt a deep satisfaction. This was all I wanted for him: room to move, a herd to be a part of, and fresh grass to eat. I leaned back against the fence, a contented smile playing on my lips.

"Well, that is a nice sight," Kinsley's voice came from behind me. She approached, crossed her arms over the top rail of the fence, and rested her chin on them.

"He's living the dream." My gaze was still fixed on the horses.

We fell into a comfortable silence, simply watching them.

After a moment, Kinsley broke the quiet. "You snuck out on me this morning."

"I know. I'm sorry," I admitted, turning to face her. "I wanted to be helpful while I'm here."

"Well, we'd better stop standing around and get the barn cleaned," she said.

With the three of us working together, we mucked out the stalls in record time, then headed up to the house for breakfast. The horses always came first.

Mrs. Jackson, as usual, had outdone herself. We filled our plates with eggs, bacon, hash browns, toast, and fresh fruit. I could get used to eating like this every day.

"I want to move the cattle to another pasture today," Kinsley's dad, Cal, said between mouthfuls. He turned to me. "You up for it?"

"You bet." I swallowed my last bite of toast.

"I'm coming too," Kinsley added and finished her orange juice in a quick gulp.

We headed back out to the barn, grabbed two ranch horses from their paddock, and got them tacked up. Riding over the range and rounding up cattle, I breathed easier. All the stresses of life on the road, trying to win all the time, vanished.

Kinsley watched me out of the corner of her eye.

"What?" I asked her.

"I like you here." She bit at the inside of her cheek.

"I like being here," I conceded, and it was the truth. If my father hadn't sold our farm, I could've given up the rodeo to manage the cattle. It was work I loved.

"Stay," Kinsley blurted out suddenly, then sucked in a breath, clamping her mouth shut.

"What do you mean?" I asked, taken aback.

"Stay with me. Work for the farm."

"Kinsley, we've talked about this." My defenses rose as I braced myself for the same old argument.

It wasn't the first time she had brought this up. Why couldn't she understand I needed to make my own way? Winning this season might allow me to save some money, but then what? Buy my own farm? Try to get ours back? I didn't know what I was going to do. I just had to do it on my own.

"I don't understand—"

"Kinsley," Cal's sharp voice interrupted, cutting through our conversation as he rode up. "There are a couple of cows falling behind over on that side. Go round them up."

"But—"

"Now, Kinsley."

I saw a flash of reluctance in her expression, but she relented and loped off after the stragglers. I exhaled a sigh of relief and dragged a hand down my face.

"Don't think you're off the hook, son." Cal turned his attention to me. "I know my daughter is pushy, but she takes after me, so now you're dealing with the big gun."

I realized then that my reprieve was short-lived. I shifted nervously in my saddle as his no-nonsense expression bore into me. He had every reason to be angry with me. I could only guess what Kinsley has told him about what went on between us. I doubted I came across in a good light and fully expected him to lay into me for hurting his daughter.

"Do you love my daughter?" he asked directly.

"Yes, sir," I answered honestly. I meant it. Despite what I'd put her through, it was never because I didn't love her.

"Lucky for you, I can see that. That's why I put up with your bullshit."

His bluntness took me aback, and I was stunned for a moment. I started to protest, but he interrupted, and I clamped my mouth shut.

"I like you, Wyatt. Kinsley has a very generous heart, and I'm glad she chose someone who doesn't take advantage of that. I can respect that you want to earn your own way, but you need to look realistically at your future. Do you want a life with Kinsley?"

"Yes," I replied without hesitation. She was the one thing I was certain of. It was just everything else…

"Well, her future is this ranch. I'm a lucky man to have two daughters who want what I've built for them. Kinsley and Abby will run this ranch together one day—God help us all. So, if you want to be with my daughter, this ranch is your future too. You best just start accepting it now. I'm not handing you anything; you'll work your ass off for this family. We'll make sure you earn it. Do you understand?"

I managed a nod, feeling as though I'd been smacked across the face with a baseball bat. I had no idea what to do with what he'd just said.

"Good. Now, get your ass in gear and get these cows moving. I don't want this taking all day."

Cal rode off towards Kinsley, leaving me with the left flank of the herd and my head spinning.

Chapter 25

Wild As Her - Tyler Joe Miller

Kinsley

I couldn't fathom what my dad had said to Wyatt, but on the ride back to the ranch, Wyatt was quiet. As we got the horses untacked and turned out, he was so lost in thought that I doubted anything short of a dynamite blast would reach him.

Watching him intently, I waited for a chance to ask what was going on.

Dad passed by, shaking his head at me. "Leave him be, Kinsley. He's processing."

"Processing what?" I called out after him, but Dad kept walking, tossing a simple "Patience, sweetheart," over his shoulder.

I exhaled a frustrated huff. All I wanted was for Wyatt to open up to me, preferably right now.

Resigned, I planted myself on a bale of hay outside the barn, waiting. My toe tapped impatiently on the dirt as time dragged on.

At last, I heard Wyatt's boots on the concrete of the barn aisle. I shot up, turning to face him. His strides were determined as he closed the distance between us, his penetrating brown eyes locking onto mine.

Before I could speak, his hands found my waist, pulling me flush against his body. The air left my lungs in a sharp exhale as Wyatt's lips crashed onto mine with an urgency that stole my breath.

I melted into his embrace, pouring every ounce of the longing that had been simmering for too long into that kiss. My fingers threaded through his hair, holding him close as our mouths moved together. Wyatt's hands roamed over my back, his calloused fingers igniting sparks everywhere they touched. When his tongue traced the seam of my lips, I readily parted them, deepening our kiss with a soft moan of pleasure. His grip tightened, pulling me even closer until there was no space left between us.

When we finally tore apart, our chests heaving, Wyatt's forehead pressed to mine. The charged air around us crackled with newfound electricity as his fingers brushed a stray strand of hair from my face, his touch featherlight.

"Finally," I breathed out, my voice shaking.

"I'm sorry. I'm a stubborn jackass," he said.

"Well, at least you're self-aware," I replied.

Wyatt chuckled and kissed me again.

"What did my dad say to you?"

"That if I want you, I have to want this ranch too and I need to earn it. And you. Here, not out there."

A small smile played across my lips. "My dad is a pretty smart guy."

"Apparently so."

"So, does this mean you're staying?" My heart fluttered with cautious hope.

He cupped my face, brushing his thumb over my cheekbone. "Let's win a few more rodeos. Then, we'll figure out what our future holds. Together."

The promise in his words warmed me to the core. "Deal." I rose on my tiptoes to brush my lips against his once more.

The rest of the evening passed in a bit of a dream-like haze. We cuddled together on the couch, watching one of Mom and Dad's old westerns, but I barely registered the movie. All I could focus on was the feeling of Wyatt's arm around me and the slow stroke of his fingers against my thigh under the blanket we shared. The restraint of being under my parents' watchful eyes only amplified my growing ache for him.

When I stole glances up at Wyatt, his face was an impassive mask of concentration, fixed on the screen. But the glaze in his eyes betrayed the battle he was waging with his own restraint.

As the credits rolled, we made a show of exaggerated yawns and stretches before bidding my parents good night.

The second we were out of their line of sight, our lips crashed together. We were a whirlwind of roaming hands and tangled limbs, desperate to touch and be touched after denying ourselves for too long. We stumbled blindly towards my bedroom, our bodies still entwined.

In our frenzied haste, I misjudged the distance, and Wyatt's head cracked against the wall with a dull thud.

"Ow!" He winced, rubbing the back of his head.

"Oh gosh, I'm so sorry!" I grimaced.

Wyatt just shrugged it off and leaned in to recapture my lips, but Dad's voice interrupted us, echoing down the hallway. "Good night, you two!"

We froze, sheepishly realizing the walls weren't nearly as thick as we'd hoped.

"We could be quiet," I whispered.

Wyatt arched an incredulous eyebrow at me. "You're never quiet," he pointed out with a teasing lilt. "Besides, I like it when you scream."

Heat flooded my cheeks, but his words sent a fresh rush of desire coursing through me. Biting my lip, I considered our options before a daring idea took hold. "Let's get out of here," I murmured.

We crept down the stairs and slipped out the front door, letting it ease shut silently behind us. The clear skies above us were a canvas of stars shining brilliantly without the interference of city lights.

Wyatt's hand found the small of my back, sending tingles dancing over my skin as he guided me towards my truck. He opened the passenger door for me, and as I climbed up, he leaned in for a brief but searing kiss that left me breathless. I settled onto the cool leather seat, my heart thundering with delicious anticipation as he closed the door and rounded the truck.

The engine rumbled to life with a roar that shattered the night's tranquil. I instinctively clapped a hand over my mouth as if that could somehow muffle the raucous sound.

Wyatt smirked knowingly at my reaction. "Should I lay on the gas and really peel out?" he teased.

I swatted his arm lightly. "Shh, you jerk! Just go already!"

With a wicked grin, Wyatt eased the truck down the long gravel driveway but then turned sharply onto a narrow dirt road that meandered through the pastures. His eyes kept darting over to me with an intensity that had my pulse kicking up another notch.

"Come on, hurry up," I urged, squirming impatiently in the seat.

"So impatient," he said, amused. Then his expression turned serious, his gaze darkening. "Take off your pants," he suddenly instructed.

I hesitated for only a second, making sure he wasn't joking, but there was no mistaking the earnestness in his expression. He wasn't kidding.

I popped open the button on my jeans and slowly undid the zipper. Wyatt struggled to keep his eyes on the road while also watching me. I lifted my hips and slid my jeans down before pulling them off. Beneath the denim, I wore a pair of plain white cotton panties printed with little horseshoes.

"Lucky underwear." I shrugged. "I guess it worked."

Wyatt let out a low rumbling laugh, the sound rich and warm. "I'd say so." His gaze drifted over me.

"So, now what, cowboy?" My voice emerged in a breathless rasp.

Wyatt guided the truck down a winding path that dead-ended near the river's edge. The gentle rush of the water over rocks drifted through the open windows, filling the air with its soothing melody. He killed the engine and headlights, plunging us into silence and darkness, save for the stars' ethereal light.

In a heartbeat, his calloused hand found my bare thigh, his rough palm sending shivers dancing over my skin as it slowly inched higher. I drew in a sharp breath as his fingers brushed against the soft cotton covering my heat.

"More," I pleaded in a whisper.

Wyatt's fingers delved beneath the fabric, finding my centre. A whimper escaped my lips as he stroked me with agonizing tenderness.

"Wyatt, please." I gasped, my hips arching shamelessly against his hand.

With a ragged groan, he surged forward, kissing me as his fingers thrust into my aching core. I cried out my pleasure into his mouth, my body quickly climbing that blissful crest as his skilled touch worked me into a frenzy.

When I shattered apart, Wyatt swallowed each desperate kiss, prolonging the tremors coursing through me with his relentless strokes until I was spent and boneless in the wake of my release.

Wyatt's eyes were dark and hooded as he watched me slowly float back down to earth. "I need you, Kins," he rasped, the rough timbre of his voice sending another shiver of need ricocheting through me.

"Then take me already, you idiot," I breathed, rising to claim his lips.

In the blink of an eye, Wyatt was out of the truck, opening my door and turning me so he was standing between my legs. His mouth moved over mine with a ferocious hunger, our tongues warring in a heated duel. My hands found their way under his shirt, desperate to map every glorious inch of his muscled torso.

When we tore apart, I quickly unfastened his belt and jeans, shoving the denim down his hips impatiently to free his straining length. I wrapped my hand around him, drawing a guttural groan from deep in his chest as his eyes slipped closed in rapture.

"Kinsley," he rasped, his voice wrecked as he struggled for control. "Can I?"

"Please," I whimpered. "I want you, Wyatt. Now."

With a ragged curse, he bent and hooked his hands behind my knees, hoisting me up and pinning me against the side of the truck. I locked my legs around his waist as he claimed my lips, groaning into my mouth as he sheathed himself fully inside me with one powerful thrust.

Our harsh pants and whimpers mingled with the rush of the river as we moved together in a fevered, frantic dance. I lost all sense of everything but the feeling of Wyatt surrounding me and filling me to the point of breaking.

When the tremors of my climax finally crested, Wyatt captured my cry with another soul-melting kiss, allowing me to shatter apart in his arms.

Wyatt's thrusts grew erratic, his harsh pants hot against my cheek as he chased his own release with single-minded earnestness. Then, with a guttural groan, he stilled, his entire body going rigid as he pulsed deep inside me.

I clung to him, quivering, as he collapsed against me, his weight pinning me to the truck in the most deliciously overwhelming way.

Sometime later, we lay tangled together in the bed of the truck, our sweat-slicked bodies still trembling in the aftermath. Wyatt nuzzled his face into the curve of my neck, placing a line of feather-light kisses along my overheated skin as my fingers idly traced patterns across his back.

"Why did we ever stop doing that?" I wondered aloud, the words a breathless murmur.

A low, husky chuckle rumbled against my throat. "Damn if I can remember, darlin', but I swear on my life I'm never going be that stupid again."

Curling closer, I smiled into the darkness. "I'm holding you to that."

"Next time, I won't have my pants around my ankles like a horny teenager," he added with a wry chuckle.

I arched an eyebrow at him. "I don't know. I kind of like that look on you."

Wyatt barked out a laugh, his chest vibrating against mine with the rich sound. "Well, I like this look on you," he rasped, letting his heated gaze roam over my naked body in the almost complete darkness.

"Obviously. I look amazing naked." I pushed him flat on his back and moved over him so I was straddling him. "Got any more in you, cowboy?"

Wyatt ran his hands up my body, over my breasts and up to my face, and tucked my hair behind my ears. "Yes, ma'am."

Chapter 26

DIRT ROAD ANTHEM - JASON ALDEAN

Wyatt

"Damn!" Finn swung off his horse, slapping the ground hard.

I followed suit, my boots kicking up dust as I landed.

He clapped me on the back so forcefully I stumbled forward. "That was our best fucking time yet!"

I grinned ear-to-ear like a damn fool, my heart thundering in my chest. The rush of rodeo always hit me hard, that high I couldn't get enough of. But the only other thing I craved was her—the tiny blonde tornado already launching herself into my arms.

Kinsley wrapped herself around me, her lean legs squeezing my waist as she smashed her lips against mine. I drank her in greedily, my hands sliding down to cup her ass and pull her harder against me.

"You're such a show-off," she said.

"It's roping. The only show I want to put on is for you." I nipped at her jawline, dragging my teeth along her delicate skin.

"Oh, really?" She raised an eyebrow at me.

"I mean in the ring, on a horse." I placed her back on the ground.

"Aww, I was hoping for a little dance, less clothing maybe."

I pretended to consider. "Maybe later," I said with a straight face.

"Ha! That'll be the day."

"Are you saying I can't dance?"

"Yes."

"You're right." I kissed her again.

"Would you two stop that? You're embarrassing me," Finn said as the three of us started leading the horses back to the barn.

Kinsley was all over Gambler, peppering that damn ornery horse with kisses and baby talk.

"Get over it," I told him.

"Must be nice to have your rich girlfriend buy you a new horse."

Those mocking words cut deep, causing every muscle in my body to seize up. I wheeled around to find that prick, Travis, leaning against the barn door, a couple of his clowns flanking him with matching shit-eating grins.

Kinsley's small hand slid into mine, giving a reassuring squeeze, but I was already losing my grip, the haze of anger clouding my vision.

"It's a *borrowed* horse ridden by a skilled cowboy," Finn shot back. "We can't help that we're better than you."

"You guys weren't that great a few weeks ago."

"Horse was slowing down; it happens to the best of them."

I didn't want to let Finn do all the talking. I wanted to say something, defend myself, but I couldn't form any words. It wasn't the horse. I'd been doing this my whole life. Kinsley hadn't bought him for me; I was doing her a favour by riding him while she recovered.

But she has recovered, I reminded myself. Should I be telling her to ride him again? If she wanted him back, she'd tell me, right?

"Is her daddy paying all your bills too?"

"Oh, shut up, Travis," Kinsley barked. "C'mon, Wyatt." She tugged at my arm.

I hadn't realised I'd stopped moving.

"Wyatt." She was looking at me, her brow furrowed.

Behind her, Travis was smirking at me like a smug SOB.

"How deep are those Jackson Ranch pockets, Collins?"

I couldn't pinpoint the moment I decided to punch Travis, but my knuckles burned when they hit his jaw. He was blindsided and hit the ground with a hard thud.

"Shit," I heard Finn breathe.

Travis's friends were already on me as if eager to be let loose. I ducked as a fist flew towards my face, but the other guy had come around behind me and stopped me from falling, only so his friend's next blow landed hard in my gut.

"Finally, Collins. I've been waiting to kick your ass." Travis rose from the dirt, rubbing his thumb and forefinger over his chin and flexing his jaw.

Then it was on.

Kinsley shrieked as we brawled. Finn's voice was letting out a slew of curses as he fought. It was three against two. At least until Kinsley decided she'd had enough and leapt onto Travis's back with her arm circling his throat in a chokehold.

"Kinsley! Get out of here!" I barked.

"Punch him!"

Fuck.

I pummelled him in the stomach, and he curled over, Kinsley going down with him, so I grabbed her around the waist and pulled her off him. She was swinging her arms and legs wildly, trying to get at Travis and deliver her own beating, but I held tight and avoided flying limbs.

A small crowd had gathered, and Grady and Rhett burst through at a run.

"Why didn't you guys tell me we were finally going to kick these pansy asses?" Grady jumped into the fray.

"Sorry, I didn't have time to make a call," I gritted through my teeth.

It wasn't long till Travis was groaning in pain, another guy was doubled over clutching his stomach, and Grady had the third pinned to the side of the barn.

"That was fun, but I was just getting warmed up. Wanna go again?" Grady asked the guy who glared at him.

"Let's go.". I released Kinsley, spit on the ground, and kicked a spray of dirt towards Travis before stalking off into the cool shade of the barn.

I was aware of my friends and Kinsley following me, but I didn't slow my steps. The adrenaline was still pumping through my veins as I leaned against the barn's wall, my chest heaving with each ragged breath. The dirt and sweat trickled down my back. My knuckles throbbed where they had connected with Travis's jaw, and my stomach ached from the blow he had landed on me.

I hated this feeling, the raw aggression that took over. It was like a switch flipped inside me, turning me into a different person—one who didn't care about the consequences of his actions.

I closed my eyes and tried to calm myself down, but the images of the fight played over and over again in my mind. Kinsley's fierce determination as she choked Travis. Finn's furious curses as he fought off his attacker. Grady's brashness as he jumped into the fray. It'd all been so intense, so primal. So out of control.

My nightmare had come true. Other competitors saw me differently now, thinking I was getting lucky because I was riding Kinsley's fancy horse. I couldn't shake the feeling that my wins weren't about my own skills anymore but because I'd taken what wasn't mine and I hadn't earned.

Chapter 27

HOME - DIERKS BENTLEY

Wyatt

As Kinsley rounded the third barrel and raced towards the finish line, her arms stretched out over Cher's neck, giving the mare all the rein she needed to soar.

My fists clenched in anticipation. I was ready to leap into the air in victory.

But as soon as she crossed the line, my eyes darted to the clock. *Damn.* She didn't post the fastest time; Maisey and three other competitors had beaten her. There was a flash of frustration on Kinsley's face as she glanced back to see her time.

"Good ride," Grady commented from beside me.

"Not good enough," Finn muttered under his breath from my other side.

I elbowed him in the ribs before walking off to meet my girl. I caught up with Kinsley as she headed back to the barn.

Throwing my arm around her shoulder, I pulled her into me. "So close," I murmured into her ear and kissed her temple.

She shot me a dirty look. "Close isn't going to cut it. With the time off I had to take, I'm behind in points. If I'm going to make it to the finals, I have to do better." Her fingers trailed through Cher's red mane, and her scrutinizing gaze fixed on her horse.

My stomach tied up in knots. The thought crossed my mind: give her back Gambler. But I remained silent. Gambler had made it clear he wasn't a fan of barrel racing, and I couldn't bear the thought of Kinsley getting hurt again. If she was considering riding him again, she'd bring it up in her own time.

"You're still getting your groove back after your accident. It'll get better," I assured her, trying to sound confident though I wasn't sure I conveyed it convincingly.

We fell into a rhythm, getting our horses settled for the night, but my eyes were on Kinsley. Her gaze kept flickering over to Gambler, her brow furrowed in thought.

My stomach twisted as if in a vise. "All done?" I asked once we had finished.

She nodded, and we entwined our fingers, walking back to her trailer in silence.

Since we returned from her parents' place, I'd been sleeping in Kinsley's trailer instead of camping out with the guys. It was a hell of a lot more comfortable than the bedroll in my tent. Also, she was in it.

She was stomping around the trailer, doing nothing in particular, except maybe making a mess.

"Do you want to talk about it?" I ventured.

"Nope." She plopped down on the couch, grabbed a magazine, and started flipping through it, not pausing long enough on any page to actually read anything.

"If you're trying to start a new interior design trend, I think 'post-rodeo chaos chic' could catch on."

Her lips twitched.

Kneeling in front of her, I ran my hands up her thighs. She resisted at first, her body tense, but I pressed my face into her stomach, and she slowly melted around me. I wanted to peel off her clothes and taste her, but I fought the urge to take things further. At that moment, I just needed to be there for her.

My phone's loud ring shattered the moment. Annoyed, I stood, pulled the phone from my pocket, and checked the caller ID. *Unknown number.* I pressed ignore and slipped the phone back into my pocket, only for it to ring again.

"Who is it?" Kinsley asked.

"No idea. Hang on." I answered the call. "Hello?"

"I'm looking for Wyatt Collins. Is that who I'm speaking with?" a female voice inquired through the phone.

"Yes, who is this?"

"Hello, my name is Emily Thompson from Maple Trust Bank. I'm calling about a farm property, 5768 Prairie Road in Cedar Valley, Alberta."

"Yeah, my dad sold that farm last year."

"No. A sale was initiated but never finalised. We still have Jake Collins listed as legal owner. Is that your father?"

My heart stopped.

Dad hadn't sold the farm? It was still ours?

Kinsley's concerned gaze met mine, her eyes asking silently, *What's going on?* I shook my head, as much in confusion as to clear it.

"Mr. Collins?" Emily's voice pulled me back from my daze.

"What?" My response was barely audible, even to my own ears.

"Is your father Jake Collins?" she repeated, more clearly this time.

"Yes, but I haven't seen him since he sold the farm, or I thought he did. I'm sorry, I'm confused. He still owns the farm?"

"For now, yes. But the property taxes haven't been paid in several years, interest has already accumulated, and foreclosure is an imminent possibility."

"Okay. How much does he owe?"

"The total amount is $17, 659."

I dragged a hand down my face. Almost eighteen thousand dollars was a steep hill to climb. I'd been doing well lately, but not that well.

"How much time do I have?"

"If you can find your father and pay the taxes by the end of the year, you might avoid a lien against the property. But I wouldn't put it off any longer than that."

Kinsley's expression was full of concern and questions, but at that moment, I was too stunned to provide any answers. The prospect of reclaiming the family farm, intertwined with the confusion about my father's actions, left me grappling with what to do next.

"Okay, thanks." I jotted down Emily's number from the bank and promised to be in touch before hanging up.

My mind raced. Where the hell was my dad?

Turning to Kinsley, who was watching me with an expectant look, I explained, "My dad never sold the farm. The sale fell through." I relayed the rest of what Emily had told me.

"Wow." Kinsley looked as shocked as I felt. "What are you going to do?"

"I guess I need to find my dad."

"Where would you even start?"

"Home. I mean, he's probably not there, otherwise somebody would've found him, but I need to see it. I can't believe we still own it.

Maybe he left behind some clue about where he went. Or maybe he goes back from time to time. That's where I'm starting."

My interest in finding my dad was secondary to the pull I felt towards home—the farm. *My home.* There was an ache in my chest that would only be eased by returning there.

"I'll go with you," Kinsley stated.

"You sure?"

"Yeah, we have time till we need to be at the next rodeo."

I nodded slowly.

Kinsley had never seen our farm, and truthfully, I felt uneasy about her being anywhere near my dad if he did show up. I couldn't help wondering what kind of shape the place was in after being abandoned for so long. Even when we lived there, when Dad could barely scrape by, the farm was rundown and shabby compared to Kinsley's family's huge, pristine ranch.

Still, her willingness to come along and face this mess with me was reassuring.

She gave my hand a little squeeze, letting me know she'd be by my side no matter what awaited us back home. Her supportive presence was oddly comforting. I realized I didn't have to tackle this on my own, like I'd grown used to doing.

I wanted her with me.

Chapter 28

THE HOUSE THAT BUILT ME - MIRANDA LAMBERT

Wyatt

"Who did Rhett get a ride home with?" Grady's voice came from the backseat of my truck, breaking the silence that had settled over us in the late afternoon.

"Missing your BFF?" Finn mocked beside him, earning himself a punch to the arm.

The guys had joined me and Kinsley on the trip to the farm, except Rhett, who had mentioned needing to get home again, though, of course, he'd kept the reason to himself.

"I think one of the other pickup men." I glanced over my shoulder as I turned onto a gravel road off the highway.

Beside me, Kinsley's knee was bouncing. I put my hand over her thigh and gave it a gentle squeeze. She had been quiet for most of the ride, but the guys more than made up for it.

"When's the last time we were out here?" Finn's question cut through the noise as we drove deeper into the countryside, the open fields stretching endlessly on either side of us.

I looked back at him in the rearview mirror, catching his eye.

"Oh, right. Never mind." He turned his gaze back to the window.

My chest constricted the moment the house came into view.

There it was. The grass was long when I pulled onto the gravel drive to the house. Too long. Weeds had pushed through, overtaking the soft blades.

Kinsley sat up straighter beside me, taking in our approach. My fingers tightened on the steering wheel.

The house, at least, still stood, though the porch sagged into the ground as if trying to bury itself away from sight. The greenish-yellow paint—an eyesore even in its prime—was now peeling badly, and the shingles needed replacing. It was even worse than I had braced myself for.

I cast a side glance at Kinsley, half-expecting to see a look of disdain. To my relief, she appeared not disgusted but merely curious.

Beyond the house, the barn seemed to be in a slightly better shape. At least the horses would be more comfortable than we would. Fences were down all over the place, but I figured we should be able to rig up some sort of makeshift corral to let the horses out tomorrow.

"I'm starving," Grady complained from the backseat. "Any chance there's food here?"

"You're welcome to anything in the fridge. Expiry dates are just suggestions," I responded.

"I filled the cooler and brought my camp stove." Kinsley rolled her eyes at me.

"You are an angel," Grady declared.

I gave Kinsley a tight-lipped smile of thanks. I hadn't even thought about what we would eat once we got here.

I parked the truck in front of the barn, and we all got out, stretching our limbs after the long drive.

The interior of the barn was damp and musty. Light filtered in through the holes in the roof, casting beams that illuminated the floating dust particles in the air. Peeking into the stalls, I sighed with relief to find them free of old manure, containing only straw and dust.

Grabbing a pitchfork off the wall, I stirred up the bedding, coughing as clouds of dirt assaulted my nose. "It'll have to do for tonight. We'll keep the door open and get the fence fixed tomorrow so the horses don't have to breathe this for too long," I said.

"I'll get a couple of bales from the truck," Finn said. "At least there's some decent grazing around here now."

Once Gambler, Cher, and Ghost were settled and munching on the fresh hay, we went to explore the house.

I retrieved the key from its usual hiding spot and unlocked the door. It wasn't until I took that first step that it really hit me. I was home. It hadn't been that long since the last time I was here, but somehow it felt like a lifetime. I honestly thought I would never see it again.

I looked around at the stillness of the house and frowned. Memories came flooding back. Most weren't good, yet I still had this unexplainable attachment to this place. With everything that had happened here, why had I wanted to come back so badly? I should've run from here the first chance I got, away from my dad and all his shit. But I didn't.

I wanted this place to be mine. And for the life of me, I couldn't figure out why.

The interior was exactly as I remembered, only layered with dust. I had braced myself for filth—dirty dishes in the sink, old food remnants—but surprisingly, there was none of that. It was ... tidy.

Opening the fridge and expecting the worst, I found it empty—a small mercy. "Sorry Grady. Nothing here for you," I announced.

"Darn, sour milk is my favourite," Grady joked.

He and Kinsley wandered around, their curiosity leading them through each room, while Finn stood inside the door, absorbing the scene with a sombre expression.

"This feels weird," Finn said. "Why does this feel weird?"

"I don't know. I'm feeling it too."

"Oh my gawd, is this you?" Kinsley's squeal drew me to her side.

I wrapped my arms around her waist and rested my chin on the top of her head. She was pointing to a picture on the wall. It was a photo of me as a child, sitting on a little fat grey pony, a big smile plastered on my face, while my dad stood next to me, holding the pony's lead and looking proud.

"Yeah, that's me." I didn't even know who'd taken the time to frame these pictures and hang them on the wall. I'd never thought about it before.

"You were the most adorable little cowboy!" Kinsley exclaimed.

"Oh, come on," Finn interjected, joining us. "That one is way cuter." He pointed to a photo next to it.

It captured a moment from our youth, me and him around twelve years old, at a rodeo, proudly showing off the buckles we had won. That was after my mom had left. My dad must've hung that one up, which was surprising.

"If you're into geeky beanpoles," I teased.

"What are you talking about? I was a handsome little devil," Finn retorted.

I rolled my eyes. "Let's figure out where we're sleeping." Dust-covered beds weren't all that appealing.

"I vote for the tents," Finn suggested.

"Agreed," we all answered.

Chapter 29

STAY - SUGARLAND

Kinsley

With no guilt, I lazily sipped my coffee in the early morning sun, by the fire, contentedly watching the guys work. After enduring their chorus of snoring all night, I felt I more than deserved this moment of peace.

They were busy fixing the corral fence nearest to the barn, preparing to let the horses out to graze on the long grass—a well-deserved treat after weeks confined in rodeo barns.

Wyatt's smile was free and easy. He was truly at home here, and although I wanted to be completely happy for him, a part of me ached at the thought. We had started to make plans, and now they were flying off track and I didn't know where we were headed.

A rumble from the road caught my attention, and I lifted my hand to shield my eyes from the sun. A truck had turned onto the drive and was heading in our direction. I quickly pulled on my boots and stood up to get a better look.

As the truck approached and stopped near us, I saw two women inside. The driver, an older woman, sported grey hair neatly pulled back into a bun, a few loose tendrils framing her face. The passenger, a girl around my age, was strikingly pretty, with chestnut hair hanging loose around her shoulders, topped by a cowboy hat.

They stepped out of the truck, and I glanced back at Wyatt, who had noticed their arrival and was walking over with a big grin. He immediately enveloped the older woman in a big hug, lifting her clean off the ground.

"Well, just look at you!" she exclaimed warmly. "Little Wyatt Collins. Not so little anymore."

"Alice, I was not little the last time I saw you. Definitely fully grown." Wyatt grinned, setting her back down.

"Maybe so, but I'll always think of you as little, just like my Gracie and Noah."

He then opened his arms wide as the younger woman approached. She stepped right into his embrace, hugging him tightly.

My fingers clenched around the coffee mug as I watched Wyatt's muscular arms envelope her slender frame in an intimate gesture.

When they finally parted, Wyatt reached over and playfully tapped the brim of her cowboy hat with his fingers, a warm crinkle forming at the corners of his eyes. "Long time, no see, Gracie."

She tilted her head back to maintain his gaze, a dimpled grin spreading across her lips. "It's about time you came home. We missed you."

"Me too."

My stomach twisted into a knot as they shared a look. I knew Wyatt had had a long-term girlfriend in the past. I could only assume it was her. I didn't know what I'd been expecting, but it wasn't *that*.

Grace was beautiful. Not that I'd thought she wouldn't be. Of course Wyatt would have had a pretty girlfriend, but she was beyond pretty.

"Thought I'd have to come check that you weren't getting into too much trouble," Gracie continued, her tone light and teasing.

Wyatt threw his head back with a rich laugh. "Me? Trouble? Now, when have I ever done that?"

"Let's see... There was riding Mr. Henderson's bulls, tractor stealing—"

"Okay, okay! That's enough!" Wyatt held up his hand, laughing.

Their back-and-forth banter rolled off the tongue so naturally, their body language and chemistry undeniable.

I shifted my weight, feeling suddenly like an outsider.

Gracie must have sensed my staring because she slowly turned her head, sweeping an assessing gaze over me from head to toe. Her lips pursed almost imperceptibly, but her eyes remained coolly guarded as they met mine.

The weight of her scrutiny made heat creep into my cheeks. I fought the instinct to look away, keeping my chin lifted as I met that stare head-on.

"Gracie said she saw a truck come up this way. Thought we better check who might be snooping around," Alice said. "Is that Finn? My, you grew up to be a lot better-looking than I expected."

"Thank you?" Finn scratched at the beard on his chin while Grady chuckled beside him.

"And I don't think I know the pretty one," Alice continued, her gaze now on Grady.

Grady clamped his mouth shut, trying to maintain his composure, as Finn let out a bark of laughter.

"This is Grady Martin, a bull rider on the circuit," Wyatt introduced him.

"You're a bull rider?" Alice appraised Grady with a frown, causing him to deflate.

"Yes, ma'am," he muttered.

"And this is my girlfriend, Kinsley Jackson."

The title "girlfriend" shouldn't have filled me with such gratification, but it made me stand a little taller. I irrationally wanted to make my claim clear.

Gracie's perfectly sculpted eyebrows rose the tiniest fraction, but she otherwise remained inscrutably cool. Alice, thankfully, was much warmer as she welcomed us both with a broad smile.

"Nice to meet you both," Alice said. "So, what are you doing back here? I thought we'd seen the last of you."

"I'm looking for my dad. Has he been around?"

"Haven't seen him. He left in a hurry. What was it? A few months ago? As far as I know, he hasn't been back. After he had been gone for a while, I came in and cleaned up the place a bit, and I check in every so often," Alice explained.

"Thank you so much." Wyatt said.

Suddenly, the mystery of the tidy house was solved.

"What's going on with the place? I thought Jake was selling, but no one ever showed up to claim it," Alice prodded further.

"I'm trying to figure that out too." Wyatt shared the gist of his conversation with the bank.

"Well, I'm happy for you. I know how much this place means to you," Alice offered sincerely.

"I'm glad you're back," Gracie added quietly.

Wyatt gave her a small smile. But was he back? I'd thought we were here looking for his dad. Wyatt wasn't moving back home.

"Well..." Alice clapped her hands together, breaking the momentary silence. "Now that I know squatters haven't moved in, I best get home. You all look like you need a good meal, so I'll expect you for dinner at five."

"That's really unnecessary," Wyatt protested.

Alice cut him off with a wave of her hand. "Nonsense. I won't take no for an answer. Come on, Gracie, let's get cooking," Alice declared, her tone leaving no room for argument.

I stole another glance at Gracie. I could sense her curiosity simmering just below the surface, like the nagging discomfort in the pit of my stomach.

Alice's home, though modest and dated, exuded a warmth and welcoming air that was comforting as soon as you walked in the door. It was on a small farm that ran next to Wyatt's property, leading me to believe that Wyatt must have spent a considerable amount of time here during his childhood.

A picture hanging on the wall inside the door confirmed my suspicions. It featured a much younger Wyatt, still tall but lacking the fullness he had now. His face bore a more youthful look, yet he was unmistakably handsome. His arm was around a little Gracie, who wore an ear-to-ear smile.

"It was a long time ago," Wyatt murmured beside me, catching me off guard.

I hadn't realised he was standing there.

"Old girlfriend I presume?"

"Umm, yeah," he admitted.

"Great, a little warning would've been nice," I grumbled under my breath as I moved further into the house, growing more annoyed with each step.

"Make yourselves at home!" Alice's voice rang from the kitchen, cutting through the awkward tension.

The four of us settled in the living room. Wyatt took my hand and led me over to a love seat covered with a blue and yellow afghan, adding to the room's cozy, outdated charm. The rest of the furniture was adorned with more knitted blankets, and a large basket of yarn sat on the floor, hinting at Alice's knitting hobby because, of course, she knitted. The house was like a portal to an earlier time, right down to the ancient-looking TV.

Finn and Grady took the couch while Gracie perched on an armchair.

"So, Gracie," Finn began, trying to break the ice. "How have you been? What have you been up to?"

"I just go by Grace," she corrected him.

"Ah, yes, all grown up. Good job on that, by the way." Finn earned a swift kick in the shin from Wyatt. "You still barrel racing?"

Grace's eyes flicked over to me. "No, I'm not. Too much to do around here. Mom and Dad need the help."

"Right. Speaking of which, where's Noah?" Finn inquired.

"He and Dad are out with the cattle. They'll be in for supper," Grace informed us.

"Noah is her brother," Wyatt leaned over to whisper to me.

I had secretly hoped she might mention a boyfriend, something to divert her attention away from Wyatt. No such luck.

"Do you still have Drifter?" Grace asked Wyatt. "I didn't see him when we were at your place."

"Oh, yeah, of course, but I retired him this year. He's staying at Kinsley's place," Wyatt explained.

"Oh. That's good," Grace responded flatly.

"Well, this is awkward," Grady remarked.

His observation was met with four sets of glaring eyes.

Chapter 30

NEED YOU NOW - LADY A

Wyatt

"I haven't seen Jake in quite a while." Ethan Harper, Alice's husband, settled deeper into his recliner after dinner with a thoughtful look. "Kept thinking he'd pop up one day, you know? He had a knack for disappearing on one of his schemes, chasing after quick cash, but he'd always circle back eventually. Heard around town that he'd sold the farm. I had no clue it was even on the market. If I'd known..." He paused, a shrug lifting his shoulders as if to shake off the thought. "We all waited for someone new to take over, or for anything to happen. But nothing did. And Jake... He never came back."

I squeezed Kinsley into my side on the couch. She had been quiet since meeting Grace. Not that I blamed her, but I didn't want her to feel threatened. Grace and I had been over for a long time, but Kinsley and I hadn't ever dealt with things like exes.

The dinner had been delicious. We ate like we'd been starving for weeks, which wasn't that far from the truth. Life on the road was hard. Good meals were one of those comforts of home you always missed.

Home was getting to be a hard thing to define. I was home, but I didn't feel it. Maybe once I found my dad and settled things, I could make it feel like home again.

I pressed my lips to Kinsley's hair. *We could make it feel like home again.*

"If I were you, I'd swing by Rodeo's End Tavern," Ethan suggested, snapping me back to the moment. "Place has changed hands. Looks different now, but you'll find some of the old guard still warming the stools. Somebody might know where Jake's at."

"Gracie, Noah, why don't you take them? You two enjoy it there," Alice chimed in.

Noah, baby-faced and barely out of his teens, perked up.

"Rodeo's End, huh?" I turned to Grace, surprised.

The Grace I remembered was more likely to be buried in textbooks than hanging out in a bar. Last I heard, she was bound for Olds College, aiming for a degree in agriculture.

"Like my dad said, it's different now."

Memories of dragging my dad from that dive did not make me eager to go.

"I was planning on heading over there tonight anyway," Noah said, his eyes lit up. "Can you fit two more in your truck?"

"I don't see why we couldn't take a second vehicle," Grace complained from the backseat, squished between Kinsley and Grady, her voice muffled.

"It's more environmentally friendly to carpool," Noah said from the front passenger seat he'd snagged, his comment triggering sighs and eyerolls from the rest of us.

"There are four people back here and only three seatbelts. This is illegal, Noah," Grace pointed out.

Glancing in the rearview mirror, I glimpsed Kinsley perched on Finn's lap.

"Hands where I can see them, Finn."

At my warning, Finn raised his hands in mock surrender, sending me a wink that had me shaking my head.

"Your girlfriend's ass is bony," he teased.

"Hey! It is not," she protested, delivering a well-placed elbow to his ribs. "Here's a bone for you."

"Ow, woman!" Finn's complaint was met with a pinch to Kinsley's side, causing her to let out a shriek.

"Cut it out, you two!" I tried to maintain some semblance of order, my focus splitting between the road and the chaos unfolding in the backseat.

"I swear there was a better joke in there, Kinsley. Bone—"

"Shut up, Grady," Kinsley cut him off.

"So, what kind of bar are we talking about here?" Grady shifted the conversation.

"Oh, it's great." Noah turned to face the back. "They expanded the place to have live music, a dance floor, and even a mechanical bull."

The thought of a bar filled with cowboy wannabes had me mentally preparing for a long night.

"Yes, I'm getting laid!" Grady celebrated, clearly excited at the prospect of showing off his talents.

The rest of us groaned in unison.

Grace was fidgeting in her seat, trying to get comfortable, her movement bringing her closer to Kinsley. The two girls exchanged an uncomfortable look, and I dragged a hand down my face, trying to focus on the road while keeping an eye on the rearview mirror.

Catching Grace's gaze, I lingered on her face, lost in a flood of memories.

Grace had been a constant during some of the toughest times of my life. Always there, always dependable. Our breakup had been amicable—a result of our lives pulling us in different directions rather than any wrongdoing. Leaving her had been hard; she was the girl I had pictured a future with. If the circumstances hadn't been what they were, if I wasn't on the road so much, maybe things between us would have been different.

The realization that I had been staring at Grace for too long hit me when my gaze flicked to the pair of livid blue eyes beside her. *Shit.*

I pulled into the bar's parking lot, and everyone piled out of the truck, but instead of heading inside right away, I leaned my back against my door, crossed my arms, and waited.

Finn was smirking and shaking his head when he walked by me.

"You coming in, Wyatt?" Noah called out.

Grace glanced back at me with concern.

"I'll be there in a minute," I assured them.

"Let's give the lovebirds some space," Finn said. "They're about to fight or fuck. Probably both."

Grace turned and walked off hastily, her cheeks turning pink.

"Are you waiting here for me or her?" Kinsley confronted me, clearly agitated, her tone sharp.

"Of course you." I tried to sound as reassuring as possible.

"Of course me? I'm not the one you were sharing long, lingering looks with in there," she retorted.

"It wasn't like that," I tried to explain.

"You could barely keep your eyes off her!" she accused, her voice rising with each word.

"We have a past. She was part of my life for a long time. She brings back memories. That's all. I was thinking about how life would have turned out if my dad wasn't such a mess, if I had stuck around home more."

"You were thinking about how you could've gone home a long time ago to be with your high school sweetheart? How the two of you lost so much time?" Kinsley's words filled with hurt, her voice cracking.

"No, Kinsley!" The frustration of the situation had me pacing now.

"Did you love her?" Her question came softly.

Her eyes shimmered, and I hated myself for causing her pain.

"I don't know! Maybe?" I admitted, my voice fraught with confusion. "We were friends for a long time, and when we started dating, it wasn't an a-ha moment; it was just expected. And, yeah, I cared about her, a lot. She's a great girl; I'm not going to lie. She was comfortable and safe. But was it love? I'm not sure. With you, though, it's different. The first time I saw you, it was like being struck by lightning. When you first spoke to me, my heart cracked wide open. There was no questioning it; I just fell. Kinsley, I knew I was in love with you the second I saw you."

Kinsley's gaze was piercing. Her lips pressed together so tightly I thought she might draw blood. Then, suddenly, she was in my arms, her hands tangled in my hair as she pulled me into a fervent kiss.

The intensity of her reaction left me breathless. I'd never gotten that hard, that fast.

Our tongues tangled together, and we clawed at each other's clothes.

"Get back in the truck," I commanded.

"Trying to tell me what to do now?"

"Kinsley. Get back in the truck."

Her expression turned from teasing to heated. She opened the back door and crawled inside, putting her perfect round ass right in my face.

"I don't know what Finn was talking about. Your ass isn't boney at all." I gave it a good smack.

She squealed, turned around, and laid back across the seat while I positioned myself uncomfortably over her, one knee on the floor and the other between her legs.

"You are too big for sex in the backseat of a truck."

"Nah, I'll make it work." My dick was already aching and straining against my jeans; if I had to put my back out to make this happen, so be it.

I kissed down Kinsley's throat, trying to take my time and not be a pig, but the little moans she made were not helping. The shirt she was wearing was low-cut, and I pulled it down to expose one breast. She wasn't wearing a bra, which I was very grateful for. I took her nipple between my teeth, and she arched herself into me.

"Wyatt," she whimpered. "Please don't make me wait."

She was already undoing my belt and unbuttoning my jeans, releasing me from the restraining fabric. She stroked my length, and I shuddered.

"Fuck," I breathed.

I made it my mission to peel the skin-tight jeans from her body. I fumbled in the small space, but I'd never needed anything more than I needed Kinsley naked right that second.

"Wyatt, hurry!" She lifted her core, seeking desperately.

"I'm trying!" I grunted with effort as I pulled her pants free from her body.

She was writhing beneath me, and my dick was throbbing. Us and trucks, it was a thing.

"Wyatt..." Her hand was between her legs. *Such an impatient girl.*

I removed her hand and pinned it over her head. "I can't let you do that."

"Then you better stop me."

I didn't hesitate. I couldn't wait a second longer either. I entered her deeply in one thrust. She gasped at the brute force.

"Better?" I asked.

"Mmm, yes." Her eyes were closed, but a smile played over her lips. Relief. "I love being filled by you."

I bit at her bottom lip. "Don't get too relaxed." I started pumping into her, slowly at first, savouring it, but then I quickened my pace, building us both into a frenzy.

We breathed into each other, deep and heavy, and sweat glistened on our skin.

It wasn't until her mouth opened in a silent scream that I let myself go in one last hard thrust and collapsed, my face buried in her chest. Her fingers threaded through my hair, stroking.

"Ow," I mumbled into her breasts.

"What muscle did you pull this time, old man?"

"I think all of them."

"Aww, poor baby." She rubbed her hands over my back. "Do you want to ask your other girlfriend if you can soak in her tub tonight?"

I raised my head to look at her. "You're not funny."

"Oh yes, I am."

I dug my chin into her chest and wiggled it, making her shriek, squirm, and trying to get away, all the while laughing.

I painfully lifted myself up and looked around the truck to make sure the coast was clear before I opened the door and stepped out into the darkness. I pulled my pants up. One of these days, I was going to get my girl into a proper bed.

Kinsley grabbed her jeans and pulled them on before sliding out of the truck, giving me a quick kiss.

"Do we have to go in there and watch Grady show off on that bull?" I asked.

"Yep. We also have some investigating to do."

Right. We're here to ask around about my dad. Did I want to know where he was or what he was doing?

"Alright. Let's go." I took Kinsley's hand and tugged her along to the door.

Chapter 31

OUTLAW STATE OF MIND - CHRIS STAPLETON

Kinsley

We walked into the bar, greeted by the sight of Grady centre stage, with a bachelorette party, teaching them how to conquer the mechanical bull. They were all fawning over him, even the bride.

Finding Finn and Grace at a nearby table, it was clear they had settled in. Finn nursed a beer while Grace played absentmindedly with her straw in an empty glass.

"Looks like we have some catching up to do." I noted the collection of glasses as we joined them.

Wyatt's arm was around my waist, an action that didn't escape Grace's notice.

"I need alcohol to endure that," Finn commented, nodding towards Grady's spectacle. "Those girls must be really drunk."

Wyatt chuckled in agreement behind me.

"You guys are joking, right?" I couldn't help but challenge their amused detachment.

"What do you mean?" Finn looked puzzled.

"Grady is more popular with the female population than the two of you combined," I explained. "There are racers with his picture in their tack trunks. The buckle bunnies adore him."

"It's a bull rider thing," Wyatt said.

"It's more a 'he's gorgeous and has a panty-dropping smile' factor," I countered, earning a mumbled agreement and a hiccup from Grace.

Her reaction drew our attention, but she just giggled into her drink.

"See?" My laughter echoed Grace's, drawing a connection between us over the absurdity.

"Okay, so where does Rhett fit into this?" Finn was curious, stirring the conversation.

"Everyone and their *grandma* has had a crush on Rhett Parker at some point," I admitted, causing Wyatt to raise an eyebrow in my direction. "It's practically a rite of passage. He's the perfect mix between rugged cowboy and Prince Charming. But don't worry; you're both plenty handsome." I patted Wyatt's cheek. Inside, I was laughing at their pouty faces.

Both guys were hot as fuck, and girls were always drooling over the two intense dark-haired cowboys, but a little humility never hurt.

Wyatt scanned the room, his demeanour shifting. Grace pointed out an older man in the corner. Recognition and distaste mingled in Wyatt's visceral reaction.

"Mark Dwyer," she identified. "Your dad used to drink with him a lot."

Wyatt nodded. "Yeah, I remember him." He scowled in disgust, lifted his hat from his head, and ran his hand through his hair. He was tense. Whoever this guy was, Wyatt did not want to talk to him.

"Want me to come with you?" I asked him.

Wyatt shook his head. "That's the last guy I want you exposed to."

"I can come." Finn stood up.

"No, if both of us go over there, he'll feel threatened and won't talk. Stay with the girls."

"Yeah, come twirl us around the floor, Finn." I tried to ease the tension in the air.

"I don't dance."

"Well then, you need another drink," I said. "Grace? Another one?"

"Yes, please," she said almost too loudly.

After Wyatt had expressed himself so ... passionately in the parking lot, I was feeling sorry for Grace. It wasn't easy to get over Wyatt Collins. Impossible, actually.

"I'll get the drinks," Finn said. "What will it be, Kins?"

"Whatever she's having." I pointed to Grace's empty glasses.

She frowned. "I don't remember what it was."

"I got it." Finn headed off towards the bar.

I sat down with Grace. "So, Finn mentioned earlier that you used to barrel race?"

Her gaze met mine, and she nodded. "Yeah, back in high school. Not at your level. I've heard of you; you're really good."

"Thanks." I smiled at her, and after a moment, she smiled too. I was about to say more, but Wyatt's form moving through the crowd caught my attention.

As Wyatt approached the man at the bar, there was immediate tension. The man, upon seeing Wyatt, stood up as if ready to bolt, but something Wyatt said made him sit back down, albeit reluctantly. Wyatt then signalled for the bartender to bring another beer for the man, who drowned his worries in the drink while stealing wary glances at Wyatt.

"So, who is this guy?" I asked Grace.

"Local lowlife. He was always dragging Jake into trouble, gambling and whatnot," she explained.

My gaze remained fixed on Wyatt, who was showing signs of agitation.

Suddenly, Wyatt's chair clattered to the floor as he stood up, the sound echoing through the bar. He grabbed the man, Mark, by his shirt, pulling him to his feet. The crowd that had gathered around them blocked my view, but I heard enough to know it was bad.

"Finn!" I called out, though I saw him already making his way through the crowd toward the commotion.

Grady was approaching from another direction. I tried to follow, but the crowd hindered any forward progress, their bodies creating a barrier I couldn't get through.

The music had stopped, replaced by shouts and the crashing of bottles and glasses. By the time I got closer, Finn had already intervened, pulling Wyatt away from Mark. Wyatt's body was rigid with anger, his fists still clenched, and a trickle of blood ran down from his nose, which he wiped away. Finn was speaking to him in hushed tones, trying to diffuse his fury.

Watching Finn's ability to calm Wyatt stirred a twinge of jealousy in me; I wished I could be that for him.

Grady and I reached them, relief clear on Grady's face that the fight was over.

"Are you okay?" I asked Wyatt, but my concern went unnoticed.

Mark was slowly getting up, grimacing with pain, unaided and ignored by everyone. Wyatt's glare was unwavering.

"Shit," Finn muttered, eyeing the entrance as two police officers made their way in.

They assessed the situation, consulting the bartender, who recounted the events. Wyatt remained stoic, his arms crossed defiantly, making Mark shrink back in fear.

In moments like these, I wished Wyatt's stubbornness would give way to reason.

He didn't resist as the officers handcuffed him and led him outside. Another patrol car arrived shortly after, and we looked on as Mark was also arrested.

"Well..." Finn broke the heavy silence that had fallen over us. "Let's go get him."

Chapter 32

CAT'S IN THE CRADLE - HARRY CHAPIN

Wyatt

I had been sitting in the jail cell for almost three hours, according to the wall clock on the other side of the bars. My stomach grumbled, and I had to piss.

Nobody had come in to talk to me. I hadn't seen a single soul since they put me in there. I laid back on the concrete bench and put my hat over my face; I was tired from going over what that jackass had said to me.

Word was Jake Collins was dead. *Dead.*

The thought churned in my mind. I would know if my dad was dead, right? But who was I kidding? Like I had some spiritual connection with the guy. I hated him. But someone would've contacted me. Except that I had no permanent address, and my relationship with my phone was an on-and-off thing. *Fuck.*

Could my dad be dead, or was Mark Dwyer a lying bastard? Both scenarios were equally possible. I was at a police station; I could file a missing person's report as soon as I got out of there. *If* I ever got out of there. I would get bail, right? Kinsley would...

Shit. I grabbed my hat and threw it across the cell. It hit the bars and fell to the ground. I dragged my hands down my face.

I had no doubt Kinsley would bail me out. That's what she did; she bailed me out of trouble.

"Fuck!"

Maybe I should stay there. Did bar fights warrant prison time? I didn't think Mark was badly hurt or anything. How bad was this? I couldn't afford a lawyer or anything, but they gave you one for free if you couldn't afford it, right?

The sound of a door opening snapped me out of my downward spiral.

A cop approached, keys in hand, and unlocked my cell. "Had a chance to cool down?" he asked in a practised, no-nonsense tone.

"Yes, sir," I replied.

"Good. Let's go," he commanded.

"Go where? What happens now?" I got up, picked my hat off the ground, and trailed behind him, apprehension and relief threading through me as we made our way down the hall.

"You're free to go. Lucky for you, we know Mark Dwyer real well around here. Most of us have wanted to punch him many times, but I don't suggest trying that again, or we'll be keeping you in there a lot longer."

"Yes, sir. Thank you." A wave of relief swept through me as I continued to follow him through the police station until he halted at a desk.

"Your friends explained the situation, and we spoke to the Harpers, who vouched for you. So, if you can promise we won't see you again, we'll let this one slide. I would not go looking for Mark Dwyer again."

"I promise." I hesitated, the weight of my next question anchoring me in place. "Umm..."

"Something else?" the officer asked.

"Yeah, I'm looking for my dad."

His expression softened.

"Could I file a missing person's report, or..." I trailed off, unsure how to broach the topic of his potential death.

"We can do that." His hesitation was clear, his eyes flickering with something akin to sympathy. "But first, would you be willing to give a DNA sample?"

"Because you think he's dead." My fingers absentmindedly fidgeted with a pen on his desk—a futile attempt to distract myself from the implications of his request.

"I don't know for sure. I made a few calls. A body was found in the river in a nearby town late last year. Never identified, no ID, nothing."

"They think it was my dad?"

"They've heard rumours but haven't been able to confirm. We can crossmatch your DNA and hear back in a couple of days."

I nodded slowly.

"I know this is hard..."

"It's fine. No problem." My response was automatic, a hollow attempt to cover up the emotions swirling through me.

"Alright. Come with me, and we'll get this sorted."

I followed him, the finality of the situation pressing down on me with each step.

After another hour of filling out paperwork and giving a cheek swab, I left the police station. Kinsley and Finn were waiting for me, perched on the tailgate of my truck. They hopped off as soon as they spotted me.

"Oh, thank goodness!" Kinsley exclaimed, rushing into my arms.

I hugged her tight, burying my face in her hair and breathing her in.

"Are you okay?" She pulled back to search my face.

"I'm fine," I assured her with a smile.

"They said you didn't need bail. I was ready to—"

"No charges. I'm good to go." I pulled Finn in for a quick hug as well. "Did the others get home okay?"

"Yeah, we drove Grace and Noah home. Told Alice and Ethan what happened. Ethan said he would make a call—"

"Yeah, he did. Thanks for that. Where's Grady?"

"In the truck. He fell asleep a while ago." Finn pointed towards the truck.

Peering through the back window, I spotted Grady fast asleep in the backseat.

I chuckled. "Well, at least someone got some rest. We'll put him to work today so we can catch up on sleep."

"Sounds good to me. Let's get back before we all collapse here and get arrested for … something. I don't know. I'm too tired. Everyone, in the truck," Finn mumbled.

I handed over the driving duties to Finn and settled Kinsley into the front seat. Opening the back door, I nudged Grady awake. "Move over."

"Hey! Look who's a free man!" Grady greeted me with a sleepy smile as he adjusted to a sitting position.

"For now. I have to report to prison in three days."

"Wait, seriously?"

"No, dumbass." I rolled my eyes.

Finn steered us into the night, driving back to the farm. The ride was quiet, each of us lost in our own thoughts.

My eyes were drooping and my head was hanging by the time we got back to the farm.

Without a word, we all headed for our tents.

Kinsley crawled in first, and I followed. I grabbed her boots and pulled them off her feet.

"Why thank—"

I crawled over her, crushed my mouth to hers, and laid her back.

"We need to sleep," she said but was kissing me back.

"This helps me sleep." I slid my hand up her shirt and palmed her breast.

I needed something to shut my brain off after the night I'd had. I needed to stop thinking about whether or not he was dead. I needed to let off some pent-up tension. I need Kinsley. I *always* needed Kinsley.

"Wyatt." Her hands roamed over my stomach, and her nails raked across my back. "Did you talk to the cops about—"

"Please, Kinsley, not now. I'll tell you everything. Just please, not right now."

My tongue plunged into her mouth. I was desperate to be inside her. I tore her shirt off, wanting to feel every inch of her skin on mine.

"Okay," she murmured before giving herself to me thoroughly and completely.

Chapter 33

BLESS THE BROKEN ROAD - RASCAL FLATTS

Kinsley

We spent the next few days lying low at Wyatt's farm, caught in a tense waiting game for any word from the police. While Wyatt and the guys busied themselves with outdoor and barn work, I took it upon myself to give the house a thorough cleaning since Wyatt had managed to get the power turned back on. Thanks to Alice's efforts, the place wasn't in terrible shape, but it still required a good dusting. I also laundered all the bedding and linens, eager for us to enjoy the simple comfort of sleeping in an actual bed.

The house was quaint—three bedrooms, a single bathroom, and a kitchen with laughably limited counter space. The furniture, outdated as it was, hinted at cosiness with a bit of effort and updating.

As I moved through the kitchen, my fingers brushed over the worn wooden table, my mind wandering to what life might be like living here. Through the window, I watched Wyatt repair the barn door, his brow furrowed in concentration and his white t-shirt clinging to him with sweat.

Was this my future? Watching Wyatt work from the sidelines, raising a family in this little home, isolated from my own family and the life I knew? The thought of Wyatt's high school sweetheart dropping by added an unwelcome twist to my musings. This wasn't the life I had envisioned for us. I cherished the rodeo's vibrancy, being close to our friends, and the warmth of returning to my family afterward.

Yet the man outside, diligently fixing what was broken, held my heart. If he hoped to stay here, to root himself in this soil...

A tear broke free and ran down my cheek. I brushed it away, scolding myself for my selfishness. Wyatt was grappling with the uncertainty of his father's life, and here I was, lost in my head over stupid little things.

Distracting myself, I turned to the groceries we had purchased the day before, trying to plan dinner despite my limited culinary skills. Cooking had never been my forte; I had always been more inclined to follow my dad around the ranch than stay in the house and learn from my mother, who was an exceptional cook.

I picked up a chicken, turning it over in my hands, clueless. The oven, an ancient relic in this old kitchen, offered no inspiration. I set the chicken back down, a nagging thought surfacing.

I bet Grace knew her way around a kitchen.

"Need help with that?" Grady's amused voice caught me off guard as he leaned against the kitchen's doorway.

"I don't cook," I admitted, a bit embarrassed.

"No shit." He chuckled, making his way to the sink to wash his hands. "Move aside."

"You cook?" I asked, surprised.

"Of course. Nobody else ever did it for me."

I averted my eyes, not wanting him to catch the flicker of sympathy that I feared might show. But it was too late.

"I don't need your pity," he said.

"No pity here. Tell me what to do, chef." I tried to steer the conversation back to safer waters, though I couldn't help being curious about his past.

I only knew that he'd been raised in foster care and had no family to speak off. He didn't talk about it much.

Grady's mood lightened as he directed me. "Grab a knife and start chopping vegetables."

Following his instructions, I laid out the knife, vegetables, and cutting board. However, I hesitated, unsure of how to proceed.

Grady, noticing my uncertainty, chuckled. "Like this." He demonstrated how to dice the vegetables.

"This is what I need. Housewife 101," I joked.

"Housewife? You?" Grady looked at me, one eyebrow raised in disbelief.

"Maybe? I don't know. It sounds kind of awful, doesn't it?" I said, the concept foreign to me.

"Not really. There's nothing wrong with a woman taking care of her home and family," he reasoned, his voice carrying a hint of respect.

"No, of course not. That's my mom—the perfect rancher's wife, the perfect mom. I respect the hell out of her," I confessed.

"It's just not you," Grady observed.

"No. At least, not yet. Maybe one day." My gaze drifted back to the window, to Wyatt engrossed in his work. "Do you think he wants to stay here?"

Grady followed my gaze and frowned thoughtfully. "I'm not sure. Even if he gets ownership, it won't be easy to get the farm up and running again."

"No, it won't be," I agreed.

"But it's Wyatt."

"Right. The most stubborn man alive." A smile tugged at my lips.

"Exactly."

"Exactly," I repeated and returned to my chopping.

Dinner was delicious—thanks to Grady because I was about as helpful as a burr under a saddle pad. We had just started on dessert, diving into some oversized cinnamon buns we'd picked up from a local bakery, when the sudden ring of Wyatt's phone sliced through the chewing sounds.

By the fourth ring, I reached out, lightly touching his arm. "Do you want me to answer it?"

Wyatt seemed to ground himself with a deep breath before shaking his head. "No, I got it." He stood, distancing himself from the table to take the call in private.

The urge to follow him was strong, mirrored by Finn's tense expression, but we held back, understanding Wyatt's need for space in this moment.

The room fell into an uneasy silence, punctuated only by the sounds of Grady gathering dishes. Finn and I helped with the cleanup, our actions automatic, but my thoughts lingered on Wyatt.

An hour passed, and my patience ran out. The need to check on Wyatt overrode my earlier resolve to give him space.

I found him outside on the front steps, the phone still clutched in his hands, his fingers white from the grip. I settled beside him, and the door creaked as Finn and Grady joined us, forming a silent, supportive wall behind him.

"He's dead." Wyatt's voice was a whisper. He didn't turn to look at me, his gaze fixed on the horizon as if searching for answers in the fading light.

Words failed me. How did you comfort someone over a loss that was as complicated as their relationship had been? Instead, I slid my arm through his, resting my head against his shoulder. When he leaned into the gesture, I breathed a sigh of relief.

Finn and Grady settled onto the nearby porch swing, its gentle creaking soothing.

As the sun dipped below the horizon, we sat together, collectively marking the end of a chapter in Wyatt's life.

Though I'd never met Jake Collins, his existence had irrevocably changed mine by bringing Wyatt into my life. Amidst the tangled feelings, there was a deep-seated gratitude for that.

Chapter 34

LONG BLACK TRAIN - JOSH TURNER

Wyatt

I was itching to put all this behind me—the endless questions, the stacks of paperwork, everything that tied me to my dad. I wanted it to be over.

The coroner listed the official cause of death as an overdose. The news blindsided me; I'd only ever thought alcohol was his vice.

Mark Dwyer, once he'd sobered up, spilled to the police how deep my dad had gotten with Richie Marcano, a loan shark he had a history with, suggesting his death had come before he completed the sale of the farm, leaving Richie to back out to avoid any legal entanglements.

The situation was a mess.

Kinsley's support was constant, almost suffocating. No matter what, she was there, always offering to help, always trying to fix things for me. She saw me as someone who couldn't handle his own problems, someone who needed her to step in and save the day. That relentless attention, though well-intentioned, made me feel even smaller, reminding me again and again that I was the one who needed rescuing because of the disaster my dad had left in his wake.

Armed with the death certificate, I met with Emily Thompson at Maple Trust Bank to wade through yet another sea of paperwork. This time, it was to take over the farm, along with the hefty debt of $17,659. I had no clue how I was going to manage that.

"Any organs you don't need anymore?" Finn joked as we stepped out into the afternoon sun, leaving the bank behind us.

I had left Kinsley at the farm, knowing she'd offer to bail me out financially if she were here. I couldn't let her do that. I also just needed a break from her pity looks, or I was going to snap.

"I think our best bet is to keep winning at rodeos," I suggested, trying to lighten the mood.

"Right. Winning. And after that?" Finn pressed.

"What do you mean?"

"Are you planning to come back here? Live here and dive back into the cattle business?"

"I haven't figured that out yet. I mean, I guess I'll come home."

"And Kinsley's okay with that? You being out here? She's moving in with you?"

"Uh..." I hadn't thought that far ahead.

Would Kinsley even want to move in with me? If I got the farm back on its feet... But it'd be a far cry from what she was used to.

"Maybe we can hit the rodeo circuit for a few more years and save up."

"I don't have a few more years. My farm's on the line if I don't head back...But, we'll do what we can to make money this year," Finn reassured me.

Back at the farm, Kinsley was nowhere in sight, and I couldn't help but feel relieved.

"I'm going to go for a ride," I told Finn, trying to sound casual.

"Now?"

"Yeah, let Kins know I'll be back soon."

"Wyatt—"

"I won't be long," I cut him off, not waiting for a response.

Heading straight for the barn, I saddled up Gambler, mounted, and rode out, hoping the distance might give me some clarity. Everybody wanted answers from me—answers I didn't have.

Dad had let everything fall apart, blinded by his habits and drowning in debt, dragging our family name and the land down with him. After he lost Mom, who couldn't stand the ranch life and left, he spiralled even faster, losing himself in drink and gambling.

Riding around, seeing all the overgrown fields and broken fences, the idea of taking on all that responsibility was overwhelming.

I gripped the reins, feeling the power of Gambler beneath me as we rode through the overgrown fields. The farm, once the center of my childhood, now lay in shambles.

As I guided Gambler around a dilapidated fence, I couldn't help but feel the weight of this responsibility pressing down on me. This place, the land that had been in our family for generations, was now mine to fix, but the task was a mountain I couldn't possibly climb.

I had wanted the farm back so badly, needing something that was mine. But now that it was, it felt more like a burden than a blessing. The bills, the repairs, the upkeep it would require—it was all too much, especially with the added pressure of keeping up with the rodeo circuit.

Then there was Kinsley. Beautiful, passionate Kinsley, who had been by my side through all of this. She wanted to help, to be a part of this new chapter in my life, but I couldn't help but feel like I was dragging her down and asking too much of her.

I slowed Gambler to a trot, letting the gentle rhythm soothe my racing thoughts.

Kinsley deserved so much more than this, more than a broken-down farm and a man struggling to keep his head above water. She was used to so much more. How could I ever give her that when I could barely keep the electricity on?

A part of me wanted to sell the place, to cut my losses and go bury myself in work on the Jackson Ranch. But the thought of letting go of this last piece of my family's legacy made my chest tighten. This farm was all I had left of my father, a man who had let me down in so many ways but who had also instilled in me a deep love for this land, horses, and rodeo.

As Gambler carried me back towards the house, I glimpsed Kinsley through the kitchen window, stirring a pot at the stove. Something was off; her movements were tense, her expression serious—a far cry from her usual vibrant self. Kinsley had grown up on a ranch, yet she seemed out of place here, like a rose in a field of weeds.

I dismounted, my boots hitting the dirt with a familiar thud. It was time to have a talk with Kinsley, to lay bare my fears and doubts. If she was going to be a part of this journey, she deserved to know exactly what she was getting into.

After I got Gambler put away, I took a deep breath and headed inside, steeling myself for the conversation I needed to have.

She looked up from the stove as I entered the kitchen, a faint smile tugging at the corners of her lips. "Hey, you. I was making a little something to eat. Hungry?"

I shook my head. "Kins, we need to talk. Where are the guys?"

Her brow furrowed, and she set down the wooden spoon, giving me her full attention. "They took your truck and drove into town for a beer or something. What's going on?"

I ran a hand through my hair, trying to find the right words. "It's ... the farm. The bank, the debt, my dad's death—it's a lot to handle. I'm not sure I can do this."

Kinsley's expression softened, and she reached out to take my hand. "Hey, it's going to be okay. We'll figure it out, I promise."

As she spoke, I couldn't help but notice the tightness in her expression. Her voice was steady, her touch gentle, but there was a hesitation in her movements that hadn't been there before. It was as if the weight of the farm's problems had already dampened her spirit.

I thought of my mother, how the isolation and demands of this place had slowly drained the life from her. I couldn't bear the thought of the same thing happening to Kinsley—the woman I loved, the woman who brought so much light and joy into my life.

"I don't want you to feel obligated to help." I squeezed her hand. "This is my mess to clean up, not yours."

Kinsley's brow furrowed, and she gave my hand a reassuring squeeze. "Wyatt, I want to help. I care about you, and I care about this farm. It's important to you, so it's important to me."

Her words, though sincere, lacked the conviction I was used to. She was holding back. Her usual passion and enthusiasm just weren't there, and I didn't know what to do about it.

"We'll finish up the rodeo season, then we'll decide. Take the time to think about if this is what you want."

"But I want—"

"Kinsley, please. Take some time to think about it." I pulled her into my arms and kissed her hair. "We'll head out in the morning, okay?"

She didn't say anything, only nodded against my chest.

Chapter 35

Amazing Grace / This is How We Roll - Florida Georgia Line (ft. Luke Bryan)

Wyatt

I sat on the tailgate of my truck, hunched over and staring down into my hands. Finn ambled over and sat beside me without a word.

"I don't want to do this," I said.

"I know."

"I hated him."

"I know."

"So, why? Why are we doing this?" I watched the crowd strolling towards the large tent set up at the Cedar Valley rodeo grounds. People were showing up. For him.

It had been a long time since I'd stepped foot in Cowboy Church—the Sunday service that took place at rodeos, usually in a tent or barn but sometimes in the arena. My dad had never missed a service when he was competing. A lot of good it'd done him.

The thought of stepping inside that tent made my stomach roil.

"You'll regret it if you don't do something. You need some sort of closure," Finn said.

"He doesn't deserve it."

"Maybe not. But you do. You deserve to say goodbye," Finn went on. "And yeah, he made a lot of bad decisions, but he wasn't all bad. He's the one who taught you to ride a horse and rope. You can love him for that, even when you hate him."

I nodded, chewing on what he'd said. "Thanks for organizing all this."

It wasn't an official funeral or anything, but Finn had spoken with one of the circuit pastors about giving my dad some time during the Sunday service, and they'd called a lot of the guys who'd known him and ridden with him, asking if they would come out. I still couldn't believe how many had agreed to show up.

"You're welcome. I had some help. You should've seen that girl of yours charming the Stetsons off those old cowboys."

A small smile tugged at my lips. Leave it to Kinsley to wrangle a group of grizzled old cowboys.

Speaking of Kinsley, I spotted her now, weaving through the crowd towards us, her sundress a splash of colour against the faded denim. Even from a distance, I could see the warmth in her eyes and the way her smile could chase away the shadows that clung to me.

She reached us, stepping between my legs, and pressed her lips to my cheek. "Ready?" she asked softly, her gaze searching mine.

I took a deep breath. "As I'll ever be." I pushed myself off the tailgate.

Finn clapped a hand on my shoulder, his grip firm. "That's my boy."

I rolled my eyes at him.

With Kinsley by my side and Finn at my back, I walked towards the tent, each step a little lighter than the last. The anger was still there, a dull ache in my chest, but it no longer felt all-consuming. Maybe Finn was right, and I needed this. Maybe saying goodbye, even to a man as flawed as my father, was the only way to let go.

As we stepped into the tent, countless gazes settled on me. The low murmur of conversations faded, replaced by a heavy silence that pressed against my skin. I kept my eyes forward, focusing on the makeshift altar at the front, adorned with a simple wooden cross and a framed picture of my father.

Hands reached out as I passed, some offering a gentle pat on my shoulder, others clasping my arm in a gesture of support. The touch of the community, the unspoken understanding in their eyes, was both comforting and overwhelming. I didn't think I'd expected anyone to care this much or at all. Each contact seemed to chip away at the armour I'd built around my heart, exposing the raw grief beneath.

Kinsley's hand never left mine, her presence a steadying force as we navigated the sea of cowboy hats and solemn faces. Finn walked just a step behind like a silent guardian watching over us.

As we neared the front, I spotted Grady, Rhett, and Maisey, their faces sombre, but they offered small smiles as we approached. They had saved seats for us, so we slid into the row beside them. Grady's hand reached over and gave the back of my neck a quick squeeze.

Their presence, the knowledge that they were here for me even amid my conflicted emotions, was comforting. For the first time since my father's passing, I felt a flicker of something other than anger and pain. It wasn't quite peace, but it was a start.

As the pastor stepped up to the podium, I took a deep breath, bracing myself for the words to come, while Kinsley's hand tightened around mine.

The pastor's voice, deep with the cadence of a seasoned preacher, filled the tent. "We are here today to remember and celebrate the life of Jake Collins..."

As I listened, images of my father flickered through my mind. The good times, the bad times, the moments of laughter, and those of heartache. It was a kaleidoscope of memories, each one a piece of the complex puzzle that had been our relationship.

Beside me, Kinsley leaned in, her shoulder pressing against mine, and on my other side, Finn sat like a stone pillar holding me up. They anchored me to the present moment.

The pastor continued, sharing stories and anecdotes from those who had known my father best. Tales of his skill in the rodeo arena, his quick wit and infectious laughter, his loyalty to his friends... With each story, I saw a different facet of the man I had called my father.

Then, one by one, some of the old cowboys stood up, their weathered faces creased with mirth and nostalgia. They shared stories of my father's wild antics, the pranks he'd pulled, and the jokes he'd told. The tent filled with laughter.

I chuckled along with the crowd, a smile tugging at my lips as I remembered the man my father had been in his lighter moments—the man who could light up a room with his presence, who could make even the toughest cowboy double over with laughter. I had forgotten about that man.

The pastor's tone shifted. He spoke of my father's struggles, his battle with the bottle, and the demons that had haunted him. That was the side of him I knew all too well, a side that had caused so much pain and disappointment. But, as the pastor said, he was free of all that now.

As the words hit me, a lump formed in my throat. The tears I had been holding back since my father's passing threatened to spill over. I blinked rapidly, trying to maintain my composure.

Kinsley's fingers intertwined with my mine. She was my lifeline, a reminder that I wasn't alone.

Then, the pastor announced, "We've got a special song today, folks. Maisey's going to sing *Amazing Grace* in Jake's honor."

Maisey stood, her face pale but resolute as she made her way to the front. She took a deep breath, closing her eyes for a moment before her sweet voice, clear and strong, filled the tent while a hush settled over the crowd. Hats came off and heads bowed, taking in every note.

As the last notes faded, I realized that my dad, for all his faults, had lived a life full of passion and adventure. He might have stumbled, might have fallen, but he'd never stopped chasing the thrill of the ride. In that moment, I knew that a part of him would always be with me—a reminder to live life to the fullest, to embrace the good times, and to never back down from a challenge. Even the ones that came from within.

The pastor concluded the service with a prayer. As the final "amen" echoed through the tent, a sense of peace began to settle inside me. It wasn't forgiveness, not yet. Just a first step on the long road to healing.

As the congregation dispersed, offering condolences, I turned to Kinsley and my friends.

"Thanks, guys." My voice was thick. "For being here, for everything."

Kinsley smiled softly, reaching up to brush a stray tear from my cheek. "Always," she murmured. "We'll always be here for you, Wyatt."

"C'mon, man," Finn said. "Let's go get a beer. It's on Grady."

"Dude!" Grady said. "We're just leaving *church*. We can't go get a beer right now."

"Sure we can. It's what Jake would've wanted," Finn deadpanned and stared off against Grady.

The corners of my mouth twitched.

"That feels a little wrong." Grady lowered his voice to a hushed tone. "He was an *alcoholic*."

I couldn't contain myself anymore. A full-blown grin erupted on my face. Finn caught my eye and smirked. I lost it. The laughter burst out of me, and I couldn't stop it.

While the others looked on in bewilderment, Finn and I laughed. Kinsley's jaw dropped, Maisey's brow furrowed, and Rhett's head swiveled between me and Finn like he was watching a tennis match, but we were too far gone, tears streaming down our faces as laughter shook our chests.

"Everything my dad did was wrong. A beer suits just fine." I clapped Grady on the back. "Let's go."

The laughter faded, but the warmth it had sparked in my chest remained. I took a deep breath, the air somehow fresher.

Kinsley's eyes met mine, questioning. I pulled her close, my hands sliding around her waist as I captured her lips with my own. In that soft kiss, I let the past, the grief, and the pain melt away, replaced by hope and possibility. Kinsley's love was a promise of a brighter future, a path forward I knew I wouldn't have to walk alone.

As we parted, both slightly breathless, I smiled against her temple and pressed another quick kiss to her head. I gently tucked a stray lock of hair behind her ear, my fingertips lingering on her cheek.

"What was that for?" she asked softly, a smile playing at the corners of her mouth.

"For being you." My voice was low and earnest. "For being here. For loving me and giving me hope."

Her smile widened, her eyes shining with a love that took my breath away. "Always," she promised.

As we turned to join our friends, my arm wrapped securely around her waist, I felt the peace take root. The memories of my father, both good and bad, would always be a part of me, but they no longer held me captive.

Everybody piled into the bed of my truck, their laughter and chatter filling the air. Kinsley and I climbed into the front, grinning at each other as I turned the key. The engine roared to life, and I immediately cranked up the music, the bass thumping through the speakers. A chorus of whoops and hollers erupted from the back as the song blasted out, and we all started singing This Is How We Roll at the top of our lungs with Florida Georgia Line and Luke Bryan.

As I pulled out onto the main road, the wind whipped through the open windows. My friends' voices were in a raucous chorus, and a grin spread across my face. This was living, pure and simple. No more dwelling on the past. I was ready to move forward.

Chapter 36

Where It Ends - Bailey Zimmerman

Kinsley

"You know you're pulling on her mouth, right?" Finn's accusation came after a practice run.

We had arrived at our next rodeo that morning, and if I wanted to win enough points this year, I needed to practise more and keep Cher in top shape. I'd asked Finn to help since he had the most horse training experience.

"Ugh, I know. I'm sorry, baby girl," I apologised, leaning down to hug Cher's neck.

"That's not like you." Finn's observation hit home.

My horse's welfare had always been my primary concern, but my desperation for better race times was clouding my judgement.

"I'll try harder," I promised.

"No. That's the problem; you're trying too hard. Relax a bit, trust her to do her job, and stop trying to force it. She can feel all your tension," he advised.

I exhaled, acknowledging the truth in his words. My competitiveness was getting the best of me, and Cherokee was suffering for it.

"Call it quits for today. Start fresh tomorrow."

"Fine." I dismounted and gave Cher a reassuring pat.

Finn walked us back to the barn, but my mind was still on the ride and how to get more speed out of my horse. Doubts gnawed at my confidence, whispering insidious suggestions of failure.

"Get out of your head, Kinsley."

"I can't help it. I want this so bad. Do you think Cher can compete at this level?"

"Yeah, of course." His assurance was swift, but his eyes darted away, betraying his words.

My stomach dropped. "You're lying."

"She's a great horse, a pro. You couldn't ask for a more consistent horse."

"Just a faster one."

"She might pull it off." Finn's tone lacked conviction.

"I'm not going to take Gambler back if that's what you're worried about."

"That's not—"

"I can see it all over your face. It's a miracle we got Wyatt to ride him. I will not mess that up—"

We'd reached Cher's stall, where Wyatt was busy tossing hay, his expression a fury of anger as he glared at us. He'd clearly overheard everything.

"The two of you just thought you would team up to solve all my problems?" Wyatt said bitterly.

"No! That's not—" Panic tightened its icy grip around my chest.

"It wasn't like that, man," Finn said.

"No? Poor Wyatt needs a horse, so you two concocted a plan to get me riding him."

The accusation stung because he wasn't wrong. Tears welled up, hot and stinging, blurring my vision.

"I'll always be a fucking charity case to you, Kinsley." With that, he stormed off.

"Wyatt, please." My tears drowned out my plea. I attempted to follow him, but Cher tugged me toward her stall, eager for her meal.

"Shit." Finn grumbled, taking off his hat and running his hand through his hair. He slumped against the stall wall. "I'll talk to him."

"No, I'll talk to him," I insisted. My heart was heavy with guilt. Wyatt's anger was directed at me, and it was up to me to make things right.

When I caught up with him, Wyatt was furiously packing his belongings into his truck.

"Where are you going?!" My voice broke, the panic rising in my throat like a tidal wave.

"Home." His response was curt as he hefted his saddle into the back. He wouldn't even look at me.

My apology stumbled out, sounding desperate. "Wyatt, I'm sorry, I didn't mean to—"

"Didn't mean to trick me into riding your horse?" His retort was sharp, cutting deep.

"You needed a horse!" I countered, my frustration mounting.

"That wasn't your problem to fix."

"I don't fucking care!" My outburst echoed between us, raw and unfiltered. The dam of my composure had broken, and the flood of fear and desperation poured out.

"What?" He seemed taken aback by my vehemence.

"When you're in a relationship with someone, that's what you do! You help each other, you figure things out together, and you sacrifice for the other person! But you can't seem to understand that! You're constantly pushing me away because you think you have to do things on your own. Well, it's bullshit! You say you love me, that you want a life with me, but it's never going to work until you pull your head out of your ass and let me in!" My words spilled out, a torrent of emotion and frustration, each sentence punctuated by the rapid beat of my heart.

He stood there across the hood of the truck, silent, his glare as intense as the emotions swirling between us. I held his gaze, my breath heavy, as my entire being screamed for him to just listen and understand.

But he only shook his head, the finality of the gesture like a slap to the face.

"No. I'm not doing this again."

I struggled to draw in air, each breath a sharp pain in my chest.

Watching Wyatt hastily throw the rest of his things into the truck was like watching the last two years of our lives being carelessly packed away.

"Wyatt, please, let's talk about this," I pleaded, my voice breaking with the effort to keep him here and make him see reason.

He paused, his hands gripping the edge of the truck bed. "There's nothing left to say, Kinsley." His voice was low and strained.

I moved closer, the gravel crunching under my boots. "I-I thought we were in this together. That we could face anything, as long as we had each other."

Wyatt looked up at me with an expression of anger and pain. "How can we be in this together when you're making decisions for me? Decisions that I should be a part of?"

I reached out. If I could just touch him...

But he stepped back, putting more distance between us.

"I love you, Wyatt. I thought that meant I should do whatever I could to help you." My voice was barely a whisper, drowned out by the sound of my heart breaking.

"I don't need that kind of help, Kinsley. I need... I don't even know what I need anymore, but it's not this."

The moment stretched on—a standstill in our personal storm. Then he climbed into the truck, starting the engine without another word.

The roar of the engine was a harsh farewell, leaving me standing there, grappling with the realization that love, no matter how deep, might not be enough to overcome some obstacles.

Chapter 37

SHE GOT THE BEST OF ME - LUKE COMBS

Wyatt

By the time I got back to my farm, it was dark. I pulled the truck up to the house and put it into park.

My head sagged. I could've fallen asleep right there behind the wheel. Somehow, I mustered the energy to drag myself out of the truck and up to the house, my fingers searching for the keyhole in the dark.

The inside of the house greeted me with an even deeper darkness, without the moon's soft glow. As I flipped the light switch on the wall, the quietness of the space struck me, but it was warm and clean thanks to Kinsley.

A lump formed in my throat as I tossed the keys onto the small table by the front door and trudged up the stairs to my room. Collapsing onto the bed, I smelled the lingering scent of sweet apple on the pillow beside me. Pulling it close, I inhaled deeply.

How could she have gone behind my back like that? I'd thought we were past these games, past the point where she felt the need to fix me. Her betrayal stung, reopening wounds I'd thought were healing.

How did we move on from this? Were we doomed to just repeat this same fight over and over again? I didn't know how much more I could take. I couldn't be with her when she constantly undermined me. But I also couldn't be without her.

When sunlight flooded my room the next morning, I groaned, reaching out for Kinsley, only to find her side of the bed empty. The events of the previous day came rushing back, deepening my groan of frustration.

Sitting up, I ran my hands through my hair. Birds were chirping outside like it was any old day and I hadn't just blown up my life again.

I checked my phone. There was only one message from Finn.

> Forgive me yet?

> No.

> Alright. I'll check back tomorrow.

Fucking Finn.

Heading downstairs, I found the kitchen bare. We hadn't known when we would be back, so we'd cleared out anything that would spoil. I considered skipping breakfast, but I was hungry and I wouldn't get much done on an empty stomach, so I grabbed my keys and headed for my truck.

I drove for about ten minutes before I realised I wasn't heading towards town or a restaurant of any kind. My stomach complained, and I turned my truck down the next mile road.

The Harper farm loomed in the distance. I inspected their pasture as I approached. It was overgrazed, early in the season too. I shook my head. It was going to be a tough year for them.

Pulling up to the house, I saw Grace on the front porch, cleaning saddles.

"Back so soon?" she greeted in surprise.

"What can I say? I'm already missing the home cooking," I joked.

"What, your rodeo queen can't cook?"

I flinched at that.

Grace turned red, looked down at the saddle, and scrubbed. "Sorry. I shouldn't have said that," she mumbled.

"It might be a little true," I admitted with a laugh.

She smiled at me. "So, what's really going on?"

"We had a fight." I shrugged, trying to downplay what had driven me here. "Kind of a regular occurrence."

Grace's next words caught me off guard. "We never fought when we were together."

"No, we didn't," I agreed, a bit taken aback by the direction of our conversation.

"I didn't challenge you the way she does."

Her choice of words made me pause. "What do you mean?"

She stopped her work on the saddle, choosing her next words carefully. "I loved you, but I think if we had stayed together, stayed here, we would've been just ... stuck. You know? Going our separate ways was hard, but I was so happy that you left. You got away from here, got away from your dad. You needed to do that. Kinsley might be a little pushy, but I think you need that too. I think she's good for you." She resumed her polishing. "And that's an opinion you did not ask for."

Her honesty took me by surprise. "Sometimes, I feel like I'm still stuck. Like the hole I'm in is too deep, and I can't climb my way out."

"Let someone lower a rope," she suggested.

After I let Alice feed me until I was ready to burst, I asked to borrow a horse to go for a ride. I did my best thinking on the back of a horse, and as much as I didn't want to admit it, Grace's words had struck a chord.

"Do you want company?" Grace watched me saddle up.

"Maybe next time. I want to clear my head a bit."

"Yeah, of course."

"Don't go out too far," Mr. Harper said, coming into the barn. "There are some dark clouds rolling in. Might be a decent storm."

"I didn't think they were calling for any weather."

"Yeah, it came up a bit unexpectedly, but God knows we need the rain."

"I noticed your pastures were looking a little sparse."

"It's been a few dry years, and we don't have enough grazing land."

My stomach was suddenly heavy and not because of the meal I had devoured. "I'll be back in about an hour." I led the big bay horse down the aisle.

"Have fun," Mr. Harper said.

Grace waved from inside one stall.

Once outside, I mounted up and urged the horse forward into a brisk walk. The air hung heavy and thick with humidity as I guided the horse through the back field behind the barn. The sky above was a canvas of shifting greys and ominous clouds. The air crackled with energy, and the distant rumble of thunder echoed in the distance.

As we moved, my horse's hooves stirred up the earth, releasing the fragrance of sun-baked soil mixed with the green undertones of nearby pastures.

Grace's words circled my mind.

'*I think she's good for you.*'

How was that possible when we fought so much? We'd broken up how many times now? Obviously, we didn't work as a couple.

That thought left a bitter taste in my mouth.

If I was being honest, I don't think I could ever walk away from Kinsley. I'd tried, and it never took. Even now, I'd been gone a day, and I missed her so much that my chest ached.

But even when she was here, when I'd brought her home to my farm, it didn't feel right. Her being here made me feel like I was dragging her into my past, and I didn't like it. She didn't belong here, and I was starting to think I didn't either.

Thunder rumbled overhead. I had been out there for at least an hour or more, and the wind had picked up, my horse's mane getting blown and tangled. I turned him and headed back in the direction I'd come.

More thunder crackled. The storm was coming in a lot faster than I'd thought.

Chapter 38

DIE FROM A BROKEN HEART - MADDIE & TAE

Kinsley

After Wyatt had left, I locked myself in my trailer for the night, and the next day, Maisey came knocking on the door several times. So did Finn, but I couldn't bring myself to open it.

The isolation had gotten to me until I couldn't take it anymore.

I found my friends, Maisey and the guys, sitting around a campfire, but Wyatt's absence was triggering, and I almost turned back. I paused, unsure what to do.

"Kinsley, how are you holding up?" Finn spotted me before I could run.

I took the last steps closer and sat down beside Maisey on a blanket. I exhaled. "I don't know. I mean, I knew he would be mad, but that— That was so much more."

Grady shifted; his gaze fixed on the fire. "Thing is, Kins, you kinda stepped over a line."

Rhett chimed in; his tone more stern than usual. "It's about trust. You and Finn went behind his back. That's not easy to forgive."

A surge of frustration ran through me. "So, what? I'm the bad guy here? I was trying to save his rodeo season!"

Finn nodded in agreement. "Exactly. Wyatt's being stubborn, but he'll see reason eventually."

Grady turned to Finn. "You know him better than anybody! It's not about being stubborn. It's about making his own choices. You two decided for him; that's the issue."

"Yeah, I do know him better than anybody, and I know when he needs to be pushed. We did what we had to do."

"You really think you had to manipulate him like that?" Grady countered.

"Yeah, I do. He had nothing left. You give Wyatt enough rope, and he will hang himself with it. I wasn't about to let that happen. Wyatt will get over it. He'll be back."

I wished I could feel the confidence in Finn's voice.

There was truth to what he'd said, and Wyatt would come back because he would never, ever walk away from Finn. But that rule didn't apply to me.

"No," Grady continued. "You guys went too far this time."

"This time?" I asked. "What is that supposed to mean?"

"It means you always do this; you always push him. And you wonder why you're always breaking up," Grady said.

"That's not— Maybe if I just—"

"Back off him, Kinsley," Rhett's voice cut through me—a tone I'd never heard from him—and it took me aback. "He needs to figure things out on his own. You can't do it for him."

"Kinsley, I think..." Maisey started quietly.

I stood up, cutting her off. "I'm not listening to this anymore. If you would all rather see him drown... I'm fighting for him—somebody should." I stomped away from the camp and heard Finn's voice behind me.

"Nice, guys," he said sarcastically. "Kinsley, wait up!" He jogged to catch up with me.

I replayed the argument in my mind, Grady's harsh words stinging. *'You always push him. And you wonder why you're always breaking up.'*

Was that true? Was I always overbearing? Controlling, even?

I chewed on my lip—a nervous habit I couldn't seem to break.

No, I refused to believe that. Wyatt needed me, even if he didn't realize it. I saw the weight of the world on his shoulders. He was drowning, and I had to throw him a lifeline, even if it meant taking matters into my own hands.

"Finn, tell me we did the right thing."

"We did the right thing."

I stopped and turned to him. "You're sure?" I bit down on my lip to stop it from quivering.

He grabbed my shoulders, forcing me to look him in the eye. "Kinsley, trust me. He'll come around."

I collapsed into him, unable to hold back the emotions that wanted to overtake me, and cried into his chest. Finn wrapped his arms around me and held me close while I let the tears fall.

"Finn?"

"Yeah?"

"This is really weird." I sniffled, all too aware of the mess I was making on his shirt.

"Yeah, I'm hoping you're almost done."

A giggle escaped me, and I pulled away from him and stood awkwardly. "We've never hugged before, have we?"

"Nope, and we probably should've kept it that way. Wyatt is the touchy-feely one, not me."

Hugging Finn was a little like hugging a grumpy bear, but the mention of Wyatt brought me back to reality.

"I need to go after him." I patted at my jean pockets, hoping to find my truck keys, but they weren't there. I never carried them around; I always left them in my trailer.

"That might not be the best idea."

"I need to tell him I'm sorry." I turned and started heading back to my trailer.

"Kinsley, he's going to need time to cool down, and he will, but—"

"No. I said I would fight for him, and I meant it." I stopped and turned in a circle, looking at my surroundings.

Where the fuck was my trailer? I was going the wrong way.

I marched off in the other direction. "He needs me to show up for him, no matter what. Even when he's mad at me or I'm mad at him, or whatever... When we're mad at each other, we always walk away. Every fight we have, we walk away. But it doesn't last because we're supposed to be together. We need to stop walking away, dammit!"

"Kinsley, wait up!" Finn jogged along behind me.

I had started running at some point. I didn't remember when, but my trailer came into view. I flung open the door, grabbed the keys off the hook on the wall, and ran out to my truck.

"Would you stop for a minute?!"

"No, Finn, you can't stop me. He needs me. I need him." I climbed into my truck and started it up. It rumbled to life.

"But I can come—"

I didn't let him finish. I slammed the door and peeled away into the night.

I glanced in my rearview mirror. Finn stood there, tossed his cowboy hat into the dirt, and ran his hand down his face.

"He'll forgive me too," I mumbled under my breath.

Right now, my only focus was getting to Wyatt.

Chapter 39

HURRICANE - LUKE COMBS

Wyatt

By the time I got back to the Harper's farm, thunder was a constant overhead, like the heartbeat of the storm. The sky had turned a dark grey, but the rain held back, teasing the too short grass that was begging for a drink.

The wind blew dirt and dust across our path and my hat right off my head. It spooked my horse, and he started crow-hopping across the field.

"Whoa, boy!" I sat firmly in the saddle and resisted the urge to pull back on the reins. He was scared, and I didn't want to make it worse. "Easy," I said in a soothing voice.

I urged him to move in a forward direction instead of the sideways movement he was doing. As we approached the barn, an open door was banging against the outer wall and the tin roof was lifting on the corner. The horse balked in response. I hopped off and tried to lead him inside, but he had his feet planted and he was going nowhere near that barn.

"Oh, c'mon, bud. We'll get you untacked, and then you can go hang out in the pasture with your friends." I gave a gentle tug on the reins, but he wasn't moving.

Another gust of wind hit us hard, and he reared up. Startled, I almost dropped the reins but hung on.

"Hold on!" Grace ran out of the barn to our side. She deftly unbuckled the saddle cinch, and as soon as it was undone, she pulled the saddle off him, ran to the gate of the pasture, and opened it wide.

I pulled the bridle off his head. He dropped the bit from his mouth and took off through the open gate towards the herd. Grace shut and secured the gate.

Thunder boomed in the sky.

"We need to get inside!" Grace yelled over the howling of the wind as we sprinted towards the safety of the house.

The gusts of wind threatened to sweep us off our feet, forcing us to lean into the storm's ferocity. When we were almost at the front door, the sky exploded with a blinding flash. A deafening crack followed as lightning streaked across the heavens. In that instant, everything became so clear, so bright.

A bolt of lightning had struck the barn behind us. The force of the impact was like an explosion. The building went up in flames and sparked to the hay shed next to it.

As the flames danced in the barn, the family rushed outside, their eyes widening.

"Oh my god." Grace's hand covered her mouth, and tears flowed from her eyes.

I put an arm around her shoulders and pulled her into my side, and she cried into my chest. All we could do was wait and pray for the rain to unleash itself and pour down onto the flames below.

While the Harpers and I continued to watch in dismay as the fire consumed the barn, the heavens responded to our silent pleas. Sheets of water suddenly cascaded from the sky, extinguishing the flames with a sizzling hiss.

The storm, now a force of salvation rather than destruction, drenched us to the bone. The raindrops, each a tiny hero, descended upon the smouldering remains of the barn.

We stood there until every last flame was extinguished and tendrils of black smoke rose into the now still air.

Grace's father clutched his hat to his chest, stepped backwards until he reached the porch steps, and sunk down so he was sitting, defeated. Alice ran over and threw her arms around him, burying her face in his neck. I couldn't tell if she was crying, but how could she not be? Grace was still sobbing into my chest, and Noah was sitting on the ground, his head between his knees.

I rubbed my hand up and down Grace's back. There were no words to say.

After a while, Grace's dad got up. "Let's go check the animals," was all he said.

This was a ranch, and the livestock was all that mattered. We went inside only to change into dry clothes, then we all headed out on foot, first to check the horses.

They were on edge and skittish as hell, but all accounted for and unharmed.

"We'll go grab a couple of quads to go find the herd," Mr. Harper said. "Looks like they ran farther into the bush."

We weren't about to make the horses work in this state, plus all the saddles, bridles, and all other equipment were in the barn. Damn, they'd lost a lot. Hopefully, they at least had their herd intact.

We searched well into the night, checked over every cow, and other than some scratches—probably from getting spooked into tree branches—the herd was more or less alright. Wearily, we headed back to the house, ready for food and bed.

"Thanks for your help, Wyatt." Mr. Harper patted my back.

"No problem." I rubbed my eyes. All I wanted was a bed.

"Crash in Noah's room; you don't need to be driving back to your place."

I nodded, too tired to argue.

Grace and Noah trailed along behind us, dead on their feet. When we walked into the house, Alice had a full spread, hot and ready on the table.

"Good timing." She looked over her family with the concerned eyes of a mother, and a part of me was suddenly wistful. When her eyes turned to me, it was like her warmth enveloped me as if I was a part of her family.

But it was fleeting. This wasn't my family.

I thought of Kinsley, and my heart ached. I wanted her in my arms.

Chapter 40

BROKEN HALOS - CHRIS STAPLETON

Wyatt

I woke late the next morning to find Mr. Harper outside, engaged in a discussion with the insurance adjuster. Grace and Noah were on the porch watching.

"You're up. You slept through half the day," Grace teased as I joined them.

I rubbed my eyes, still experiencing the drag of exhaustion from the storm and the fire. "Guess I needed it," I admitted as I sat down next to Noah.

I pulled my phone from my pocket. It was only 10 AM, hardly half a day gone. I also noted that I had no calls or messages.

Noah elbowed me. "You missed Dad's showdown with the insurance guy. It was something to see."

I glanced at Mr. Harper animatedly explaining the extent of the damage to the insurance adjuster, who listened while occasionally jotting down notes. "Looks like they're figuring things out."

Grace nodded in agreement. "Yeah, it's a relief. The insurance will help, but it won't replace everything. We're going to have to rebuild and find more hay."

Watching Mr. Harper and the adjuster, I realized the magnitude of the challenges that lay ahead. Rebuilding the barn and recovering from the losses seemed impossible.

After the insurance adjuster had finished his assessment and left, Mr. Harper joined us, his expression tight. "Well, it's not everything we hoped for, but it's a start. We'll get through this, like we always have. Now, I need to make some calls to hay suppliers," he said, the stress clear in his voice.

It was hard enough to get the bare minimum of hay needed, never mind more after losing that much.

Grace, Noah, and I began sifting through the debris, although hope was slim that the fire had spared anything. The barn, once filled with dry hay, had stood little chance against the flames.

It wasn't long before vehicles started pulling into the farmyard; word had gotten around the community about what had happened, and people were showing up to help with whatever they could.

All day, friends and neighbours worked to clean up the fire site. Alice kept food and cold drinks flowing from the kitchen to the yard, feeding every person who showed up.

"Grace!" Alice called out at one point. "I need you to run to the store! I'm running out of everything!"

"On it, Mom!" Grace hurried off.

"Wyatt, come drink something. You look parched," Alice then shouted to me.

Wiping the sweat from my brow, I put down the shovel I was using and wandered over to the porch. My mouth was dry and coated in dust. I grabbed the pitcher of freshly squeezed lemonade Alice had left out and poured a glass. I sat down beside Mr. Harper, who had also been forced into taking a break.

The sun was hot as I took a sip of the lemonade. It was a welcome relief from the heat.

"Thanks for the help, son." Mr. Harper wiped sweat from his forehead with a worn cloth.

I nodded in response. "I can't believe all these people showed up to help."

Mr. Harper chuckled, his gaze sweeping over the busy scene around us. "If you have the ability to help someone in need, you do it. That's the way things work around here, what community is all about. They all know we'd do the same for them in a heartbeat."

Leaning back, I took in the sight of our community in action. It was powerful seeing everyone pulling together.

"I guess I've never seen that before. I don't like to rely on anyone else," I admitted.

Mr. Harper offered a knowing smile, the lines around his eyes deepening. "There's no shame in accepting a helping hand. It doesn't make you any less strong; it just means you're smart enough to know when you need it."

I let out a sigh, his words sinking in. "I've always thought I had to do things on my own. Like, if I accept the help, it doesn't count."

He laid a reassuring hand on my shoulder. "We're not meant to go through life alone, son. We're part of something bigger—a community of family, friends, and neighbours. Accepting help doesn't make you weak; it makes you human. Your dad wasn't there for you the way he should've been, so maybe you don't expect anyone else to be, but if you keep pushing everyone away, you're going to wind up all alone, and we humans are not designed to be alone. We come together, we help each other, and love each other—that's how we live our best lives."

Mr. Harper's words were turning over in my mind. My gaze drifted to the people working in the yard, their laughter and chatter mingling with the sounds of tools and machinery. They were here, giving their time and energy, not because they had to but because they wanted to. Because they cared.

I thought back to all the times I'd pushed people away, insisting I could handle everything on my own. The long nights spent working on the farm, scrimping by on the bare minimum because it was all I could afford. I'd worn my independence like a badge of honour, a shield against the world.

But now, watching this community come together, I wondered if that shield had become a prison. Had I been so focused on proving my strength that I'd forgotten the power of connection?

The memory of Kinsley's face, hurt and frustrated by my stubborn refusal to accept her help, flashed through my mind. I winced, realising how many times I'd done that to her.

I took another sip of lemonade, the tartness lingering on my tongue. Maybe it was time to see things differently, to open up and let people in. The thought terrified me, but it also sparked a flicker of hope.

What if I didn't have to carry everything alone? What if I learned to lean on others, to trust them, to be part of something bigger than myself?

I glanced at Mr. Harper, who had the look of satisfaction over a life well-lived. A life built on community, on family, and on love. I wanted that. I wanted to build something real, something that would last.

I couldn't do it alone.

I thought of Kinsley with a pang of regret. I had been an idiot to let my pride get in the way of our relationship. The fact was, I needed her in my life.

"Have you found any hay yet?" I asked, shifting the conversation.

Mr. Harper's face fell. "Not yet. But something will come through."

"I have an idea."

Chapter 49

NEVER SAY NEVER - COLE SWINDELL & LAINEY WILSON

Kinsley

The sun was low on the horizon when I pulled up to Wyatt's house. There was no sign of him or his truck. Hesitation gripped me for a moment; I was caught between the urge to turn back and the resolve to wait it out, intent on making things right.

The door was unlocked. He'd obviously been here, so I opened it and stepped inside. I recognized the smell of the place—leather and sawdust. It was just like him, rough around the edges but holding a certain charm.

"Wyatt?" I called out but received no response. I thought about calling his phone, but I knew he wouldn't answer.

Choosing to wait, I stepped onto the porch, letting the evening breeze and the fields' earthy aroma wash over me. As time passed, my anxiety grew, fear whispering that I might have missed my chance.

As doubt took hold, the crunch of gravel under tires caught my attention.

Wyatt's truck rounded the bend, and my heart raced.

He parked and stepped out, his weary gaze not finding me until he was close. Surprise flickered across his face, followed by an emotion I couldn't quite place. "Kinsley," he breathed.

The way he said my name sent a shiver down my spine.

I drew in a deep breath, steeling myself. "Wyatt, we need to talk. I can't let things end like this."

He nodded. "I can't believe you're here."

"I'm so sorry. I shouldn't have tricked you like that. It was wrong, and I—" I tried to keep my voice as steady as possible, not letting my emotions betray me.

"No, Kins. I'm the one who was wrong. I've been stubborn and stupid. I'm always stubborn and stupid." He lifted his hat and ran his hand through his hair.

"Maybe I pushed too hard," I conceded, that guilt still making my stomach turn.

He shook his head, a small smile touching his lips. "Maybe I needed it. Maybe I needed someone to push me off a cliff."

I laughed despite myself. The sound was a welcome release.

He went on, "I don't want to face anything alone anymore. I want to do everything with you. You're my family, my everything."

His words hit me like a tidal wave. It was everything I had been waiting to hear from him, almost too good to be true.

"What does that mean, Wyatt? Where do we go from here?" I bit my lip, the uncertainty creeping back in.

If he asked me to stay here, I didn't know what I would say. I couldn't lose him again, but could I tell him what I really wanted?

"It means we go home. To your ranch. When we're not on the rodeo circuit, at least." His words painting a future I hadn't dared to hope for.

Warmth spread from my chest into each limb until I was flushed from head to toe.

"Do you mean it?" My voice was barely above a whisper; I was too afraid that if I said anything too loud, I'd shatter the moment.

"You could use another ranch hand, couldn't you?" he offered, a hint of playfulness in his tone, all the conflict that normally plagued his expression gone.

"What about this place?" I gestured to the acres and acres of land, the house, and the barn—everything that was now his. "You got your home back."

He took a step closer, his voice earnest. "It's not my home anymore. You are." The conviction of his words took my breath away. His love shone through every syllable.

"But—" My mind grappled with the enormity of what he was offering, of the sacrifice he was willing to make for me, but he placed a finger to my lips, and I clamped my mouth shut.

Wyatt told me about the storm, the fire, the community pulling together to help Grace's family, and the losses that they had to deal with.

"Omigosh." My eyes widened in disbelief as I processed.

"Grace's dad can't find more hay, so I offered my grazing land. It'll be more than enough to get them through this year," Wyatt continued.

Admiration for the man standing before me swelled in my chest. I was so proud of him. "Wyatt, that's amazing."

"He said he would use part of his insurance money to pay the back taxes on the farm. It will also serve as a down payment."

"A down payment? You're selling the farm?" Shock rippled through me, my mind struggling to comprehend the magnitude of his decision.

"Yes, ma'am." He said it with such certainty, such resolve, that any doubts I'd had about his commitment to us vanished in an instant.

"Are you sure?" I had to ask and give him one last chance to rethink this.

"I've never been surer of anything in my life. Except for the fact that I love you more than anything, including this land."

I closed my eyes, letting his words wash over me. All the struggles of our past wiped clean.

"I love you too." My voice trembled, and I didn't bother trying to hold back the tears.

Wyatt pulled me into his arms. I buried my face in his chest, inhaling his familiar scent. It was a scent that meant home, safety, and love. In his embrace, I felt whole, like all the broken pieces of my heart had finally been put back together.

"I can't believe this is happening," I mumbled into his shirt, my voice muffled by the fabric.

He chuckled, the sound rumbling through his chest. "Believe it, darlin'. I'm done running from what matters most."

I pulled back, looking up at him. "What about your dreams? I thought..." Internally, I was kicking myself for questioning him even more, but my head was trying to catch up to what my heart had already accepted.

"My dreams have changed." He brushed a strand of hair from my face. "I realised that my biggest dream is to be with you, wherever that may be."

"And mine is to be with you," I whispered.

I gazed up at Wyatt. His eyes shone with a lightness I had never seen in him, and before I uttered another word, he leaned down and kissed me. The kiss was electrifying, igniting that spark deep within me. His lips were soft yet firm, and I melted into his embrace, savouring the warmth of his body against mine. My fingers tangled in his hair as I pulled him closer, desperate to deepen the kiss.

Wyatt's hands roamed over my back, his touch setting my skin on fire. Each caress was a promise, a vow to cherish and protect me. His kiss grew more passionate, more urgent, as if he were pouring every ounce of his love into this moment.

His stubble grazed my cheek, adding a delicious roughness to the tenderness of his touch. I parted my lips, inviting him in, and our tongues danced. A soft moan escaped my throat as Wyatt's kisses trailed along my jawline, leaving a path of fire in their wake. He nuzzled the crook of my neck, his breath hot against my skin and sending shivers down my spine.

Time stood still, the world fading away until there was nothing but the two of us. In that moment, I knew without a doubt that this was where I belonged—in Wyatt's arms.

As our lips parted, I gazed up at him, breathless and utterly captivated. His eyes looked at me with a love so pure, so deep, that it threatened to undo me. Without words, he had conveyed everything—his devotion, his longing, his promise of forever.

I beamed up at him full force. "So, you ready to be a full-time ranch hand?"

He grinned. "As long as you're ready to be stuck with me."

I laughed. "I think I can handle that."

Hand in hand, we walked into the house. As I looked around at the place that had been Wyatt's home, I felt a twinge of sadness for what he was leaving behind. But then I looked at him, at the love and certainty in his eyes, and I knew that home wasn't a place. It was a person.

I had found my home in him, and we would never walk away from each other again. This time, when I said never, I meant it.

Chapter 42

SIMPLE - FLORIDA GEORGIA LINE

Forgive me now?

That was a jackass move.

Yeah, I know.

Alright, then.

Cool

Epilogue

SETTLING DOWN - MIRANDA LAMBERT

Wyatt

The warm summer breeze carried the scent of freshly cut hay as Kinsley and I rode across the fields of Jackson Ranch. The sun's rays warmed our backs, and long shadows stretched out before us.

I glanced over at Kinsley as she effortlessly guided her new mare, Wildfire. The horse's sleek chestnut coat glistened with each stride. Red mares were now her go-to type, not black demon horses.

Kinsley's eyes sparkled with excitement, a wide grin spreading across her face as she caught my gaze. "Isn't she incredible?" Kinsley gave Wildfire an affectionate pat on the neck. "I can't wait for next year's rodeo season. With Wildfire and Gambler, we're going to be unstoppable."

"I still have to convince Finn to give me another season."

"We'll work on him."

I looked down at Gambler. The once unruly gelding had become an extension of myself. Our partnership had grown stronger with each passing day. Meanwhile, Drifter got to enjoy his retirement in horse paradise.

Kinsley urged Wildfire into a gallop. Not one to be outdone, I pushed Gambler forward, matching her stride for stride as we raced across the open field. The rhythmic pounding of the horse's hooves on the ground filled my ears. It was my favourite sound.

As we neared the edge of the field, Kinsley slowed Wildfire to a trot, turning to face me with a glint in her eyes. "Race you back to the barn?" she challenged, her competitive spirit shining through.

I couldn't resist the opportunity to push Gambler's limits. With a grin, I nodded, and we were off once more, our horses' hooves thundering against the earth.

After cooling down the horses and turning them back out into the pasture, I took Kinsley's hand, and we strolled leisurely toward our new home—her grandparents' old house.

As we approached, our friends' familiar voices drifted through the open windows.

"Well, if it isn't the slackers," Grady hollered, emerging from the front door with a wide grin. "C'mon, we're doing all the heavy lifting while you two were off gallivanting."

Finn poked his head out, a smirk tugging at the corners of his mouth. "He's right, you know. The least you could've done was greet us properly."

I shook my head, pulling Kinsley closer as we approached the porch steps. "You guys said you'd be here after lunch."

Rhett leaned against the doorframe, arms folded across his chest. "We figured if we got here and to work before lunch, then you would have to feed us."

"We've been working so hard," Finn added with a pout.

Kinsley laughed. "We appreciate every bit of sweat you boys are putting into it. Lunch is on us."

"And supper," Grady said.

"And supper."

The money from selling my farm would help us fix up Kinsley's grandparents' old homestead and make it our own. The place was in good shape but needed some updating. With our friends' help, we were slowly transforming it into our dream home.

We stepped inside, tools and construction materials were scattered about. In the living room, Grady and Finn had already begun sanding the hardwood floors, while Rhett worked on stripping the old wallpaper from the hallway.

"You boys have been busy," I remarked, surveying the progress.

"Yeah, so get your ass in gear," Finn said.

Kinsley's enthusiasm was infectious as we gathered around the kitchen table with her Pinterest account on the laptop.

"I want to paint the cupboards to look like that." She pointed at a picture of a sage green and oak kitchen.

As they discussed the details, I watched her. I'd never imagined I'd settle down in such a beautiful house, let alone on the Jackson Ranch, but with Kinsley by my side, it felt right. Like I was finally home.

I admired the way her brow furrowed in concentration as she scrolled through more pictures. She caught my gaze and smiled, her hand finding mine under the table and giving it a gentle squeeze.

"What do you think, Wyatt?" she asked, her voice soft. "Is that okay?"

I brought her hand to my lips, pressing a kiss to her knuckles. "Whatever you want darlin'."

Kinsley's smile widened, and she leaned in, planting a kiss on my cheek. "I can't wait to make this place our own. Imagine waking up every morning in this house together."

"It'll be perfect." I pulled her close and kissed her neck.

"Alright, lovebirds, save it for the bedroom." Finn pushed back from the table. "We've got work to do."

As we set about our tasks, a sense of contentment washed over me. This was the life I'd always wanted, even if I hadn't known it until now.

I swiped the back of my arm across my forehead, wiping away the sweat that had gathered there after a productive morning's work. The rest of the crew was taking a breather too, gulping down water in the shade of an old oak tree.

The roar of an engine shattered the peaceful ranch silence. I turned toward the noise, squinting against the sun's glare, as a sleek, cherry-red sports car came barreling down the long driveway towards Kinsley's parents' house.

"Who the hell drives a car like that out here?" Finn grumbled, shaking his head in disbelief.

Grady let out a low whistle. "Rich jackasses, that's who."

"Oh, that'll be Evan," Kinsley remarked with an eyeroll.

Rhett's eyebrow quirked upward. "Evan?"

"My sister's boyfriend." Kinsley did not hide her disdain. "Asshole with more money than brains."

"Isn't he a lawyer?" I asked.

"My statement still stands."

I stole a glance over at Grady, who had gone unnaturally still and quiet beside me. The usual playful glint in his eyes was nowhere to be seen, replaced by a guarded look as the passenger door swung open.

Abby Jackson stepped out in a sundress, her dark hair blowing in the breeze.

The sports car peeled away in a cloud of dust, leaving Abby to make her way towards the house alone. Grady's eyes tracked her every movement, his jaw tightening almost imperceptibly as she entered her home without so much as a glance in our direction.

I knew that look all too well; I'd worn it myself over the last couple of years more times than I cared to admit, and there was no mistaking the flicker of wistful tenderness passing over his features before he could hide it.

At first, I hadn't thought much of Grady's little crush on Kinsley's sister. We all got starry-eyed now and then around a pretty face. I'd figured it would blow over once the next rodeo rolled around and his head was back in the game. But seeing him now, the way his eyes stayed glued to the house even after Abby had disappeared inside... It made me rethink just how deep those feelings might run.

Before I could dwell too much on my friend's reaction, the vibration of Grady's phone cut through the silence. He fished it out of his back pocket, brow furrowed as he read the screen. In the next moment, the tense look on his face melted into one of pure elation.

"Fuck yes!" Grady let out a whoop of surprise and joy, leaping up from where he'd been sitting on the grass. "I just got an invitation to the PBR Canada Tour!"

The rest of us were on our feet in a heartbeat, crowding around to slap him on the back as we offered our congratulations. This was the big break he'd been chasing, a chance to prove himself on one of the biggest stages in bull riding.

But even as the celebration swirled around him, I couldn't help but notice Grady's eyes drifting back towards the house where Abby was.

A sinking feeling settled into the pit of my stomach. I recognized all the signposts on the road to heartache.

As happy as I was for Grady's success, I couldn't shake the feeling that his luck might take a turn for the worst with Abby Jackson.

Don't miss a single book in the Bad Luck Cowboys series! Visit my website and be sure to sign up for my newsletter! Thank you so much for reading!
https://chelseyfay.com

Acknowledgements

First of all, a big thank you to every reader that takes a chance on my book! Thank you!

This book wouldn't exist without the love and support of many wonderful people.

To my family and friends, thank you for your constant encouragement. Mom, thank you for always believing in me and my dreams.

A huge thank you to my critique group: Brianne, Aimee, Moa, and Holly. Your feedback, support, and friendship have been invaluable throughout this journey.

Evelyn, thank you for the stunning cover that perfectly captures the heart of this story.

Nina, your meticulous editing and unwavering enthusiasm have been instrumental in bringing this book to life.

And most importantly, to my incredible husband, Chris, and our two amazing boys, Charlie and Cole: you are my world. Thank you for being my biggest cheerleaders, for your patience and understanding, and for always inspiring me to chase my dreams.

About the author

Chelsey Fay, a romance author from Manitoba, Canada, crafts stories in both contemporary and fantasy settings. A wife and mother of two boys who are her greatest joy and achievement, Chelsey draws inspiration from family life and the beauty of the nature. When not writing or cherishing moments with her family, she enjoys cozy time with a good book or spending time with her horse.

Manufactured by Amazon.ca
Bolton, ON